BLC

A Medieval Murder Mystery

by

Stephen Wheeler

BLOOD MOON

First published in 2011 by

The Erskine Press, The White House, Eccles, Norwich, NR16 2PB
WWW.ERSKINE-PRESS.COM

Text © 2011 Stephen Wheeler
Illustrations © 2011 Stephen Wheeler
Cover photograph © Philip Moore
This Edition © 2011 The Erskine Press

ISBN 978 1 85297 111 3

The moral right of the author has been asserted

A CIP catalogue record is available from the British Library

No part of this book may be reproduced in any form,
by printing photocopying or by any other means
without the prior written consent of the Publisher.

Typeset by Esme Power
Printed by CLE Print Ltd, St Ives, Cambridgeshire

East Anglia in 1214

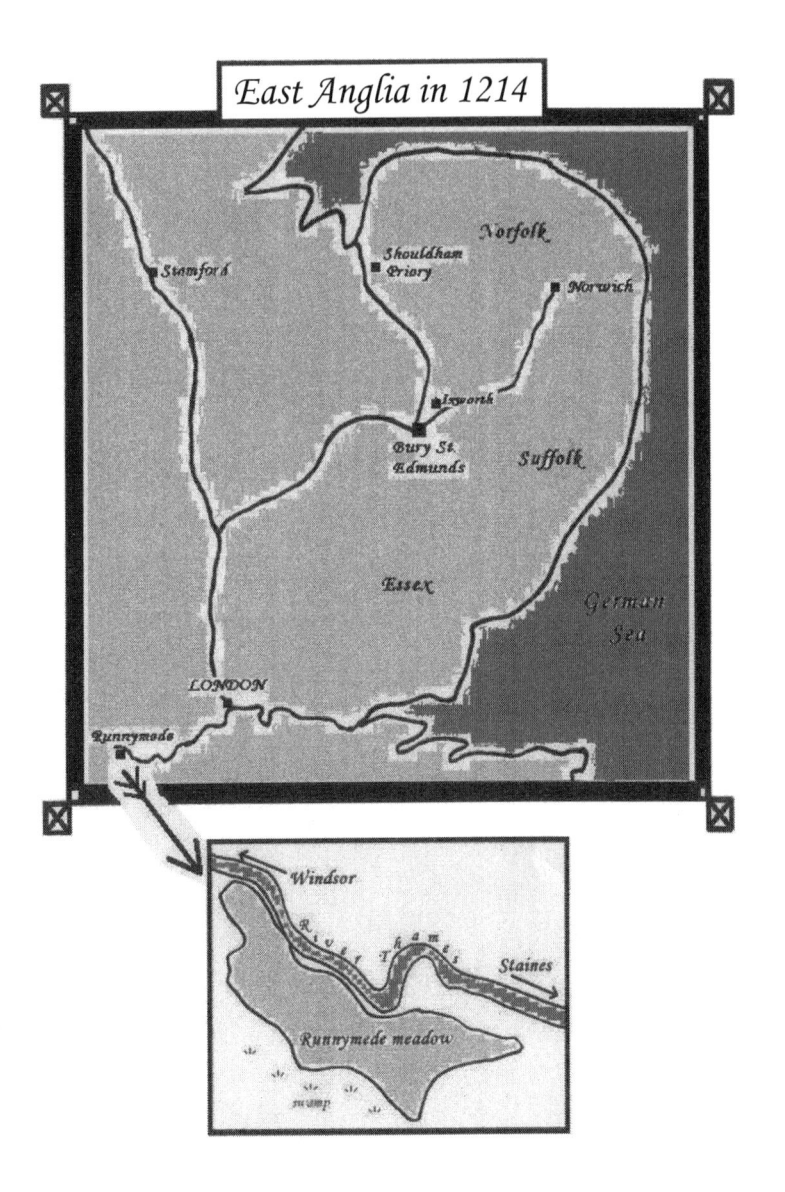

Saint Edmund's Abbey in 1214

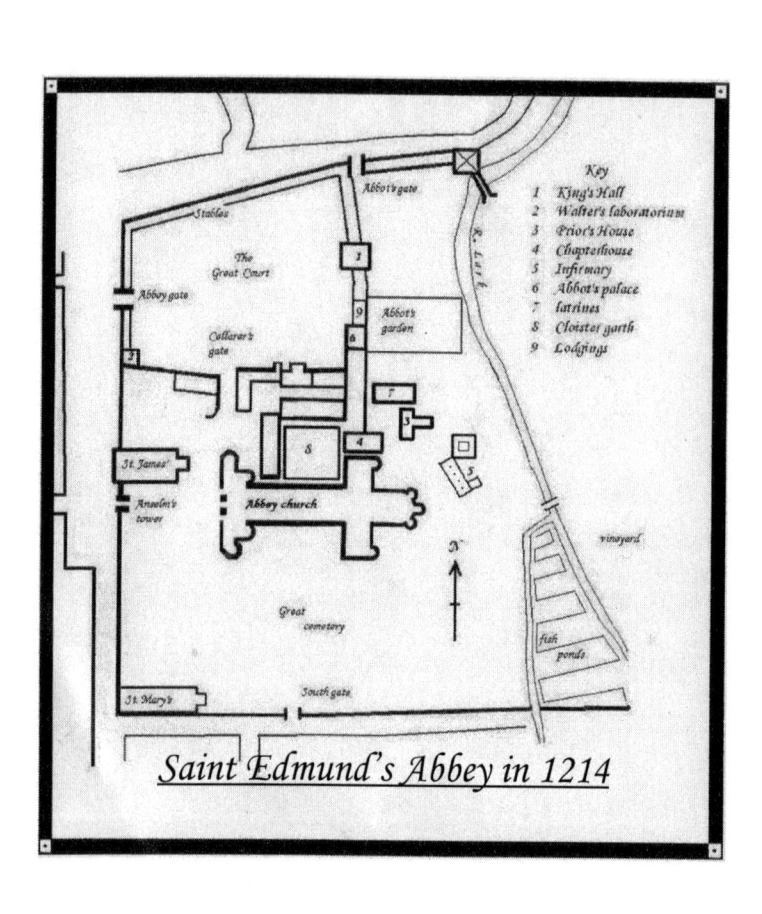

Key
1. King's Hall
2. Walter's laboratorium
3. Prior's House
4. Chapterhouse
5. Infirmary
6. Abbot's palace
7. latrines
8. Cloister garth
9. Lodgings

Prologue
Chapterhouse of St Leonard's Priory, Stamford, Lincolnshire
15th October 1214

The conspirators fell silent as they tried to tell from the sounds alone if the news was good or bad. They heard the clatter of the horse in the yard; heard its rider dismount; heard the crunch of his boots as he crossed the yard. Entering, he brought with him the cold of the night and the smells of the open road. He quickly searched among the anxious faces in the room until he found the one he was looking for and then dropped to one knee.

'Well?'

'My lord marshal, he has escaped.'

At this the room erupted, but the marshal put up his hand for calm. 'Thank you John, you have done well. Go now to the kitchens and eat.' He then turned to the man seated next to him. 'So your grace, what now?'

The archbishop thought long and hard. Finally he shrugged. 'We have no choice. We carry on.'

Now another man stepped out from the shadows and the archbishop reluctantly met his eye. 'You know the people of Suffolk, my lord?'

'Indeed I do, your grace. We are old friends.'

The archbishop nodded. 'Then you know what must be done.'

PART ONE
The Crime

Chapter One

BEGINNINGS

On a cold and blustery autumnal afternoon in the year of Our Lord 1214, while war raged and empires were being lost and made, there arrived in our little town of Edmundsbury a seemingly inconsequential party of travellers consisting of a young man, his heavily pregnant wife and a maid. The husband was of sufficient rank to be lodged in the abbey and they were duly allotted rooms adjacent to the abbot's palace. The girl was close to term and a bumpy day in the saddle had its inevitable results with her waters breaking, inconveniently, in the middle of the night. Being the abbey's physician I was summoned shortly before lauds to attend the delivery.

Now, as a monk used to ministering to the needs of seventy other monks my expertise in the science of midwifery is at best rudimentary. What the girl needed was a clutch of nuns fussing about her with pails of hot water and yards of linen, but our nearest Benedictine sisters are twelve miles away at the convent of Saint George in Thetford, and even had they been summoned straight away by fast rider the earliest they could have got here would have been noon of the following day and that would have been far too late. So for better or worse what the lady got was me - with the doubtful aid of my young assistant, Dominic, whose bleary-eyed knowledge of the sacred mysteries of childbirth was even less than mine. Fortunately she did not have to suffer at our hands too much because by the time I managed to haul my protesting limbs out of my cot and get them to the lady's bedside she had done most of the hard work herself and presented me with the product of her night's efforts: to wit, a beautiful pink baby girl with a face like a wrinkled prune and a mouth big enough to swallow a cabbage.

The miracle of new life is always a source of wonder and joy and something that happens all too rarely in a house of irredeemably male servants of God – indeed, to my knowledge it has never happened before in all the twenty-seven years I have been here. More used as I am to lancing boils than severing umbilici, when it comes to babies I admit to a little nervousness. Short of making sure the cord was securely clamped there was little I could do other than wiggle a finger in that cavernous mouth as it protested noisily in my arms. In so doing I was perhaps a little neglectful of the mother who, after all, had had the worst of the night. One thing I do know about giving birth is that it can be a long and arduous affair. I well remember the arrival of my cousin's firstborn. His poor wife had been utterly exhausted after many hours of exertion, at the end of which she looked as though she had simultaneously scaled a mountain and swum a river, drained as she was of energy and drenched in sweat. From what I could see of this young lady however, she seemed quite serene and rested - astonishingly so after her efforts. I could only admire the fortitude which singles out a daughter of the higher ranks of our society.

'How are you feeling, my child?' I said, carefully replacing the babe back in its cot. The proud father standing nervously to one side answered for her:

'She is well, thank you brother, as you can see.'

I nodded. 'Indeed, remarkably so. Please accept my congratulations, sir. May I ask, is this your first child?'

'Yes,' the young man answered curtly.

We stood about in awkward silence while the baby wailed.

'Nothing wrong with her lungs at least,' I chuckled.

'I expect she's hungry.'

I raised my hands in supplication. 'Of course. My apologies. Whatever was I thinking of? We will withdraw and allow you some privacy to, erm…yes indeed. Dominic, what are you standing there gawping for? The door, boy, the door!'

And that was that. Mother and child seemed healthy enough, so I left the couple to their own manifestly adequate devices. In a couple of hours I was due to leave for my home at Ixworth Hall, and with the sun already beginning to lighten the horizon above the abbey walls I promptly forgot all about the young family in the lodge and instead concentrated my mind on my impending expedition into the wilds of Suffolk. It was to be the start of a journey that would take me half way across East Anglia and into the pages of history.

*

Visiting my family home is a prospect I both relish and dread. *Relish* because who does not delight in revisiting the scenes of happy childhood memories? And *dread*, because my mother still lives there. It is in answer to her summons that I have come. My mother is no longer a young woman. Exactly how old she is I have never had the impertinence - or the courage - to ask, but I am in the fiftieth year of my life and she was not in the first blush of hers when she bore me. That makes her very old indeed. She has always been a hearty woman but no-one can put off the imperatives of time for ever, and recently she has been sending word to the abbey that her health is failing and that she wishes to see me. This has been a matter of some embarrassment to me for along with everything else we monks give up when we enter the cloister we are supposed to sever our links with our earthly families, joining as we do instead the Family of Christ. That being said, the Benedictine Rule is not unsympathetic. Occasional contact is still permitted with kinfolk but for this the protocol is quite clear: It is for the family member to visit the monk and not the other way around. But whoever wrote that rule never had to deal with the Lady Isabel. On the pretext of her great age and increasing immobility, she has been badgering the prior to allow me out to visit her and each time he has replied in the negative, insisting instead that she should come to us. But that merely prompted further messages from her, each more urgent than the last, until it became a battle of wills and one which Prior Herbert was determined not to lose. In the end I think he gave in from sheer exhaustion. It seems I am to be allowed to leave the abbey after all - for one night only - and that on the strict condition I am back at the abbey in time for compline the following night. And so it was that I came to be saddling my mule in the abbey courtyard so early on this bleak October morning in readiness for the short ride to Ixworth Hall.

The hall is barely six miles from the abbey by road but a span as wide as the world apart in philosophy. The Lady Isabel does not approve of monks. That is an awkward state of affairs for me and is the reason I say that while I am always pleased to see my mother, as any dutiful son must, I am not entirely regretful of the rule that places limits on the opportunity to do so. Still, I could not help wondering as I ambled my way along the leaf-strewn lanes of Suffolk if this time she might really be as ill as she was making out and if perhaps this visit was indeed to be the Final Reckoning. I should have realised it was nothing of the kind.

'How is your arthritis, mother?'

'Pah! There is nothing wrong with my joints. If faking illness is the only way a mother can get to see her only child then I will hobble on two sticks before that buffoon of a prior. Come, kiss your mother.'

I lightly pecked the proffered cheek and sat down to look at her. She had once been a great beauty – I know, I've seen the portraits. But now she is wizened with a mouth drawn tight with pain and the weariness of living. Dressed these days from head to foot in black she resembled nothing so much as a malevolent old crow.

Oswald, our ancient family retainer, hobbled in carrying two goblets of hot mulled wine on a silver salver. 'You shouldn't be too angry with Prior Herbert,' I said taking mine, 'he has much on his mind at the moment.'

'Ah yes,' she grinned. 'Who is to be the next abbot? Have you monks managed to come to a decision yet or are you still debating? After all, it has only been three years since the last one died.'

I shifted uneasily in my chair at her mocking. 'A name has

been revealed to us,' I replied cautiously, 'by God's grace.'

'Cha!' she snorted. 'By the pope's you mean - Hugh Northwold. But the king doesn't approve.'

'The king...' I said eyeing Oswald hesitantly '...is in need of persuasion.'

'The king is in need of a choice. What you monks gave him was a *fait accompli.*'

I frowned irritably. 'You are remarkably well-informed of abbey business, mother. Do you have spies in the abbey cloister now?'

'I like to keep abreast of events,' she sniffed. 'God knows I've little enough to engage me stuck out here in this wilderness.'

That at least I could appreciate, for, despite appearances, the Dowager Lady Isabel de Ixworth is no simple country widow. Indeed, there was a time when men of learning sought her out to discourse on every subject from religion to mathematics. In her youth she had been determined to pursue an academic life and had even gone to study at the cathedral school of Notre-Dame in Paris for a while when it was still possible for a woman to do so, and there she attained something of a reputation as a scholar. It meant giving up any thoughts of marriage, naturally, since no-one can sully the sanctity of learning with the profanities of married life. Meeting my father put an end to all that. Not because he disapproved of her intellectual aspirations - on the contrary, he found her propensity to question everything a stimulating challenge, even though having a wife cleverer than he would have tried the patience of a lesser man. No, it was matters *domestique* that altered the direction of her life – the eternal female dichotomy. She wanted a family and my father was the first man she had met whom she considered worthy enough to furnish her with one – a decision for which I am understandably grateful. Even so, the mechanics of conception proved to be no simple task and it was not until their fifth year of marriage that I finally made my way into the world. And what a disappointment I turned out to be. She had hoped for another Peter Abelard. What she got was a barely adequate physician and monk. Of my first choice of career Lady Isabel approved, but not the second. She had, after all, rejected for herself the life of a religious contemplative, and now here was her son doing the self-same thing. I don't think she ever quite forgave me for it.

'It's a pity you could not have got yourself nominated to the post.'

I guffawed at the suggestion. 'Me? Abbot of Edmundsbury?'

'Why not? You are as qualified as any.' She frowned and tapped her stick irritably. 'You've no ambition, Walter. That's been your trouble. You'll always be stuck in this backwater physicking to a lot of smelly old bachelors.'

I would hardly call one of Europe's richest abbeys a backwater, but she was being deliberately provocative and I wasn't going to rise to the bait.

'I've plenty of ambition,' I said pushing my legs out in front of me. 'And the welfare of my brother monks is a more than worthwhile calling – a calling, I might add, from God. Besides, the post of abbot is too…political.'

'Politics is the only calling worth having. The great affairs of state, the wars in France, the king…'

I pulled a face and looked pointedly at Oswald. These were dangerous times, and it is never wise to discuss such matters in front of servants, even lifelong retainers.

'Oh, don't mind him,' she said flapping a hand at the man. 'He's as deaf as a post – aren't you Oswald?'

'Yes, my lady.'

Oswald finished banking up the fire and left the room.

'So,' I said when he'd shut the door and we were alone at last. 'Since it isn't my candidacy to be the next Abbot of Edmundsbury, and you are clearly not at death's door, why am I here?'

She leaned toward me. 'You've had some visitors: A young nobleman and his wife.'

My mouth dropped open – an unfortunate habit of mine that happens whenever I am taken by surprise and one I have never been able to conquer. 'How on earth did you know that? They only arrived yesterday.'

She waved away my objection. 'What do you know about them?'

'Not much. The boy is called Raoul, his wife is Adelle and they are from Norfolk. That's all I know.'

She nodded. 'The boy is a de Gray - you know the name, of course.'

'Not unless you mean John de Gray, the Bishop of Norwich.' I looked at her face. 'Oh dear, you do mean Bishop de Gray.'

'Bishop, sometime Justiciar of Ireland, sometime Archbishop of Canterbury - and one of King John's most trusted servants.'

I shrugged. 'So?'

She fixed me with a quizzical eye. 'The girl is pregnant?'

'Not any more,' I smiled, pleased at last to know something she didn't. 'She gave birth to a female child in the early hours of this morning. I know. I delivered it.'

Her eyes widened. 'You were there? At the birth?'

'I was indeed - well, within a minute or two. Don't look so surprised, mother. I am the abbey physician.'

'But the birth - it was normal?'

'Perfectly. A completely normal healthy baby girl, not a finger more nor a toe less than the required number - I counted them all myself. And a very healthy pair of lungs, too,' I added, remembering those wails.

Her frown deepened. 'How did she look? The mother, I mean.'

'Radiant - exceptionally so as a matter of fact.'

Lady Isabel went quiet. Not a good sign. I knew my mother, she was calculating something, the gears of her mind turning like those of a windmill. I could almost hear the cogs connecting.

'Are they still at the abbey?' she asked at last.

'Don't you know? You seem to know everything else.'

She tapped her stick impatiently. 'Just answer the question.'

'I doubt it. They're on their way south. They'll almost certainly be gone by the time I get back.' I yawned. The subject was beginning to bore me.

'Then you must stop them,' she said pushing at my thigh.

'Oh? And how exactly am I supposed to do that?'

'You're a doctor, think of something, some *medical* reason to keep them at the abbey.'

I had no intention of doing any such thing. As far as I knew they had every right to come and go as they pleased, but to say so would only lead to further argument. It would soon blow over and she would forget the matter. And I knew there was no point in asking her *why* she wanted the de Gray family to remain in Bury for she wouldn't have told me – or worse, she'd have made up some lie. For the moment, though, she seemed satisfied.

'Come,' she nodded holding out her hand. 'There's something I want to show you.'

What now? I supported her under the elbow as she hobbled over to the other side of the room. Old people do get fixated. Perhaps she wasn't as well as I'd supposed after all. Perhaps her mind was going. Despite her protestations I knew she suffered with her joints. She had a podagra of the hip - a condition I'd diagnosed long ago and for which I have prescribed many remedies none of which she has ever heeded. It made her slow to get moving especially if she'd been sitting for a while. I could only imagine how long it must take Oswald to get her out of bed in the mornings.

We stopped by a wooden chest that filled half the length of one wall of the room. I knew this chest well. It had been standing in that exact same spot for all of my lifetime and probably most of hers too. Made of sturdy English oak and fixed to the floorboards with six heavy iron screws, it was where my mother kept all her most important items - all the estate accounts, her jewellery, private documents and much more. No-one was ever allowed so much as a glance inside without her say-so. Not that they hadn't tried - tool marks around the locks betrayed signs of attempted entry in the past. But all had failed. I knew also that this was *not* where she kept her most highly prized secrets of all.

She took from her belt a ring of iron keys to undo the three heavy locks on the chest. 'Turn around,' she said to me.

'Why?'

'So that you can't see which key fits which lock, of course. Now don't be tiresome Walter, do as I ask. Turn around and close your eyes.'

I didn't turn around. Instead, I reached over to an obscure object standing in shadow on a shelf just above the oak chest. It was an unattractive and seemingly valueless old crucifix affixed to a plain wooden stand - something that no self-respecting thief would look at twice. Even so it was a holy rood, a representation of Christ's passion on the cross and I kissed my fingers before touching it. Then with a deft twist of the wrist I turned the upright of the cross to the left which produced a click in the stand at the bottom from where a drawer popped out on a spring. Without hesitating, I reached inside the secret compartment and withdrew the contents.

I must say I did enjoy the look of surprise on that shrivelled old face of hers — or as much of it as I could see behind the wimple. She looked like she was chewing a particularly tough piece of gristle.

'If you are going to disparage the one true religion, mummy dear,' I explained in answer to her unspoken question, 'you would do better than to have its symbol so prominently displayed. In this room - with you - it's incongruous. Besides, Joseph and I have known about your secret hiding place ever since we were children. It's where you always hid our presents and where you stored the love letters from my father when he was courting you.'

'They weren't love letters,' she growled. 'They were marital negotiations.'

'They were love letters. I read them.'

'Then you shouldn't have.'

'Then you shouldn't leave them where I can find them.'

She snatched at the item I was holding but not before I'd

taken note what it was. It was a letter made of thick vellum folded much smaller than is normal and heavily embossed with the Ixworth seal. She stood turning it over in her hands for a minute thinking. Then just as suddenly she thrust it back into my hand again.

'Here, take it.'

'What is it?' I said with surprise feeling its thick, luxuriant richness in my fingers.

'Since you're so clever,' she smirked, 'divine it for yourself.'

I shook my head. The parchment was too thick to hazard a guess as to what it contained. It could be anything. There was no point in trying to guess.

'What am I supposed to do with it?'

'You are to deliver it to the new abbot.'

'To Hugh?' I said with astonishment. 'Is that why you've brought me here, to be your messenger?'

'There's no-one else I could trust.' She squinted warily up at me. 'Can I trust you?'

'Clearly not enough to tell me what's in it.'

'Hm,' she grunted, but still she wouldn't be drawn. 'Into Hugh's hands, mind, and no-one else's. Do I have your oath on it?'

'Mother, you astonish me. I -'

She grabbed my arm. 'Your oath. Do I have it?'

I looked at her gnarled face. Something in those old eyes told me she was in earnest. 'You do,' I sighed. 'But its deliverance may have to wait a while. Hugh is not even in the country at the moment.'

'Don't you think I know that? He's with the king in France still trying to persuade him he's the right man to be abbot.' She saw me fingering the seal. 'Oh, don't bother trying to open it. Hugh will know if you do. And more importantly, so will I.'

I reluctantly placed the letter in my belt pouch while she hobbled over to the window and looked out into the gathering dusk. Already the moon was rising, big and full in the night sky illuminating my mother's face with its stark cold light.

'What month is it?'

'October – as you very well know.'

She nodded. 'That's a Hunter's Moon up there – or to give it its old name, the Blood Moon.' She glanced over her shoulder. 'Do you know why they call it that? Because it gives the huntsmen a few more hours of light in order to chase down their quarry. A few more short but vital hours,' she said wistfully, then shook herself. 'The chase has begun. The question is, who will be the hunter and who the hunted? Let us hope we know the answer before too long.'

Chapter Two
ONETHUMB AND THE PRIOR

Blood Moon indeed. I had no idea what my mother was talking about and cared less. Perhaps she was losing her mind after all. But then, she has always delighted in tying me up in these metaphysical knots and watching me struggle to unravel them. Over the years I've learned not to try. Whatever her true purpose in bringing me out to Ixworth I assumed it would become obvious in time. Still, she seemed satisfied with the way our meeting had gone and spoke no more of secret letters. I therefore spent the following morning touring the estate villages and re-acquainting myself with old friends and tenants I had not seen for years until it was time to begin my lonely trudge back to Bury.

My mother's behaviour may seem a little odd but these were strange times. King John had been on the throne for fifteen years and for much of them England had been at war - with France, naturally, but also with the church. The French war was over at last, *Deo gratias*, but John had been forced to return home in disgrace having lost nearly all his overseas possessions and for the first time in nearly a century and a half England was an island nation again. John's humiliation was made all the more painful by the intransigence of his own barons, many of whom had refused to fight or even pay for a war that seemed to them increasingly expensive and irrelevant. This did not bode well for future relations between the king and his courtiers.

There was, however, better news coming from Rome. Pope Innocent had finally lifted the yoke of interdict he'd imposed on the English people six years earlier as punishment for King John's refusal to accept Cardinal Langton as Archbishop of Canterbury, and we were free once again to ring the bells, to say mass aloud and to rebury the bodies of the dead in consecrated ground - including that of our former abbot Samson of Tottington who, despite having died three years earlier, we were only now able to lay to rest in the chapterhouse amid much veneration and tearful thanks. Joyful as that occasion was, Abbot Samson's interment highlighted the other great matter that had been concerning the abbey lately, namely the election of his successor. My mother had unfairly blamed us monks for our vacillation but in truth we had little choice for during the interdict all such elections were prohibited. But with the king once more reconciled with the Holy Father we were permitted to make our selection, and after much prayer and careful consideration Hugh Northwold, the subcellarer, was chosen. Alas, this has not been the end of the matter for King John has so far refused to ratify Hugh's appointment and with half the monks favouring the king's position and half opposed, stalemate has ensued.

The one beacon of light to shine amidst all this gloom concerned my brother Joseph. Joseph and I are not really true brothers; we just call ourselves that having grown up together in my father's house. Both our fathers had been medics during the wars in the Holy Land, albeit on opposite sides, and when the wars ended they returned to England together to carry on with their work. Joseph and I were born in that house, Joseph first and me three years later. We both inherited our fathers' enthusiasms for healing the sick but whereas I went to the best medical schools in Europe Joseph had to be content with opening an apothecary shop in Bury town. With an Arab father and Jewish mother he could not practice the mystic arts of the physician since his heathen prayers, so vital an ingredient in the healing process, would naturally be useless. Happily though, his apothecary business has flourished - so much so that when he asked for my help in finding him an assistant I had no hesitation in recommending my old friend Onethumb.

What Onethumb's birth-name was no-one has ever discovered or even whether he ever had one. His nickname was given him when he was a child living – or rather *surviving* – on the streets of Bury, for in addition to being mute he was also born with a deformed right hand which has a normal thumb but four pea-sized stumps in place of fingers. Despite these handicaps Onethumb manages all the skills necessary to the apothecary trade, so much so that Joseph now swears he cannot do without him. Indeed, it is largely because Onethumb is so very good at his job that I see so little of my brother. I no longer have to visit Joseph's shop in order to replenish my stock of oils and potions for by the time I've noticed that I require them Onethumb has anticipated my need and appears as if by magic at the door of my Laboratorium with the items already measured and invoiced. And that was where I found him when I returned from Ixworth that evening. With everything else that had been happening I'd completely forgotten that I'd arranged to meet him, a dereliction that I realised as soon as I saw him waiting patiently in the gathering gloom.

'What hey, Onethumb!' I greeted him heartily and pointed to the bundle lying next to him. 'My goodness, what have we here? Half my brother's stock by the look of it. Did we, erm, agree that you should bring it tonight?'

The question was rhetorical of course, for being mute Onethumb couldn't reply; but his features, mobile and expressive as ever, were eloquence itself. He was not taken in by my false bonhomie.

'Yes, you're quite right,' I nodded humbly. 'I have no excuse. I admit it, I forgot you were coming. My apologies, my friend, for keeping you waiting.'

I could have blamed my mother for my lapse of memory, I suppose, but that would have been unworthy. Besides, I knew well enough how to soothe Onethumb's temper.

'Tell me,' I beamed at him, 'how are the lovely Rosabel and little Hal? Still beautiful and thriving I trust?'

At the mention of his wife and son Onethumb's frown instantly evaporated and his face split into a shy grin as I knew it would. But it faltered a moment later as he looked over my shoulder and cocked a warning eyebrow. I turned to see in the gathering twilight another figure gliding silently towards us across the expanse of the Great Court like a hawk falling upon its prey. Prior Herbert, his beaky nose twitching with disapproval, was the first to speak and from his tone I could tell his mood was not placatory:

'Brother Walter, there you are.'

'Indeed I am, Brother Prior,' I smiled affably.

He tutted disapprovingly. 'Do you know the time? It is past compline. Did we not agree when we allowed your visit to your mother it was on the understanding that you would be back by now?'

I shrugged. 'But I am back by now.'

'I meant back in time *for* compline brother, not *after*. We were fearful that something might have happened to you.'

I shrugged again. 'What could have happened?'

'Well that's just it, we don't know, do we? And that is the danger of allowing these…excursions.'

Oh dear. I could see he was still smarting over losing his fight with my mother. If only the Lady Isabel realised the havoc she left in the wake of some of her battles.

Prior Herbert continued with his peroration: 'Do you not realise that we monks are innocents in a wicked world, brother. Within these walls we are, so to speak, oysters secure in our shells. Out there…' and he encompassed half the town in the sweep of his arm '…are many predators waiting to gobble us up.'

'Crabs, Brother Prior?'

Behind me I heard Onethumb snigger.

'I speak of the Devil, brother. The Great Tempter assumes many guises – as the wolf prowls at the edge of the camp, or even in the smile of a pretty girl. That is why I resisted your mother's request in the first instance. You must see now that I was right to do so however imploring her entreaties.'

Imploring? My mother? I think not. But I knew where this was leading:

'Rules, brother, are not made from caprice. It is rules that keep us safe. Far greater minds than ours have devised them and we disregard them at our peril.' He cleared his throat. 'Take, for instance, the Rule of Silence.'

Oh dear. This was one of Herbert's favourite topics but I was in no mood to be lectured to tonight. It was late and I was tired after my journey and Onethumb needed to get home to his family. But Herbert would not be deterred. And I suppose in essence he was right for the bedrock of a monk's life is indeed the list of rules devised by the founder of our order, Benedict of Nursia. But Benedict never meant his rules to be rigid, merely suggestions to be modified as circumstances demanded. What may be sensible in the dry heat of Italy did not necessarily apply to the cold damp of a Suffolk fen. But that argument, I knew, would not wash with Herbert. As far as he was concerned a rule is a rule, unbreakable and immutable. Not for the first time I lamented the passing of Abbot Samson. For all his faults he would not have been so pedantic. It indicated a petty mind and why *Prior* Herbert would never be *Abbot* Herbert.

He peered hard at Onethumb. 'I believe I heard you greet this man just now.'

'Of course. He is a friend of mine.'

'Yes,' Herbert frowned painfully, 'but *out loud*, brother. Was it really necessary? A simple raising of the hand would have sufficed. Like this.' He lifted his own hand to demonstrate what he meant.

'It's night, Brother Prior. I didn't think Onethumb would see me if I'd simply flapped my hand at him.'

'Then you adapt the movement to the prevailing conditions,' persisted Herbert. 'Watch again.'

This time he brought his hand up with much exaggerated aplomb and then repeated the gesture a third time just to be sure I had caught it. Resignedly, I copied the movement to Onethumb who in turn copied it back to Herbert. Unfortunately Onethumb used his mizzened hand whose single upturned digit gave the gesture a somewhat different meaning to the one Herbert had intended.

Herbert squinted suspiciously at Onethumb. 'Yes, well I think I've made my point. Meaning can be conveyed without the need for the spoken word – provided, of course,' he added spitefully, 'one is fully equipped with the tools that God intended.'

That was unfair. Onethumb couldn't help his malformation. Now it was my turn to bristle.

'Perhaps the meaning behind the gesture is more important than the gesture itself, brother,' I said haughtily. 'Or else it may be open to misinterpretation.'

'My point entirely,' agreed Herbert. 'The voice conveys far more complexity with its inflexions, tones...*etcetera*...while a hand gesture, clearly given, is eloquent in its simplicity.'

I was growing more and more tired of this nonsense and drew breath to defend Onethumb. But I had no need, for Onethumb was more than capable of answering for himself and now he did just that with a breathtaking extemporization of rapid speed-signing that went on for several seconds. Being dumb from birth, Onethumb had no option but to sign if he wished to communicate at all - a skill he mastered long ago with his characteristic thoroughness and has even attempted to teach me a little of it. His needs being far more extensive than merely to ask for the salt to be passed or to be excused to visit the necessarium, his "vocabulary" is far more extensive than anything we monks have devised. And since Onethumb's language of signing is entirely his own invention, Herbert understood not one word of it.

'What's he saying?' frowned Herbert alarmed by Onethumb's violent arm movements.

I couldn't follow them completely either, but the signs for "pig" and "arse" were in there somewhere.

'He asks if we may conclude our business soon as it is late and he has to get home in time for curfew,' I interpreted loosely.

Prior Herbert nodded. 'Quite so. Well, I think I've made my point. Do try to remember it - and to be on time in future, brother. That's all I ask.'

With that he swooped off again into the darkness. It seemed not to have occurred to Herbert that nothing of the sense of his lecture could have been conveyed using mime alone, nor that the only person who might have been able to do so was Onethumb.

If I sound less than courteous towards Prior Herbert then I am sorry. He is, after all, the most senior member of the abbey, at least until a new abbot is enthroned, and as such I owe him deference and a duty of obedience. But the truth is I don't much like the man. He was forced upon us by Abbot Samson as one of his last and uncharacteristically misguided decisions. Put it down to an old man's fancy. But I thought at the time it was a wrong decision and I was not alone in that opinion. To put it bluntly, Herbert is a schemer. Take this business over the election of Hugh as abbot. Half the monks are in favour and half against – there are honourable arguments for both points of view. But Herbert wishes to keep a foot in both camps hoping to jump to the winning side once he's worked out which it is. That's no way for the spiritual leader of our community to behave. We need firm leadership even if occasionally it is wrong. It is yet one more reason why we need to resolve the question of the new abbot as quickly as possible.

I turned back to see the smirk on Onethumb's face and wagged an admonishing finger at him.

'I understood your mime, my young friend,' I said sternly, 'don't think I didn't. Prior Herbert is a very important man. You should show him more respect.'

Onethumb cocked a sceptical eyebrow as if to say "like you?".

'Yes well, enough of Prior Herbert. We never finished our conversation. You were telling me about lovely Rosabel and the little fellow. Both are well I trust?'

Well enough, he signed, and mimed rocking the baby in his arms. His mime was excellent and I could almost believe that he had a real child in his arms. It reminded me of that other babe born only yesterday and its mother just a few yards away across the Great Court in the abbey lodge. I told Onethumb about them including my own part in bringing the little girl into the world. But his reaction was not at all what I expected. Instead of rejoicing with me at the miracle of new life, Onethumb frowned and shook his head.

'What's this?' I chided him. 'Not jealous, surely? That's not like you.'

At first he merely shook his head, but pressured by me he pursed his lips then started to sign again, slowly now so that I could follow him. It seemed it was the father, Raoul, who was concerning him. I was surprised that Onethumb knew of him and asked him to elaborate. He did so. He'd seen him, it seemed, in the town taverns.

I laughed with relief. 'Is that all? I expect he was celebrating his good fortune at becoming a father. Surely you do not begrudge him that? This child is his first-born. Celebration is natural, is it not? You were the same when Hal was born, don't pretend you weren't. I well remember the dancing - and the drinking.'

Onethumb merely shrugged, but if I am honest I'm not sure I was entirely convinced by my dismissal either. There was some mystery over this family – my mother's unusually keen interest in them for one thing. On the surface all seemed perfectly normal – a young couple arrives in a town on a donkey, the wife heavily pregnant. Her waters break after the arduous journey and overnight a child is born. What could be more natural? Indeed, there are precedents. I'm quite sure that had the shepherds and the wise men not visited the Holy Stable when they did Joseph would have been off to the taverns of Bethlehem to wet his baby's head – a more justified occasion for celebration could hardly be imagined.

But I am being flippant. There were other similarities between this birth and that of the infant Christ of a more disturbing nature. Others knew of that event, too, people who did not wish to celebrate it but had murder in mind. Not wishing to take the analogy too far, I did wonder why this couple had crept into town unheralded with no baggage to speak of and no help other than that of a single maid. Why travel at all when the girl was so far advanced in her term? Unless like the Holy Family they too had a special reason for doing so.

Chapter Three
EE-MA-MUM-MA

The key to a monk's life is repetition. Each day is like the one before which is like the one before that, each with its regular round of devotion, prayer and study, always constant, never wavering until that special day dawns when Christ will come again in glory and that will be the end of time. In the course of this journey a monk forswears the world of Man with its trifling concerns, seeking instead those higher rewards that come from growing daily ever closer to God.

So why then am I so bothered by what happens to this family which is lodged in the abbot's palace? They will be gone in a day or two and I will be able to return to my life of utter predictability with only the occasional gumboil or cracked thumbnail to tax my increasingly atrophying brain. The reason is my mother. Like a worm she has burrowed into the soft flesh of my imagination and planted there the seed of doubt. Yesterday the de Grays were an object of mild curiosity; today they are one of intense intrigue. Even so, I was determined to resist getting involved partly because I had better things to do but also in order to prove that she does not pull my strings like the fairground puppet she thinks I am.

What changed my mind was that comment of Onethumb, for if Raoul de Gray truly has been carousing about the town at night then that would mean the Lady Adelle has been left alone and unattended and that cannot be good for a young mother and her newborn babe. As abbey physician both are nominally in my care whilst here and I do feel a certain proprietary responsibility having been midwife, as it were, to the birth. And then of course there is curiosity, plain and simple. I admit it, I am naturally nosey. The problem is that I have no real reason to visit them again. Childbirth is not an illness. In all probability mother and baby are perfectly healthy and in no further need of my services. But it wouldn't do any harm just to pop my head round the door just to satisfy myself that all is well - and in so doing I might just learn what has got my mother so interested in them.

Before I did, however, I thought I'd just clear it with our guest-master since all who stay at the abbey are ultimately his concern. The current holder of that office, Brother Gregor, is a Scotsman who takes the role rather seriously. Exceptionally so. He is also one of Prior Herbert's appointees and shares his master's appetite for rules and their adherence. Yes, better get him on board first so as not to tread on too many toes. I managed to catch up with him next morning immediately after terce.

'Good morning, Brother Guest-master,' I hailed him heartily. 'How are you today, and how fare our guests?'

Gregor was just leaving the lodge where the de Gray family were staying but stopped abruptly in the doorway blocking my entry and squinting short-sightedly at me.

'Master Walter,' he replied in his soft Caledonian brogue. He glanced over his shoulder. 'It is the young couple anon with the wee babby you'll be referring to, I take it?'

'Do we have any other guests?' I beamed.

'Aye, we do. Two young roustabouts arrived late last night. I put them in the loft above the stables where they can disturb no-one else.'

'Rowdy pair, are they?'

He made a snorting noise in his nose and muttered some Gaelic invective. 'Out till all hours and then hammering on the gates demanding to be let in. If they weren't pilgrims on their way to visit the shrine of Our Lady of Walsingham I'd've shown 'em the toe of m'boot. And I'm sorry to say, yon young man was with them.'

I looked up. 'You mean Raoul de Gray? He was out in the town as well?'

'Aye, he was.'

So, Onethumb had been right. A worrying state of affairs considering his wife's condition.

'What of the Lady Adelle?'

Gregor's thin lips widened into something approximating a smile. 'Ah now, she was quite a different kettle of fish. A very quiet, very *respectable* young lady I'd say, not at all like her husband. And,' he added pointedly, 'no doubt not wishing to be disturbed.'

'By two roustabouts on their way to Walsingham?' I suggested with a grin.

He leaned towards me. 'By anyone.'

'Oh, quite so, quite so,' I frowned and nodded. 'I thought as much myself the other night.'

Gregor looked uncertain. 'You've met the wee couple?'

I nodded. 'I delivered the baby. A healthy bonny wee girl,' I chortled mimicking his accent. 'Or so she seemed. Mind you, you can never tell with children, can you? They're prone to so many ailments.' I frowned, took out my vademecum that I keep hanging from my belt and fingered it absent-mindedly.

Gregor glanced at the intimidating array of charts and diagrams in my hand. 'The bairn seemed well enough to me just now,' he said suspiciously.

'Oh, to be sure. But they always do, don't they? To begin with. And then we turn our backs for a minute and – *poff*!'

'*Poff*?' frowned Gregor.

I nodded seriously. 'I don't envy you the responsibility, I must say - especially the daughter of such an important family. You know that Raoul is the nephew of the Bishop of Norwich? That would make Bishop John...let me see...the baby's uncle - no tell a lie, her *great* uncle. Assuming she lives, of course.'

'Aye, I suppose it would,' agreed Gregor worriedly. His frown deepened and he bit his lip in thought.

I squinted up at the window. 'Well, I'll get up there while things are quiet,' I said taking a step forward. Gregor hesitated for an instant but then relented stepping reluctantly to one side and leaving the slightest of gaps between him and the door-jamb for me to squeeze though. I managed to get past with difficulty and was up the stairs before he could object, but as I approached the de Grays' bedchamber I still had no idea what I was going to say to the lady inside or how to explain my visit. For inspiration I said a silent prayer to Saint Margaret of Antioch, the patron of women in childbirth - and another to Saint Jude, the patron of hopeless causes - before letting my knuckles fall tentatively upon the door.

It opened at the first knock and before me stood a creature I certainly had not expected to see: A young girl dressed in servants' attire. For a moment her appearance threw me but then I remembered the couple had arrived in the town with their own maid. This must be she. I had not seen her the night of her mistress's labour - presumably off somewhere organizing the abbey servants. A not unpretty girl, I thought, if a bit young and she did look rather pale and drawn. With just her to provide for all the wants of her mistress and her husband *and* cope with the new baby, I was not surprised she looked tired. I gave her my most avuncular of smiles:

'Good day to you, my child. Is your mistress awake? I know the hour is early but I...erm...oh...!'

I got no further with my speech before the girl pulled me inside and quickly shut the door behind me. Startled, I turned to admonish her for her forwardness but she had already disappeared back into the shadows. Indeed, I couldn't see very much at all with the shutters being closed, but a movement to my right caught my eye. As it adjusted to the gloom I could just make out the bed with the Lady Adelle lying upon it and the baby asleep in her arms. There was no sign of the husband, I noted with regret - presumably not yet returned from his revels. Sometimes I despair of the youth of our country. Here was the man's wife, fragrant, young, delicate, newly delivered of her first child and yet left entirely to her own devices in a strange town with only this slip of a maid for protection while the husband goes off to revel in the town with other young fustians - and no doubt bragging about his achievements as a father into the bargain. I took a tentative step closer to the bed but to avoid any suspicion of impropriety I maintained a respectable distance.

'Forgive the intrusion, madam,' I began, but once again my words cut short as the lady placed a warning finger to her lips.

'Ah, I see now,' I said lowering my voice. 'The baby is asleep. Of course - I should have realised. All is well with her, yes? No colic or indigestion? She suckles well?'

Inwardly I cringed at my own clumsiness and began again on a less delicate tack:

'May I ask - have you decided on a name yet?'

'Alix.'

'Alix,' I beamed delightedly. 'A charming name, charming – and one, if I'm not mistaken, that our dear late Queen gave to one of her own daughters - by the King of France, I hasten to add. Not that that would have been the reason for your choosing it, I am sure, aha...' My voice faded away. I was beginning to sound ridiculous to my own ears. 'A family name was it - Alix?' I blundered on. 'Your mother's perhaps? Of course she will have to be churched before you go, but that can wait a day or two yet.'

I prattled on in this nonsensical fashion not really knowing what I was saying while my eyes roamed round the room searching for anything unusual. But nothing caught my eye. All seemed perfectly normal. But then there was a sudden rush of air as the door behind me opened again and before I knew it I was flat on my back on the floor with Raoul de Gray on top of me and a dagger at my throat. It was as if the Devil himself had entered the room. I yelped which caused the maid to scream which in turn awoke the baby who started to wail. Suddenly all was bedlam.

'I have him!' barked Raoul de Gray at his wife. 'Are you all right?'

'Of course she's all right,' I choked back. 'It's me, Brother Walter. Get off me you oaf!'

We grappled for a few moments more with his arm round my neck, his weight on my chest and that knife perilously close to my nose. He stank of ale which probably explained his behaviour. But through his drunken haze he did seem at last to recognize me.

'You?' he frowned.

'Yes me!'

'What do you want?'

'If you'll let me up I'll tell you.'

'Tell me now.'

I tried to push him off but he was too strong. I gave in. 'I was concerned for the welfare of your wife and your daughter,' I said and added pointedly, 'who you seem to have abandoned.'

He frowned looking about him. 'Effie. Where's Effie?'

'You think it sufficient to leave your wife in the care of a mere child?'

'Yes – *no*.'

'Oh, for goodness sake, will you let me rise?'

At last he came to his senses and released me. 'I'm sorry, brother. I thought you were... I'm sorry. Here.' He put out his hand to help me up.

I pushed his arm away. 'You thought I was what? A murderer?

Most ridiculous thing I've ever heard of!'

I got up by myself and dusted myself down feeling as I did so a sharp pain in my shoulder where he collided with me. He was frowning, evidently still trying to make sense of what had happened – alcohol no doubt dulling his already dull brain.

'You came to see Adelle?'

'Yes.'

'And the baby.'

'Of course. What else?'

'I see,' he nodded. 'Well, I'm here now, so there's no need for you to stay.'

'That, I think, is for your wife to say young man.'

I looked expectantly at Adelle but to my dismay she seemed to acquiesce in her husband's boorishness. In fact she seemed quite unperturbed by his behaviour – doubtless used to it. But he was right; there was no longer any need for my presence. Mother and baby were self-evidently well and to satisfy myself of which was my reason for coming – ostensibly at least.

'I'm sorry if I hurt you, brother.'

Raoul went to the door and opened it for me to leave. But I hadn't quite finished with him yet.

'Is that all the apology I get? Rest assured, sir, I shall be reporting all I have seen here today.'

Bold words, but what would I report? That Raoul had been in the taverns, yes - but he had returned to find an uninvited guest in his wife's bedchamber and proceeded to defend her honour. That was how it would appear. And I could just imagine Prior Herbert's reaction. No, perhaps I had better leave now before any worse harm was done – to me as much as to anyone. But what of the other thing? At the door I took one last look round.

There was nothing here. Whatever it was that had inspired my mother's concern about these people was invisible to me. I was going to have to leave knowing no more than I did when I arrived.

But then something did catch my eye. In the commotion I hadn't really taken much notice of the maid. Her initial behaviour when I arrived had been a bit odd and now that I could see her more clearly she still looked troubled – shock from the violence of a few moments ago perhaps? Her eyes seemed transfixed upon the mother and not in that adoring way of women presented with a newborn baby, but with an intensity that frankly made me uncomfortable.

'Are you all right, child?' I said to her laying a hand on her shoulder.

At my touch she jumped and turned to face me seeming to see me fully for the first time. I smiled encouragingly and thought she was about to speak but at that moment the baby cried and drew her attention away again. She clammed her mouth shut. I sensed something was wrong but had no idea what. I would have liked to quiz her more but Raoul was already pushing me out the door and a moment later I found myself out in the passageway with the door firmly shut in my face.

Frustrated and confused, I stood on the landing outside the door fuming for a few moments trying to decide whether to knock again. I wanted to go back inside and demand to know their secret for I was sure now that they had one. Whatever my mother's other failings she was no fool. If she took this much interest in something it was for a reason, and after that little performance I was inclined to agree with her. The problem was

I knew not what questions to ask or even if I had the right to ask them. I stood staring at that closed door. It was no good. Reluctantly I started to descend the stairs.

But maybe all was not yet quite lost for as I got to the bottom I heard footsteps behind me and I turned to see Effie rapidly descending the stairs after me:

'Effie, my child,' I said stepping smartly back to meet her. 'Thank God! What is it? What's wrong?'

She was out of breath from her effort and took a moment to recover. 'Brother...please...I must tell you...'

'Yes yes,' I encouraged with growing excitement. 'I'm listening. Take your time.'

I waited for her to catch her breath, but before she had a chance a voice echoed down the stone stairwell:

'Effie, what are you doing?'

The girl caught her breath and drew back into a corner.

'Effie please!' I whispered but she just shook her head, too petrified to speak as Raoul descended to our level still drunk but dangerous.

Thinking quickly, I tried to make light of the moment. 'Why thank you my child,' I said taking a small crucifix from my robe and holding it aloft for Raoul to see. 'I must have dropped it in the scuffle. Thank you for returning it to me - aha.'

A weak excuse that fooled no-one, least of all Raoul. He gave a drunken lopsided smile and put his hand on the girl's elbow. She flinched at his touch and I knew then as I knew nothing else that he would beat the girl as soon as they were behind closed doors again.

'Effie,' I begged, 'if there's something you want to tell me, say it now,' but, terrified, she just shook her head. She had clammed up tight again just as she had in the bedchamber.

'Very well,' I said through gritted teeth, 'but I will be looking out for you. Mark me well, I am a doctor and know my art. I will know if you are...harmed in any way.' This last I said looking directly at Raoul.

'Harmed?' he sneered. 'Why should she be harmed? Come along, Effie,' he took her by the elbow. 'Your mistress awaits you.'

He started to pull her gently but firmly towards him and she went, albeit unwillingly, with him. I could do nothing to help her. I had to step aside and watch them slowly ascend the stairs.

But before she finally went up Effie turned and mouthed something at me. She did it quickly and only the once before disappearing from view, but the memory of it was seared into my brain. I caught my breath and watched them slowly ascend the stairs away from me as I tried to force the girl's mime into recognisable words. But they made no sense. What I thought she said...that is to say, what it *looked* like she said was...

Ee-ma-mum-ma.

I mouthed the phrase several times to myself:

'Ee-ma-mum-ma, Ee-ma-mum-ma.'

No, I could make nothing intelligent of it. I wanted to run up the stairs and ask her to repeat it out loud but I knew that would probably end with her getting an even more severe beating from her bullying master than I was sure she was about to get. But I could tell from the look of urgency on her face it meant something to her, and whatever that something was, she desperately wanted me to know it.

Chapter Four
A NOSEBLEED

Ee-ma-mum-ma. What did it mean? I found myself muttering the phrase over and over to myself. It clearly meant something to Effie, something important enough to risk her master's displeasure in order to tell me. But for the life of me I could not make out what it meant.

Ee-ma-mum-ma.

Maybe I was saying it wrong. Maybe if I tried a different emphasis the meaning would leap out at me. I tried again out loud:

'*EE*-ma-mum-ma. Ee-ma-*MUM*-ma. Ee-*MA*-mum-ma. Ee-ma-mum-*MA*...'

'Are you all right, brother?'

'Ma...ha...Eh? What?'

I spun round to find Prior Herbert standing behind me with a curious look on his face.

'Herbert. You frightened me near to death,' I said holding my hand over my heart.

'Well, we certainly wouldn't want that, would we?' he smirked. 'I was merely asking if you were well. You seem a little...distracted.'

'Thinking, brother, that's all - I was thinking.'

He shook his head. 'No brother, you were *talking* - to yourself this time.' He sighed. 'It seems you cannot hold your tongue even when alone. Well I'm glad to have caught you. I wanted to make sure you'll be at Chapter this morning.'

'Is there any reason why I should not be?' I said recovering myself.

'No no,' he smiled. 'I just wanted to be sure, that's all. Until later then.' And with that he was gone again.

I didn't like that smile. Whenever Herbert was pleased with himself it usually meant bad tidings for someone else. What was he up to? And why did he want to know if I'd be in Chapter today? I was always there unless I had a pressing need to be somewhere else - a patient requiring my urgent attention. Besides, Chapter was something most monks would wish to attend since it is the one time of the day when we all come together to discuss the important business of the abbey. The rest of the time we are dispersed about our duties. Chapter is also the time when disciplinary matters are dealt with, which can on occasion be...I won't say *entertaining*, but certainly *distracting*. Closer to heaven than the common herd we may be, but monks are still men, and since only God is perfect it is inevitable that even the most saintly among us errs on occasion. It is therefore a central tenet of our calling that we correct our transgressions if we are to progress along that spiritual journey of which I have already spoken. For 'if the Devil tempted Christ in the desert, what man is there that will not be tempted?' Or so wrote Cesarius of Heisterbach.

Anyway, the point is that Chapter is our one opportunity for us monks to own up to our faults in a spirit of true humility and that in the full scrutiny of our brother monks. This is necessary for occasionally we are not even aware that we have sinned. And where this is the case, or if we deny or refuse to self-accuse, someone else can usually be found to do it for us. We are reminded that this is done not from spite but out of compassion and as such we are not to bear a grudge against our accuser who, as it were, like the razor of God shaves us of the unsightly hair of sin. Of course, this gives plenty of scope for vexatious allegation - although no-one would suggest that a brother monk could be capable of such base motive. In any event, this was of little concern to me for I had not, so far as I was aware, been guilty of any wrongdoing recently that would attract the censure of my brother monks. I therefore went into Chapter with a cheerful heart and a clear conscience.

Prior Herbert opened the session with the usual prayer of supplication:

'The Peace of the Lord be with you and may He give His blessings on these our solemn deliberations.'

We rejoined with a resounding 'Amen', all seventy monks in unison, and sat down on the stone benches that line the walls of the chapterhouse to hear the day's business. When all were settled Brother Michael read the daily chapter from the Rule of Saint Benedict which today was Chapter 53 – appropriately enough in light of our visitors from Norfolk, viz: *Let all guests who arrive be received as Christ, because He will say: 'I was a stranger and you took Me in'*. Brother Michael then sat down and Prior

A NOSEBLEED

Herbert rose to address us.

First, he related more of the details of the war in France and the distressing news of the defeat of King John's allies in Flanders. Prior Herbert did not linger over this for too long except to extend the hope that now that the King was back on English soil he might at last find time to devote to specifically English matters – by which we all understood he meant Hugh Northwold's bid to be our new abbot. But for once, mercifully, even that matter was allowed to rest there rather than to rehearse the arguments yet again with all the usual acrimonious disagreements between the brothers. I presumed the reason for this self-restraint was out of courtesy for the stranger in our midst whom I'd already noted sitting at the front of the room when we filed in - a tall, rather sickly young man not above twenty summers, thin and pale of complexion. This man Prior Herbert now brought forward to present to us.

'Brothers, I would ask you to welcome today into our midst Brother Eusebius.' He extended his hand towards the young man who stood up for our inspection.

Herbert then continued: 'Brother Eusebius is a member of the Priory Church of the Holy Cross and Blessed Virgin at Shouldham in our neighbouring county of Norfolk. As many of you know, the canons of Shouldham are not Benedictines like us but follow instead the Rule of Saint Augustine of Hippo – hence his rather exotic attire.'

Herbert was referring to the young man's tunic of black wool which was unusual, covered as it was in a white cloak and hood and therefore quite different from our own robe of plain black wool. Herbert's comment was meant as a light-hearted jest designed no doubt to put the stranger at his ease, and we duly responded with polite laughter.

Herbert then concluded his introduction: 'Brother Eusebius will be staying with us for a while and I hope you will welcome him into our family in the usual way.'

At this there was a general murmur of agreement among my brothers and many went up to the stranger with 'smiles and tears of joy in their eyes' as befitted such a welcome.

I should just mention here that there is nothing unusual in having a guest religious from another order come to stay at the abbey. Monks often spend time away from their own houses and for a variety of reasons: for study or reflection, or simply to give the man a break from his normal routine. The monastic life, though rewarding in so many ways, is not an easy one. Some men, especially the young, find the discipline difficult. It is often the first time in their lives that they have been away from their families and homes. And however welcoming we may be, a house composed entirely of men with no female around to soften the corners of our harsh masculinity can be very intimidating, especially for a boy brought up at his mother's side.

There can, however, be a very different reason for such a visitation to Saint Edmunds. We are occasionally asked to host men whose behaviour has been, shall we say, *problematic*. Far from being intimidated by their new lives, such men are themselves disruptive to it. I speak here of those who are lucky - or perhaps unlucky - enough to have been granted visions that are denied to the rest of us. Often these sensitive souls - *Euphorics* as they are called - are apt to behave in ways not entirely conducive to communal living. They may, for instance, cry out to God at inappropriate moments – during the singing of the office, say, or at night. Small communities of a dozen or so men find it difficult to accommodate such unsettling behaviour and the monk concerned is sent away to a larger house such as ours which has the space and numbers to absorb such unsettling behaviour without restraining it. Of course, the cause of such disruption may be nothing to do with spiritual sensitivity but something else entirely. I well remember the unfortunate incident a year or two back when Gaspard, our pet billy-goat which used to have free range of the cloister, one night got into the dormitory while the monks were asleep. What with the late hour when the mind is at its most susceptible, one or two of our more sensitive brethren reacted badly to the invasion. To be fair, it was the height of the Interdict when nerves were already frayed and we were feeling somewhat cast adrift in a Godless world. In the terror of the midnight hour when all manner of evil stalks the land, they glimpsed the horns and the cloven feet, felt Gaspard's beard and hot breath on their cheeks and came to the inevitable conclusion. The eviscerated remains of poor Gaspard were discovered next morning strewn across the cloister garth. To this day some of my brothers still maintain that the Devil was vanquished that night.

That being said, there are genuine religious sensitives and such men are to be venerated and cosseted. Often a period away from their own houses and the guide of a sympathetic chaplain will still their troubled minds and give them the strength to return to their communities refreshed and repaired in body and soul. If not then they may decide to move on, perhaps to a different order or possibly out of the cloister altogether. I wondered if this young man was one such.

The business of the day concluded we awaited the Verba mea

which marked the end of Chapter and we could all return to our daily tasks. But then Prior Herbert held up his hand once more for silence.

'Brothers, before we disperse there is the small matter of our customary discipline at this hour.'

Oh dear, I'd feared as much. That smirk on Herbert's face when we spoke earlier - someone was for it.

Herbert recited the usual formula: 'He who is in error having grievously sinned against God and Saint Edmund step forward and receive due punishment according to the tenets of our order.'

We waited. No-one moved.

Herbert continued: 'He who has knowingly sinned should freely admit his fault now - or be exposed by others.'

Still no-one moved.

Herbert clearly had someone in his sights and I pitied the poor fellow. Whoever he was he must be hoping that another will step into the breach - there's usually someone who will volunteer. Brother Mathias, for instance, was forever admitting to the most trifling foibles. Last week he accused himself of not chewing his food the required fifty times. But not to today, it seemed. We waited on, the tension becoming oppressive. I leaned forward a little in my seat and glanced surreptitiously along the line of brothers to see if anyone either side of me was about to rise, but no-one seemed to be. I leaned back again.

'Very well,' said Herbert at last, 'then I must name him myself.' And then I heard the words that every monk dreads: 'Master Walter de Ixworth, step forward please.'

My jaw fell open. Me? Surely there was some mistake. I looked around the house but every eye was avoiding mine. No, it seemed I had not misheard. It was me all right. But what had I done? My mind raced but I could think of nothing.

'Master Walter – if you please,' said Herbert again, more forcefully this time and fixed me with his eye.

Involuntarily I felt myself begin to rise desperately trying to think and slowly made my way to the front where Prior Herbert was waiting with the expression on his face hovering between sadness and satisfaction.

'Brother Walter de Ixworth,' he intoned loud enough for the furthest and deafest among us to hear, 'confess your sin before your brothers, receive your due punishment and beg forgiveness of our lord God who knows all that is in our hearts.'

God may well know it, but I did not. My lips moved but no sensible sound emerged.

Herbert leaned forward and whispered in my ear, 'Tongue-tied at last, brother?'

No, surely that wasn't it? Not the business in the courtyard with Onethumb? That minor infringement didn't deserve the punishment it appeared I was about to receive for I now saw behind Herbert's chair the bundle of willow rods used to beat transgressors. That particular penalty is usually reserved only for serious offences such as fighting, murder or sodomy. But it seemed Herbert was determined to use it on me. From the expression on his face I'd almost say he was enjoying the prospect.

'Kneel brother if you please, and remove your robe.' He signalled to the subprior to hand him the rods.

Still confused and in a state of shock, I obeyed pulling my habit over my head so that I was dressed now only in my shift and braies. I thanked God it was not summer or I might well be completely naked before my fellows. I knew what I was supposed to do next: Confess the sin for which I was indicted. But confess to what?

'Brother Prior,' I announced at last. 'I do freely confess that I am a woeful sinner and humbly beg forgiveness,' and then added quietly, 'if you could just remind me what exactly it is I have done?'

Herbert exploded with fury. He swished the rods through the air several times to flex his wrist thus making a pleasant, if unnerving, whistling sound as they passed my ear.

'Brother, you compound one transgression with another,' spat Herbert. 'You know your sin. Contrition should be your watchword now. *Contrition.*'

'Oh I am contrite, brother,' I agreed. 'Erm - perhaps if I knew the name of my accuser I might better repent the sin?'

'*I* accuse you, brother,' he growled.

'For speaking out loud?'

Herbert snorted with contempt. 'No, not for speaking out loud, brother. For consorting with a woman, the Lady Adelle de Gray.'

His voice rose as he spoke these last words eliciting a few genuine gasps of horror from my brother monks. Put like that I suppose it did sound shocking. It is absolutely the worst crime in the calendar for a monk to have any dealings with a woman within the bounds of the abbey. In this case there were mitigating circumstances which given the chance I might have been able to explain. But it didn't look as though I was going to get the chance.

'Do you deny it brother? Before you answer I warn you, there is a witness.'

A NOSEBLEED

A witness? Ah yes: Brother Gregor. No doubt he would have gone straight to Herbert with the news.

'I don't deny that I visited the lady,' I began awkwardly, 'but -'

'You hear that, brothers? Brother Walter does not deny visiting the woman alone in her bedchamber while her husband was absent,' interrupted Herbert.

More murmurings of disapproval. Herbert was clearly savouring every moment. I couldn't help thinking he had been looking for a reason to do this ever since he lost his battle with my mother. This was his way of paying her back. Well, he was about to have satisfaction at last. The 'crime' having been admitted, he raised the bundle of canes high above my shoulders and I braced myself for the blow. But before he could bring them down again there came a commotion from the opposite side of the chamber. A cry of anguish rang out with brothers rushing from their seats. We all turned to look and we saw that at the centre of the upheaval was Brother Eusebius.

In the confusion that followed I remained on my knees while Herbert jiggled his collection of canes impatiently not knowing what to do. But the focus had already shifted from him to the side where a crowd of monks had surrounded Eusebius. Even from my kneeling position I could see that blood was pouring from the young man's face. Being the only medic present it was clearly my place to deal with the situation. But equally clearly as a penitent about to be punished I could do nothing without permission of the prior. Several of my brother monks pleaded with Herbert to release me so that I could attend to the patient. Herbert looked on the verge of apoplexy. Finally he conceded defeat. He made a rapid sign of the cross:

Brother Walter, consider yourself absolved – this time. Oh,

do what you can for the boy.'

So saying, he stormed out of the chapterhouse hurling from him the bundle of rods that clattered harmlessly against the wall.

Chapter Five

BROTHER EUSEBIUS

'How are you feeling now, my son?'

'Still a little light-headed, master.'

I chuckled. 'Hardly surprising since it is from your head that the blood escaped. Half its weight is now lying on the floor of the chapterhouse!'

Eusebius looked alarmed.

'I jest, brother,' I reassured him. 'Where blood is concerned a little goes a long way. Come, lie down and raise your feet. We will soon put the colour back into your cheeks.'

We were in my laboratorium where I'd taken Eusebius to recover. If I thought he looked pallid before the nosebleed, he looked almost ghostlike now. But I was confident that with a little rest he'd be fine. Nosebleeds are a not an uncommon event in religious houses. They are particularly frequent among younger men new to a life of austerity. The sudden change in diet in particular disrupts the balance of the body's humours resulting in a build-up of surplus blood which is then expelled through the most convenient orifice – in this case, the nose. When this happens, the initial treatment is to sit the patient down and place something cold and dry on the forehead – something like the large iron key which is what I had used on the boy in the chapterhouse. This temporarily cools the hot and moist blood thus stemming the flow. But it is only a temporary solution. The excess blood would have to be siphoned off later using either leeches or a drain in the arm. But it is a simple enough procedure with no lasting ill effects.

I began preparing a warm suffusion of burdock and figwort in lime juice for Eusebius to drink.

'Have you had emissions like this before?' I asked him.

'I've always had them ever since I've been with the Gilbertines.'

'And how long is that?'

'Since I was oblated at the age of ten. Why do you ask, master?'

I smiled. 'Oh, it's just my questions. A doctor has to ask these things.'

In fact the boy's answers confirmed my suspicions. By his own admission he was not new to the Gilbertine order but had been with them for I calculated to be at least ten years – more than enough time to adapt to the regimen, I would have thought. No, something more fundamental was amiss here. I would need to study his birth chart to be certain of my diagnosis, but in my experience those most susceptible to frequent nosebleeds are, by definition. of a sanguine nature and are usually outgoing, sociable and rather jolly people often given to corpulence. Eusebius, by contrast, struck me as being melancholic, introspective and painfully thin. This mismatch of humour and type was worrying.

It could, of course, simply be a lack of nourishing food that was the cause. The Gilbertines are few in number and known to be very poor - I believe there was even a revolt a while back among the Gilbertine lay brothers against their poor food. But if I had to guess I'd say in Eusebius's case the source of the problem lay much deeper and be of a spiritual rather than physical nature. That would explain his presence here. Something of the sort must be the case else why was he here at all? Whatever his problem, however, I wanted to do my best for the boy grateful as I was for his having saved me from my own ordeal at the hands of Prior Herbert, for had he not cried out when he did it might be me now lying on the couch nursing something rather more painful than a mild headache.

'Here, drink this,' I said, handing him the suffusion of burdock and figwort. 'It will revive you.'

He sipped it and pulled a face. 'Urgh! Sour.'

'Nevertheless you should persevere,' I insisted sternly, but then softened my tone. 'I'll ease its passage with a little honey in deference to your youth. I know the young like sweet things.'

I watched while he drained the cup.

'Have we met before?' I asked as he handed it back. 'Your features seem somehow familiar to me.'

'Not unless you have been to our priory at Shouldham. This is my first time away.'

'No, I have never been to a Gilbertine house. I think I would have remembered if I had.'

'You disapprove?' he asked hesitantly.

'Of monks and nuns cohabiting together?' I shook my head. 'I confess I find the concept strange, but I would be loath to condemn that which I do not fully understand.'

'It is not difficult once you try it – men and women living and praying together in modesty as God ordained Adam and Eve before the Fall. It is not a new concept.'

'But one that must cause…difficulties,' I suggested gently.

He looked at me shyly. 'You fear the carnal desire, master. But if you live in the love and devotion of the Lord Jesus Christ and his Holy Mother the Virgin Mary then all earthly temptation is conquered.'

'Noble sentiments,' I conceded. 'Perhaps the faith of Gilbertines is stronger than ours. We Benedictines prefer the certainty of geography and locked doors to ensure our chastity.'

'Oh, we have locks too,' he insisted. 'And walls to keep us apart - even inside the priory church itself. The nuns and the canons can hear each other, but not see. We have separate dormitories, separate refectories, even separate cloisters. There is no contact between us at all - other than for spiritual purposes.'

I shrugged. 'Then I fail to see the point. Why not go the whole hog and separate totally into different houses?'

He frowned trying to explain: 'It is a matter of historical precedent. The first Gilbertines were nuns. But since nuns cannot celebrate the mass or hear confession a community of canons was added to serve them. Then a community of lay sisters was added to serve the needs of the nuns and finally another of lay brothers to do the heavier work.'

'Goodness me!' I chuckled. 'Not *two* houses but *four*.'

He lowered his eyes. 'You mock us, master.'

I shook my head. 'Not at all. But you have to admit, it does sound a little…complicated.'

'Not if the rules are obeyed. If correctly followed the arrangements work well enough. Although...'

'Although?'

He stiffened a little. 'No doubt you have heard the tales.'

I had indeed. I didn't like to mention it, but as is so often the case with even our noblest of intentions, human behaviour has a habit of tripping us up. There was one particular case I knew of - a Gilbertine nun who was seduced by one of their lay brothers. When the other nuns found out they forced the girl to castrate the brother concerned and to consume the severed parts - or so the story had it. The disgraced nun was then locked away to bear her shame alone. But all was made well in the end for during her lonely sojourn in the dungeon cell the nun had a miraculous visitation from the Archbishop of York, no less, who spirited away both her chains and her unborn child thus saving the girl from everlasting damnation - and Holy Mother Church from everlasting disgrace, of course. I am not saying such things never happen among Benedictines, but the opportunity must be all the greater with so many men and women living together cheek by jowl.

'We are none of us perfect,' Eusebius was saying shyly. 'We are all tempted at times.' He looked up. 'Even you, master.'

'Me?' I was stunned by the sudden personal reference. 'Oh well - when I was your age, perhaps. I'm not sure I have such feelings anymore. Not for a while at any rate.'

'But did I not hear the prior correctly,' Eusebius persisted, 'that you visited a lady privately in her bedchamber? Isn't that why you were being disciplined in the chapterhouse this morning?'

I grimaced. 'I'm afraid Prior Herbert's imagination sometimes runs away with him. It is true that I paid a visit to the lady concerned, but in my capacity as her doctor. She has just given birth to a baby daughter which I delivered. It was concern for her health and that of her child that attracted my interest, not her feminine charms.'

He went quiet. 'Did I hear correctly that the lady in question was Lady Adelle de Gray?'

'You've heard of her?' I asked suspiciously.

'I know the name. Bishop de Gray is our bishop.'

Of course, that would be it. Shouldham was in the diocese of Norfolk - Bishop de Gray's diocese.

'You would agree, though,' said Eusebius, 'that it is the animation of carnal lust which damns us?'

'Erm – well yes, I suppose so,' I agreed somewhat reluctantly as I rinsed out his bowl.

He nodded. 'Guiges of Chartreuse says that it is not possible for a man to hide a fire in his breast or touch pitch without getting stuck. And Gerald of Wales advises that if we are tempted by the desires of the flesh we should visualize coupling with a corpse, for what can be more disgusting than stinking, rotting flesh?'

I laughed awkwardly at his extreme imagery. It was clear the boy was both well-read and deeply serious. His devotion to the Virgin was also commendable if a little severe in one so young. I thought I was beginning to understand why Eusebius had been sent to us.

'I find a dip in the cold waters of the Lark has the same effect,' I said trying to lighten his mood.

But the boy was not to be deterred so easily. 'No, master.

Abstinence is the only safe way. The Holy Mother showed us by her example; the only truly virgin in thought as well as in deed. Only by following her supreme example can we achieve full redemption. Her chastity is the light and the purity, whiter than snow, clearer than glass, more brilliant than the sun!'

Well, that certainly brought the colour back to his cheeks. His eyes were bright with adoration. I could only hope that a few weeks with us might calm him - perhaps by mixing with some of the other young men in the novice house would bring him back down to earth. But I seemed to have discovered what was ailing my new young friend and what had brought him to seek solace at the foot of Saint Edmund's tomb: terror of his own humanity.

Chapter Six
AN OLD ENEMY RETURNS

Strictly speaking Eusebius wasn't my responsibility at all except in the general sense that the health of everyone within our walls was the concern of the abbey physician. But he did have a physical problem which required my attention and to this end I had a quiet word with Brother Nigel, the fraterer, to see if the boy might benefit from a diet richer than we monks are normally used to, just until he built up his strength a little. Nigel was sympathetic to my request but asked me to clear it first with the prior since the dietary regime was another one of those areas covered by Herbert's precious rules. I'd had a feeling he might say that. I agreed to try but frankly after the fiasco in the chapterhouse any suggestion coming from me would probably get short-shrift from Prior Herbert. I therefore decided to put off approaching him for a day or so to allow muddied waters to settle and hurt pride to heal. When I did

AN OLD ENEMY RETURNS

see him I would need all my powers of charm and delicacy to plead the boy's case and no doubt Herbert would enjoy every squirming, wriggling moment of it before refusing - doubtless with much heart-felt sorrow and regret.

In the meantime I got on with my regular rounds of sewing wounds, setting bones, easing bowels and letting blood. I saw no more of the de Gray family who I imagined if they hadn't already left the district soon would, although I was surprised that baby Alix hadn't been baptized in the abbey church before leaving. Being one of the blessed sacraments, baptism is essential if a child is to be protected from everlasting damnation should the worst happen and it did not survive its first few months of life. The latest thinking on the subject is that the souls of those infants who die without being baptized do not go to Purgatory like everyone else since they have had no opportunity yet in their brief lives to have committed personal sin. But they are guilty along with the rest of us of *original* sin – that offence against God perpetrated by Adam and Eve and which devolves upon everyone simply by dint of being human. It is thought, therefore, that their souls go instead to somewhere called *limbus infantium* - or Limbo of the Infants - a place at the edge of Hell where they suffer no physical torment but are denied seeing the face of God, which is punishment in itself. This state is similar to, though distinct from, *limbus partum* - or Limbo of the Patriarchs - which is reserved for those Old Testament Fathers like Noah and Moses who lived before the advent of Christ but who nevertheless died in special friendship with God. *Limbus partum* is a place milder than Purgatory for their souls to repose until Christ comes to redeem them. Dead infants, on the other hand, can avoid Limbo altogether by the expediency of being baptized while still alive. Given this simple precaution I was surprised that the de Grays had not taken advantage of it.

All this I would have liked to discuss with Prior Herbert given the opportunity, but unusually he seemed tied-up with abbey business and was out of circulation. Though not an entirely regrettable state of affairs in itself, his inaccessibility was becoming something of an inconvenience. I did try once or twice to get in to see him but each time I failed, either because he was too busy or was not in his office when I called. After my third failed attempt I began to wonder if this unavailability wasn't deliberate and frankly I had better things to do than keep trudging back and forth to his house on a fool's errand. I also thought when I did eventually manage to pin him down that I'd take the opportunity to smooth ruffled feathers over the Lady Adelle incident – or at least to put my side of it. It did the abbey no good to have its pastor and its physician at loggerheads with each other especially at a time when there was already enough bad feeling within the community over the election of the new abbot. As things turned out, it was a thought I rather wish I'd never had.

The prior's house is a fine-looking two-storey building set well away from the main abbey complex within its own walled garden on the sleepy banks of the River Lark. Compared with the common dormitory, or even the few individual cells such as my own, it is a luxurious dwelling but not one begrudged of the second highest office-holder in the abbey. He rightly needs space to accommodate his large household of servants and clerks as well as suitable surroundings in which to entertain important guests. Or so he maintains.

AN OLD ENEMY RETURNS

Herbert's office is on the upper floor of this rather grand pile and is guarded by his faithful secretary, Jephthet, a clerk in minor orders who sits at the foot of the stairs screening his master from unwanted visitors. Like all petty officials Jephthet likes to exercise what little power he has to its limit. I could not but again reflect on the contrast with Abbot Samson whose door had always been open, literally as well as metaphorically, to anybody who wished to see him - once you made it up the staircase that led to his study, of course.

On my approach Jephthet had a sudden coughing fit, loud enough certainly to be heard in the room above.

'Ah, Jephthet – good man,' I greeted him amiably. 'Your master is in I take it?' and started to go round his desk.

A skeletal hand shot out barring my way. 'You have an appointment, master?'

'Yes – well, no actually. Do I need one?'

'The prior is a very busy man.'

'Oh, my business is not great. A minute or two of his time is all I crave.'

Jephthet smiled as I imagine Aesop's fox smiled when it first spied the grapes. 'I can give you a minute…' he ran an ink-stained finger down a list on his desk '…a week on Tuesday - in the fore-noon.'

I smiled back at him. 'Perhaps I'll come back when he's less busy.'

'Please do,' smiled the fox.

I started to leave but turned back. 'By the way, that's a nasty cough you have there, Jephthet. I do hope it doesn't turn into anything sinister.'

I did try to get to see Herbert on several more occasions

but each time Jephthet had a different reason for not allowing me to pass. The man is a Cerberus guarding the gates of the Underworld, and like that multi-headed monster his eyes and ears are everywhere. I don't believe he possesses a bladder for I have yet to go to the prior's house and not find him sitting hunched over his desk scratching away at some scroll or other.

Subterfuge was called for. The next time Jephthet refused me access to his master I intended to accidentally upset his ink horn over his precious scrolls and in the confusion mount the stairs before he had a chance to stop me. I was quite looking forward to executing my plan which I had timed for late one evening when I was sure Herbert would be at home. However, I was to be disappointed for when I entered the hallowed sanctuary of the entrance hall I saw that for the first time ever since I had been coming to the house Jephthet's desk was empty. Indeed, so neatly arranged and tidied was it that I decided he must have been dismissed for the night – as I later discovered to be the case.

The hallway was in darkness but there was the faintest glimmer of light coming from the next level and I began to climb the stairs. As I got to the top I could hear subdued voices coming from the other side of Herbert's office door - it seemed Herbert already had a guest. My immediate reaction was a mixture of relief that the unpleasant confrontation could be put off for another night, and irritation that I had been frustrated yet again. I was about to turn and go when I heard something that made me halt. Until that moment the only voice I'd heard coming through the door was that of the prior - a distinctive nasal whine. But when his companion replied the sound of the voice sent an involuntary shiver down my spine. I was unable to distinguish individual words but the timbre and inflexion were unmistakable. It had been many years since I'd heard that voice and yet I knew it better than I knew my own.

What I did next was something I have never done before in my life: I went down on one knee and peeped through the keyhole. It was dark inside the room and it took me a moment to focus on the occupants, but when I did I nearly fell backwards in shock. It was him all right: Geoffrey de Saye, the man who had once tried to murder me.

It was coronation year, 1199. King John had come to Bury to give thanks at the shrine of Saint Edmund for his accession to the throne. But the visit had coincided with the murder of a fourteen-year-old child – the son of a local fuller. The child's body had borne all the signs of ritual murder for which the Jews were blamed, and one Jew in particular. The accused man was eventually exonerated but not before his own life had been forfeit and his family destroyed. It subsequently transpired that the real murderer had been Geoffrey de Saye and for reasons nothing to do with religious sacrifice but everything to do with money and corruption. As the investigating officer at the time, I had been responsible for exposing de Saye, in revenge for which he tried to murder me too in Thetford Forest. But unbeknown to me, my life had been in double jeopardy because of an older connection between our two families about which I knew nothing. As I subsequently discovered, my own father had killed de Saye's uncle - the infamous Geoffrey de Mandeville, the so-called *Scourge of the Fens* - thereby ending a reign of terror by that had blighted the lives of the people of East Anglia for two years. All this happened years before I was born, even before de Saye was born, but as a consequence he had harboured a grudge against my family. And when he learned that I was the one responsible for exposing him as a murderer his vengeance knew no bounds. That time his attempt to kill me failed, but would he fail again?

Geoffrey de Saye and I are both a decade and a half older now - I am fifty and he must surely be sixty. But even in the dim candlelight of the office there was no mistaking the man. And yet how could it be? As a result of his murderous activities all those years ago he had been exiled to the Welsh Marches *for life* - or so I had thought. It had always aggrieved me that he had never been brought to trial, but his was a powerful family. His nephew was the then Justiciar of England, Earl Geoffrey Fitz Peter, and such people never fully answer for their crimes. Exile was the best we could hope for. It had been one of the conditions exacted by Abbot Samson for not prosecuting de Saye that he was never to be allowed to roam free again but be confined to his nephew's manor in distant Shropshire. But both Earl Geoffrey and Abbot Samson were now dead and with them had gone the last two guarantors of de Saye's banishment. Now he was back and there was no-one to prevent de Saye finishing the job he'd started all those years ago – and this time, it seemed, with Prior Herbert's blessing.

So engrossed was I with my memories that I hadn't noticed that the voices in the room had stopped. There were two quick steps, the door to Prior Herbert's office swung violently open and suddenly de Saye was standing in the doorway glowering in the half-light. Fortunately, I had managed to scamper away into the shadows just in time. He didn't see me, but I saw him

– older, greyer than I remembered. But if I had any lingering doubts about his identity they were dispelled by the reaction of my own body: I felt physically sick.

De Saye glared along the dark landing but I remained absolutely still not daring to even breathe until he gave up and went back inside again, closing the door behind him.

Chapter Seven
THE HANGED MAN

I managed to return to my cell although I have no recollection of how I got there. One moment I was teetering at the top of the prior's stairs and the next I was collapsing onto my own cot.

My mind was spinning with questions. Why was de Saye here? What did he want? Surely there was only once answer to that: to finish the job he'd started fifteen years ago. Geoffrey de Saye was no respecter of rank or position; certainly my tonsure would not protect me from his wrath. I know because he had once come within a whisper of slicing through my gullet and would have succeeded had one of my mother's servants not been on hand to stop him. This time I had no such guardian angel to protect me. Indeed, the one person who I should have expected to shield me, whose duty it was to care for all among his flock, Prior Herbert, appeared to be in collusion with the man.

I needed time to think - and more importantly, someone to think with.

THE HANGED MAN

*

Another of those rules of which Prior Herbert is so fond is that monks are not permitted to leave the abbey grounds after compline, the last office of the day. But the gate-keepers are used to my comings and goings at odd hours on some medical emergency or other and readily open up when I approach.

'Someone fainted, have they?' the man asked as he unbolted the wicket door to let me out.

'Something like that.'

'You don't look too good yourself, brother. Seen a ghost, have you?'

The town's curfew bell was already tolling as I started up Abbeygate Street but I knew my way well enough to Joseph's shop in the moonlight - the Blood Moon-light as I reminded myself with a shudder. But I didn't get as far as Heathenman's Street for coming down the hill towards me was Onethumb.

Blessèd boy, I have never been so relieved to see him. He must have just finished his work for the day and was on his way home. Seeing me, his face lit up in greeting, but his smile soon faded as I explained my presence. He had reason to remember Geoffrey de Saye as well as I did from his own brush with the man during those terrible events of fifteen years ago and was shocked to hear that the old enemy was back in town again. But the street was not the place to discuss such matters especially with watchmen prowling, eager to fine those still out after the curfew bell. Taking my arm, Onethumb led me to an ale-house he knew would still be open, The Hanged Man as it was ominously called, and located in a thoroughly unsavoury part of town. Normally I would never think to frequent such a place but Onethumb enticed me with the promise of a warm fire and liquid refreshment, and frankly I was too weak to resist.

Are you sure it was him? he signed once we'd got our drinks and found a bench.

'Older, fatter, uglier - but yes, it was him all right.'

But I thought he'd been banished?

'He had been – he *is* banished. But with Justiciar Geoffrey and Abbot Samson both in their graves who is there left to enforce it? He's somehow got loose from his shackles and it seems his anger has not mellowed. He's back to send me to join all his other victims - in Hell. I know it - Oh!' I groaned with my head in my hands.

Onethumb looked sceptically at me. *Are you certain that's why he's here?*

'What other reason could there be? De Saye has no connection with Suffolk. His family are from Essex – a Godless county if ever there was one!'

But as Onethumb pointed out, fifteen years is a long time. If de Saye had truly wanted me dead, why wait till now to do it? He could have had me disposed of any time during those years without the need come in person to do it. Indeed, what better alibi could he have being confined to a manor two hundred miles away?

It was my turn to sign as I demonstrated with my hands around an imaginary throat. 'Maybe he just likes the idea of placing his own hands round my neck.'

But would he risk further banishment - for the sake of a monk?

'Not just *any* monk,' I said peevishly. 'You forget, our quarrel goes back many years and is enduring. These old family feuds, you know, they go on until the last man standing. An eye for eye, a tooth for tooth, a hand for hand - oh, I'm sorry,' I grimaced awkwardly at Onethumb's mizzened stump.

But there are other things that might explain his presence here, he signed.

'Like what?' I looked at him suspiciously. 'What have you heard? You've heard something, haven't you? Tell me.'

Mute of speech he may be, but there was nothing wrong with Onethumb's ears. Working in Joseph's shop, he picked up all sorts of titbits from customers and tradesmen – gossip, fact, opinion – most of it trivia but with the occasional nugget of interest. It is a common enough truth that men converse more freely in front of servants and shopkeepers than they ever would in front of their own wives, especially those for whom they have contempt - like a Jewish apothecary or his dumb assistant. Onethumb was very good at playing the fool when it suited him, smiling at their insults while soaking up their loose chatter. It was the way a dumb and crippled street-urchin learned to survive.

Something is happening, he signed cautiously. *Something important.*

I looked at him doubtfully. 'In what way "important"?'

He looked around the tavern surreptitiously as though wary of being overheard - although "overheard" was hardly the right term for it. Even so, his signing was restraint itself.

It happened a few days ago, he signed, while Joseph was away visiting suppliers and Onethumb was alone in the shop. Two men came into the shop - Londoners he was sure for they spoke of the guilds of merchants who congregated up on the hill of that great city and how they were looking forward to getting back amongst them again. They had just been to Stamford in Lincolnshire on business but had left that town earlier than planned because of the troubles there. They were congratulating themselves on having had a lucky escape.

'Troubles?' I queried. 'What troubles? I haven't heard of this.'

Apparently there had been some kind of important meeting in the town. The men didn't say what it was about but while it was going on the town gates had been locked and guards were posted allowing no-one to enter or leave.

'They told you this? These London merchants? They spoke so freely?'

He shook his head. At first they spoke in low voices, but once they realised Onethumb was, as one of them put it, 'nought but a Suffolk idiot' they became less guarded. They were full of speculation about what the meeting was about and were competing with each other to drop names of those they recognised.

'Such as who?'

Onethumb shrugged. Lord this and earl that - the names meant nothing to him. But their rank was noble, of that he was certain. It seemed the two men had managed to bribe their way out of the town - at considerable cost to their purses, Onethumb was pleased to say - and were making their way back to London by a circuitous route, which was how they came to be in Bury.

I took a mouthful of my ale. The story didn't amount to much in itself and if he'd mentioned anywhere other than Stamford I probably wouldn't have taken any interest. But Stamford was a well-known meeting place situated conveniently half way up the old north road between London and York. Gatherings had taken place there since time immemorial - Harold Godwinson was said to have assembled his army there on his march north to defeat Harald Hardrada at Stamford Bridge, and once again on his way back south to lose to the Conqueror at Hastings. More importantly, it was just two days' ride from Bury - a fact that prompted my next question:

'These men of noble rank - was Geoffrey de Saye among them?'

They hadn't mentioned the name. But that didn't mean he wasn't there. Geoffrey de Saye had been out of circulation for a long time - those London merchants might not have known of him. But if he was at this meeting in Stamford, and it was as clandestine as Onethumb suggested, that might explain why he arrived here unannounced like a thief in the night. I was rather hoping he had since it meant his presence here might have nothing to do with me after all and so Onethumb might well be right: I'm really not that important. But what it didn't do, of course, was explain why de Saye was here at all - or the nature of Prior Herbert's involvement with him.

'Is there anything else you want to tell me?' I urged Onethumb. 'Anything at all?'

He shied impishly. Not really - except to say that while round the back of the shop filling the Londoners' orders he had pissed in the bottles of perfume they had bought for their wives in payment for their insults and then charged them double for the privilege.

'Oh, did you just? And what do you think that will do for my brother's reputation, his cologne stinking of piss?'

Onethumb grinned and shook his head. He didn't think the Londoners would be back. They thought Bury a very dull place and couldn't wait to leave. And I have to admit the thought of them getting back to London and unstopping the bottles of perfume for their wives to inhale the fragrance made me smile.

I could just imagine their reaction.

We were interrupted by a disturbance at the far end of the room. Someone was being thrown out by our host.

'Oh good lord,' I muttered under my breath. 'No, don't look. It's Raoul de Gray. What's he still doing here? I thought he'd gone.'

It was Raoul all right. He was drunk again, and this time it wasn't the arrival of his new baby he was celebrating. He had his arm around the neck of one of the whores and seemed to be trying to take her with him as he was being ejected. The girl clearly didn't want to go with him and was protesting angrily, trying to free herself from his grasp while two other men attempted to help her. I had to remind myself that this was the nephew of His Grace the Bishop of Norwich and tutted to myself. Noble rank is evidently no guarantee of noble bearing - or maybe this behaviour was what passed for it these days. At any rate, one of the men punched Raoul in the stomach winding him and eliciting more whoops of laughter from other customers. But it did mean he released her long enough for the other two men to bundle him out through the door and into the night. But Raoul wasn't to be deterred so easily. Barred from coming back inside again, he started shouting abuse from the street. The two men jeered and threatened him with the beadle if he didn't go home which only made Raoul even more belligerent and he tried to get back inside the ale-house again. But he was no match for the two burly men who pushed him back every time he tried to get in. Most of what he was shouting was the incoherent nonsense of a drunkard, about a man's rights and the fact that he had paid good coin to get them. This brought more jeering particularly from the girl he had been pawing who yelled abuse back at him. Doubtless it was the regular sort of banter that occurs in most alehouses on any night of the week, but I thought it was just desserts for the way he had treated his maid the previous day and I secretly applauded the girl's spirit. This was one female he was not going to be able to bully.

Entertaining though the exchange might be, a rowdy ale-house is no place for a monk and certainly not a senior obedientiary of the abbey. It wouldn't do for me to be on the premises when the beadle arrived. So I signalled to Onethumb that it was time we were leaving and pushed my way out of the ale-house nearly knocking Raoul to the ground in the process. Fortunately he was too drunk to notice who it was shouldering him. He went down hard and didn't look as though he was about to get up again too quickly. Frankly, I'd have been happy to leave him there, but ever a slave to my own scruples I could not leave the boy lying in the gutter where he might be robbed or beaten or worse. Certainly leaving him would not help the Lady Adelle and her child. So reluctantly, and with Onethumb's assistance, we lifted him up and half carried, half dragged the boy down the hill to the jeers and cheers of the ale-house clientele.

By the time we got to the abbey grounds Raoul was barely conscious. He'd either drunk an inordinate amount or - more likely - his young head was simply not used to strong ale. Either way the night porter would never allow us to bring him back inside in his condition, and heaven alone knew what Brother Gregor would have made of it, so we heaved him up over the wall as quietly as we could – no mean feat for a one-armed apothecary's assistant and a feeble old monk – and hoped he didn't break his neck on the way down the other side.

Chapter Eight
A BODY IN THE MARKETPLACE

Raoul didn't break his neck, more's the pity, but then I didn't really think he would. I've seen enough drunks to know that they rarely hurt themselves in a fall, ale seemingly able to turn grown men into rag dolls that flop harmlessly onto the hardest surface. It was my back that felt broken for, rag doll or not, Raoul was no light-weight and it took the combined strength of both Onethumb and me to get him over the abbey wall. I sent Onethumb home and hurried back inside the monastery grounds hoping no-one found Raoul before I got to him. I found him on the other side of the wall still among the bushes where he'd landed and had to summon Dominic to come and help me haul him back to my laboratorium where we left him to sleep off his excesses on the floor. It would have been impossible to return him to his own rooms without rousing the entire monastery, and I didn't think the Lady Adelle would have thanked me for trying. I left Dominic to watch over him for the rest of the night while I took myself off to my cell where I collapsed exhausted onto my cot.

*

Next morning I went straight down to my laboratorium where I found Dominic fast asleep on the cot. Apart from a few scuff marks on the floor and a suspicious-looking puddle, there was no sign of Raoul.

'I take it since he isn't here he must have survived the night,' I said to Dominic once I'd wakened him. 'What time did he leave?'

'I'm not sure,' yawned Dominic rubbing his tonsured pate. 'I rose to sing lauds at daybreak and he was still here then. By the time I returned he was gone.'

'It doesn't look as though you got any more sleep than I did.'

Dominic shook his head. 'I slept badly. He snored noisily and eructed odorously throughout the night.'

'Eructed?'

'Belched. He also vomited copiously.' Dominic indicated some sour mess on the floor covered with a cloth.

'I see. And did he also go on a murderous midnight rampage?' I nodded to a dead cat that was lying on the bench.

'Oh that. I found it among the bushes,' said Dominic stroking the animal's pelt. 'Such a shame. I rather like cats. One of God's gentler creatures, I always think.'

You wouldn't say that if you saw what they bring in from the garden, I thought. 'What were you doing out among the bushes at midnight? I thought I'd asked you to stay with our guest.'

'We are all slaves to our bodily functions, master. I was in need of micturition.'

Micturition? Eructation? I'd forgotten Dominic came from an educated and aristocratic Norfolk family. Doubtless the whole lot of them spoke to each other in such esoteric terms.

'Well, what I want you to do now is go over to the abbot's lodge and make sure our guest got back safely.'

'Yes master. Master?'

'Yes?'

'Who was our guest?'

'Don't you know? The Bishop of Norwich's nephew. And let that be a lesson to you to avoid having a bishop as a relative if you can possibly help it. Now off with you.'

I pushed him out the door before the question I could see forming on his educated brow made it as far as his aristocratic tongue.

While Dominic was gone I cleaned the place up a bit – I didn't want patients slipping on puddles of sick while I was trying to treat them. There was a particularly pungent smell to Raoul's vomit I noticed as I scooped up the mess into a bucket and placed it outside the door for the servants to dispose of. I presumed it was the particular mix of drinks that he had consumed at The Hanged Man the previous night. It must have been quite a cocktail to have had such a potent effect.

Damn the boy! Why was he still here? I thought he and his family would have gone by now. At least my mother would be pleased they were still here though not by my hand. And frankly I had enough to worry about now with Geoffrey de Saye looming over everything. Assuming Onethumb was right about him and it wasn't to torment me, why was he here? There had to be a reason. And what was the significance of his meeting with the prior? His *secret* meeting with the prior. Was it connected at all with the one in Stamford that Onethumb mentioned? And then there was this letter my mother wanted me to deliver to Hugh Northwold. What was that about? My eye lighted upon where I'd hidden it on the shelf above the preparation bench. I'd almost forgotten it was there. What message did it contain, I wondered? Something important to be sure, something that couldn't be entrusted to a regular messenger to deliver. Well, there was only one way to find out. I jumped up and went resolutely over to the shelf where I had hidden the letter, and pulled it out.

Turning the letter over in my hands I had a terrible sense of *déjà vu* for it reminded me starkly of the last time I was entrusted with a sealed document like this. That time I had resisted the temptation to open it considering it a breach of trust to do so. Had I done so then and acted on what I found much of the subsequent tragedy might have been avoided – a man's life saved, his home and family kept intact and a murderer apprehended sooner. The murderer then, as if I needed to remind myself, was none other than Geoffrey de Saye. My timidity that time had haunted me ever since and I didn't want to repeat the same mistake again.

Still I hesitated. I placed the neat little white oblong on my lectern and studied it carefully. It looked such an innocuous thing sitting there with its huge embossed imprint of the great seal of Ixworth in bright red wax obliterating half of one facet. My fingers itched to open it, but that red seal was daunting. Red for danger - isn't that right? I'd seen it affixed to so many documents in my lifetime. It was as powerful an injunction not to violate its sanctity as would a decretal from the pope himself. Once broken it would be impossible to put back together again, and no-one would believe I'd done it accidentally. Summoning all my courage and with trembling fingers I gently eased the knife-blade under the seal.

But before I could make the final irrevocable cut I was halted by a pounding on the door. God in heaven, were my mother's spies even here in the privacy of my own laboratorium now? With a stifled yelp, I dropped both knife and note on the floor and swung round just as the door fell in and Dominic appeared in its frame, his eyes wild with unspoken horror.

'What is it, child?' I gasped. 'What's happened?'

'The Lady Adelle!' he panted.

'The Lady Adelle?' I repeated stupidly. 'What about her?'

His mouth was working but no sound was coming out.

'Breathe boy,' I urged, 'or we shall be here all morning.'

He took a deep breath, held it, and let it out all in a rush: 'Murdered!' he managed at last.

No, it couldn't be! Another sealed note, another murder, and Geoffrey de Saye all together at once? The coincidence was too much to bear.

I realised my mouth had dropped open and I snapped it shut. 'The Lady Adelle has been *murdered*?'

Dominic shook his head. 'No, not her.'

'Then who?' I said impatiently.

He gulped more air. 'Her maid. She's…it's…' he panted pointing high in the air. 'Oh…!'

'Come along,' I said shuffling him out the door. 'Show me.'

'Oh master, it was horrible!'

'Fortitude lad,' I said pushing him ahead of me. 'Don't faint on me now.'

*

A BODY IN THE MARKETPLACE

In the marketplace a crowd had gathered in the south-east corner - a dark, uninviting place furthest away from the market cross. From the gasps of people as they pushed forward to catch a glimpse of the horror it was clear that this was where the body lay. They were being held back by the beadle, a rotund breathless little man with a thick black beard that hid much of his blotched features, and wielding his mace of office at the more determined gawpers.

'Keep back, please! Back I say! Stand clear please madam! I'll thank you sir not to touch. Hey, you there! What you think you're doing?'

I'm afraid I was no better than the rest for while the beadle's back was turned I quickly sneaked a look for myself. I only had a moment or two but managed to take in most of what there was to be seen: The body lay face down in the muck but was unmistakably Effie - I recognised her clothing. But there was something else. I winced as I saw the thing that was lying next to her: A severed hand – Effie's *left* hand, presumably, since her right was visible. It looked as though it had been chopped or chewed off by something very big, and lying next to her was the probable culprit: An extremely fat sow, its neat double row of teats prominently displayed on the underside of its belly. It too was dead, pole-axed by an outraged onlooker who was still strutting around and boasting about what he had done. That was as much as I was able to glean before the beadle put his hand on my shoulder:

'Now brother, you should know better than that. Step aside, if you please.'

I was about to move away when someone else blustered into the confusion: The owner of the pig, apparently, shouting angrily and demanding to know who had killed his prize porker. The guilty man readily owned up and there ensued a bit of a tussle between the two of them with a lot of pushing and shoving but no actual blows being exchanged while bystanders took sides depending on whether they sympathized with the pig-murderer or the pig. The overwrought beadle now had the added problem of trying to separate this warring pair and while his attention was diverted a second time I took the opportunity to have another look at the body.

Unfortunately for the pig the pole-axing appeared not to have killed it outright for a lot of its blood had pumped out of the wound and pooled beneath Effie's chest. But something else amongst the shambles caught my eye. I picked up a stick and lifted the object clear of the mess. It was dripping with congealing blood but there was no mistaking what it was: The cap that Raoul had been wearing when Onethumb and I saw him in the tavern the previous night — or if not his cap then one identical to it. And attached to it — that is, holding on to it — was that severed left hand. As I lifted the grotesque object the hand dropped off and a woman in the crowd fainted. But something about it wasn't quite right. I couldn't for the moment think what was wrong and it was while I was puzzling over this that I heard something else that made my own blood run as cold as the pig's:

'Bone-breaker!'

I froze. Those words and that voice uttering them. I knew instantly who the owner was and turned to see Geoffrey de Saye standing just a few feet behind me surrounded by his usual posse of brutish-looking thugs. I suppose it was inevitable our paths were bound to cross I just wished it hadn't been so soon.

Such was my shock at seeing him that I'd forgotten I still had Raoul's cap suspended from my twig. With a flick of his glove de Saye signalled one of his men to prise the stick out of my hand and I wasn't quick enough to stop him.

'Aow!' I cried as he nearly twisted my hand off too in the process and walked towards de Saye with his trophy carefully held out in front of him. I was so furious that despite my shock I turned on de Saye:

'You've no right!'

'I have every right,' he growled and added with a snarl, '*bone-breaker.*'

But then something curious happened. I'm not sure if it was the epithet itself or the way he uttered it so contemptuously but it must have tickled the fancy of someone in the crowd for they gave a nervous laugh. 'Bone-breaker,' I heard them whisper and then chortle. That made someone else giggle which in turn made me start to laugh. Put it down to nerves but I couldn't help myself. Laughter is infectious. And others must have found it so too for more and more of them started to laugh until pretty soon practically everybody in the crowd was laughing. The one person who wasn't laughing was Geoffrey de Saye who looked as though he was about to have a fit turning a mixture of purple and blue. He clearly didn't see the joke and somehow that just made it even funnier. And suddenly I could see him for what he really was: No longer the ogre of yesteryear but simply an old man to whom years of soft living had given a paunch and jowls, and what little hair he had left on his head was grey and wispy made all the more obvious by the contrast with the puce of his cheeks. None of this I had noticed the previous night as I crouched before the prior's study door with my eye to the keyhole.

Laughing was both the best and worst thing I could have done for while it eased the tension it humiliated de Saye, and a mocked man is a dangerous man. If he resented me before he must surely loathe me now. He looked as though he'd have liked to kill me. He did take a step towards me but it is difficult to maintain a menacing stance when all around you are collapsing with mirth. Finally with a roar he spun on his heel and barged his way through the crowd followed by his bodyguard who collided with each other in their confusion and haste to leave.

Chapter Nine
PRIOR HERBERT DIPLEASED AGAIN

I received my summons to the prior's study later the same day. Funny how impenetrable the place was before when I wanted to get inside it and how permeable now when I did not. Jephthet was back at his post fiddling with quills and parchment as usual and looking this time not so much like a fox with the smell of sour grapes under his nose as the cat that got the cream. As I passed his desk I gave him the briefest of nods which he answered with a self-satisfied smirk. That smirk confirmed what I already knew: There was trouble ahead.

Hearing voices on the other side of the door, I knocked and waited. There were hurried whispers followed a few moments later by Herbert's nasal whine:

'Come!'

I composed my features into a blend of sycophancy and innocence, took a deep breath and put my head round the door.

'You wished to see me, brother prior?'

If the size of a man's office reflects his level of self-importance then Herbert was a very insecure man indeed. His was enormous, at least thirty feet long, and he sat alone at the far end of it – that is to say, there was no-one else in the room. But the door to his private chapel stood slightly ajar behind him. Since I'd distinctly heard voices before I entered and there was no other exit I guessed whoever it was Herbert had been speaking to had now retreated to the chapel. No prizes for guessing who that might be.

Herbert's eyes narrowed and he beckoned me towards him with a manicured forefinger. It felt a bit like the old days when I was often being hauled before Abbot Samson to receive a dressing down for some misdemeanour or other, although Samson's study was barely a quarter the size of this one. Herbert had Samson's same air of displeasure but none of the Norfolk Trickster's cunning.

Dispensing with civilities, he launched straight in to the attack:

'You in the marketplace today, Walter. Why?'

'My assistant summoned me. He heard there had been an accident and thought I might be able to help – in my capacity as abbey physician you understand.'

'The girl was already dead.'

'But I didn't know that until I got there. You'll be surprised how many corpses spring back to life again once they've had a chance to recover. These difficult diagnoses are best left to the experts, don't you agree?'

Herbert made a growling noise in his throat. 'You insulted my Lord de Saye.'

He spoke the name clearly and with due deference thus confirming my guess had been correct and the man was indeed in the chapel a few feet away and listening to every word.

'Did I? I'm sure I didn't mean to. I don't actually remember saying anything much to him.'

'You laughed at him.'

I shrugged. 'Lord de Saye made a joke and I laughed. Everybody laughed. It was a good joke.'

Herbert wagged his head slowly. 'Walter, you undermine his lordship's authority with your impertinence.'

'In that case I apologize. Had I known he was going to take such a personal interest in the case -'

'Lord de Saye does not take a personal interest in the case,' Herbert interrupted abruptly. 'How could he? He'd happened to be passing through the market on his way to see me when the body was discovered. It was only natural he should take charge.'

That was a clumsy lie. A cleverer man would have passed off de Saye's earlier visit to the priory as a courtesy call instead of trying to pretend it never happened. It just confirmed to me that skulduggery was afoot. But more interesting to me was why someone of de Saye's rank should take any interest in the death of a mere maid.

'Not just any maid,' said Herbert reading my thoughts. 'The murdered girl was a member of an important household. The Bishop's household. These things need careful handling.'

'How astute of his lordship to have divined all that merely from a casual glance at the body as he happened to be passing by.'

I thought I heard another angry growl this time coming from the chapel. Herbert glanced briefly over his shoulder before turning back to me.

'You'll gain nothing by being clever, Walter. Lord De Saye has graciously offered to resolve this appalling business - with my full approval I hasten to add - and it is the duty of all of us to try to help him if we can.'

The thought of my helping Geoffrey de Saye almost made me choke. 'In what way could I help him?' I asked.

'You're one of the few people to have had dealings with the family. You must have met the murdered girl on one of your visits. How did she strike you?'

I shrugged. 'A pleasant enough girl. A bit young to be a maid, perhaps.'

'What about the Lady Adelle.'

'As you would expect of someone of noble birth: a lady of refined manners and sensibilities.'

'Could she have murdered the girl?'

I nearly guffawed. 'Of course not! She has just given birth, virtually bed-ridden.'

He nodded. 'What about the boy?'

I had to be careful here. I didn't want to give too much away about the previous night's activities.

'Like all young men these days,' I answered carefully. 'Selfish, inconsiderate…'

'Violent?'

I hesitated before replying. In all conscience I couldn't deny that I thought Raoul was capable of violence - after all, he'd grappled with me on the chamber floor and Effie had clearly been terrified of him. But being capable of committing murder was one thing; actually carrying it out was quite another. Unfortunately my hesitation only confirmed Herbert's suspicions. He smiled knowingly.

'Oh, now wait a moment,' I protested. 'You can't just assume —'

'He threatened the girl. Brother Gregor confirmed as much.'

'Every master disciplines his servants,' I countered. 'It is only natural. An ill-disciplined household is a weak household.'

'But not every master murders them.'

'There's nothing to suggest Raoul did, either.'

'His cap was found at the scene.'

'Which could have put it there by anyone.'

'For what reason?'

'To incriminate him, of course.'

He snorted. 'And who would want to do that?"

'I don't know. Perhaps you should ask Lord de Saye since he seems to have the answers to everything else.'

Herbert's eyes lit up at that. It was a hasty remark to have made and I cursed myself for my impetuosity. I hadn't actually accused de Saye but I'd come pretty close to it, and him just feet away in the chapel listening to every word. Frankly I should have been surprised that he didn't emerge from his hidey-hole right then and there and have me hauled off to some dungeon. He would have been perfectly justified to do so. In light of what I know now, of course, I can see why he didn't. But at the time I wasn't thinking clearly. I was too angry at being forced to defend the boy. Raoul de Gray was a brute and a bore and I didn't much like his morals. But I liked Geoffrey de Saye's even less.

'If you're so sure he did it,' I said rowing back a little, 'why don't you arrest him?'

Herbert smiled his weasely smile. 'We have. Lord de Saye

detained him this morning immediately after the discovery of the maid's body and placed him in the abbey gaol.'

The news stunned me. I hadn't anticipated things would move so quickly. 'What will happen to him?'

'He will be taken back to Norfolk for trial.'

That shocked me even more. 'Why not try him here? Surely it comes under the abbey's jurisdiction? You being most senior in the order have the authority,' at least until the new abbot is appointed, I could have added.

Herbert grimaced painfully. 'Unfortunately I am unable to give the matter the attention it deserves. You know our situation over this election. I'm far too preoccupied with that. And it wouldn't be proper for me to begin proceedings only to have to hand the case over to the new abbot while still in midstream. Far better for the boy if Lord de Saye takes him back to his home in Norfolk and carry out proceedings in full there. He'll receive a fairer hearing that way.'

'If he makes it that far.'

Herbert glanced quickly over his shoulder as though expecting de Saye to be there. 'Walter, this continued antagonism towards Lord Geoffrey does you no credit. I know you and he have had your difficulties in the past. But that is ancient history now. If Lord de Saye is willing to work with you over this tragic affair you should do the same. It is, after all, your Christian duty to turn the other cheek.'

'It's also my duty to correct an injustice when I see one.'

'Not this time. Your duty is to obey me. And I'm telling you to leave well alone.' He sighed heavily. 'Remember what happened last time. I refer, of course, to that child murder back in '99. I was new to the cloister then, only two years monked, but it made an impression on me. It was quite a fiasco, as I recall. The murderer escaped and ended up killing himself and his wife while his accomplice got clean away. We wouldn't want that happening again, would we?'

'That's not quite what happened,' I objected, and was tempted to add that far from getting 'clean away' the true murderer was apprehended - by me - and was at that moment standing barely five feet away from us.

'Be that as it may,' Herbert said waving his hand in the air. 'This time you are not to get involved. That is a direct order - do you understand?'

I didn't reply but simply lowered my eyes. So he repeated himself more forcefully: 'Do you understand, Master Physician?'

I nodded curtly.

'Besides,' he added enticingly, 'I have another job for you.'

I looked up. 'Oh?'

'Yes. This Gilbertine canon.'

'What about him?'

'You tended his wound after the incident in the chapterhouse, I gather?'

'Hardly a wound. He had a nose bleed.'

'Which you managed to stop - impressively I might add. The boy was very grateful.'

'I am heartened to hear it.'

'Indeed,' Herbert nodded. 'You know why he's here, of course?'

'I believe he's something of a euphoric.'

'One of the chosen.' Herbert smiled. 'I envy him.'

'Do you?'

'Of course. It must be wonderful to feel the spirit moving so strongly.'

I looked at him sceptically.

Herbert continued: 'The boy is alone here. In need of a chaplain.'

Oh, now I could see where this was going. 'Brother Prior -'

'And since he knows and trusts you -'

'Prior Herbert, I have my duties...'

'...which need not conflict.' He smiled beguilingly. 'Just keep an eye on him, that's all I'm asking. You've already recommended a change of diet – a recommendation, by the way, which I have approved. Now I want you to continue your interest and mentor the boy fully.'

I shook my head. 'Out of the question. I'm far too busy.'

Herbert sighed heavily. 'Walter, please don't make me go to the Bishop.'

I was trapped. It was obvious what he was doing. He wanted to keep me so preoccupied that I wouldn't have time for the murder. If I refused he would appeal to Bishop Eustace of Ely as our temporary pastoral director while the abbacy was vacant. Ironically, that role would normally belong to the Bishop of Norwich - Raoul de Gray's uncle; but Bishop John was out of the country. I knew Bishop Eustace well enough but even if I managed to persuade him to relieve me of this duty it would involve a lengthy trip to Ely in Cambridgeshire. By the time I returned de Saye would have Raoul half way across Norfolk. It was a shrewd move on Herbert's part - uncharacteristically so. More likely it was Geoffrey de Saye's idea. I was angry and frustrated which probably explained what I said next:

'What if I can prove Raoul's innocence?'

Herbert's eyes narrowed. 'Be careful, Walter. I haven't yet

forgotten your indiscretion with the Lady Adelle. Don't add to your woes by providing a spurious alibi for her husband.'

'The girl's body was found in the early hours of this morning - yes?'

'So I believe.'

'So she was murdered some time last night - agreed?'

He didn't reply, so I continued:

'In which case, Raoul de Gray definitely could not have killed her.'

'Oh? Why not?'

'Because he spent all of last night on my laboratorium floor with me.'

Chapter Ten

THE BEADLE, THE WHORE AND THE VAGRANT

Stupid, stupid, stupid to admit that Raoul had been in my laboratorium. I should have kept it to myself. It was a disciplinary offence although I could possibly have claimed he was ill and in need of my services. But I was angry over his arrest and even angrier over the way I was being manipulated. And I couldn't resist seeing the look on Herbert's face when I told him. The sin of vanity, you see? It clouds the clearest of judgements. Herbert was furious practically accusing me of being the boy's accomplice. I could only repeat what Dominic had told me that Raoul was in my laboratorium at the start of lauds but had gone by the end of it. There was the possibility, I suppose, that Dominic could have fallen asleep thus allowing Raoul to slip out of the abbey, murder Effie, dump her body in the marketplace and then slip back into the abbey again without Dominic or the gatekeeper noticing, but there didn't seem much likelihood of that. As a sop to Herbert's vanity I told him that had I known about the murder beforehand I would naturally have handed Raoul over to him. I don't think he was much impressed. Fortunately he was too stunned to make any response. Anyway, I left his office before he could accuse me of anything else - or worse, confine me to the abbey precinct as punishment.

What intrigued, though, me was why de Saye was so keen to be involved. I didn't believe he 'happened to be passing through the market' when Effie's body was discovered - he'd arrived too smartly and too well-prepared for that. But why sully his boots over the death of a maid, even a maid to such an illustrious house as de Gray? It was the Matthew case all over again. Then, too, there had been a murder and then, too, de Saye had attempted to fog the evidence in order to blame someone else, someone who later turned out to be completely innocent. I was loath to let the same thing happen again. But how to prevent it? Clearly not by wasting my time with the Gilbertine boy. This was just Herbert doing what came naturally to him: hedging his bets in order to keep in with the rich and powerful and doing whatever they say. Once again I yearned for the days of Abbot Samson. Trickster he may be, but he was in thrall to no man - certainly not the likes of Geoffrey de Saye.

The truth is I wasn't entirely convinced of Raoul's innocence either. Given his maltreatment of Effie I was almost inclined to let matters take their course and let him prove his own innocence if he could. Before Geoffrey de Saye's appearance I might have done just that. But with de Saye there is never any chance of fair play. The truth was that Raoul could not have killed the girl between leaving the tavern and the discovery of the body because for all that time he was never out of someone's sight - either me, Onethumb or Dominic. That didn't mean he didn't kill her, only that he couldn't have done it overnight. The only time, in fact, available to him was the period before the tavern incident, and I had an idea about that.

I decided to speak first to the town beadle, the man who had been trying to control the crowd when the body was discovered. I found him in his office beside the guildhall dozing behind his desk. He woke up with a start as I entered.

'What? Oh it's you,' he said squinting hard at me. 'You're the monk who got me my black eye.' He gingerly prodded a discoloration on the side of his face.

'That's a nasty bruise you've got there, my friend,' I tutted and went over to him. 'I'm a doctor. Let me look at it.'

He flapped me away. 'No - thank you brother, leave it. You've done enough. You'll only make it worse.'

'Quite right,' I said taking a step back again and putting my hands behind my back. 'Better to let it heal naturally. I'll send my assistant over with something to ease the discomfort. A potion of my own concoction…'

He shook his head. 'No, it's really not necessary -'

'…of fermented apple wine suffused with citrus and honeydew. I can only spare a gallon or two, you understand, as it's potent stuff. It is the least I can do for causing that fracas in the market place this morning.' I smiled beguilingly.

He grimaced uncertainly. 'Lord de Saye's men have such sharp elbows,' he grumbled rubbing his arm. 'They really hurt me, you know? If only you hadn't laughed at him...'

'*Mea culpa*,' I said, bowing. 'It was my fault entirely. I can only apologize profusely, my very dear friend.' I stepped forward and carefully patted him on the shoulder making him flinch involuntarily.

'Yes, well...' He thought about that for a minute gingerly prodded his eye with a fat finger. Gradually his frown faded and he began to chuckle. 'Mind you, he did look funny.'

'Didn't he just!'

'Snarling at you like that!'

'I know!' I flapped a negligent wrist.

'Bone-breaker!' he guffawed and rolled his eyes - then winced fingering his tender eye-socket again. 'Apple and citrus, did you say?'

'With honeydew.'

He sniffed. 'Well, perhaps for medicinal purposes.'

I smiled benevolently. 'I will get my assistant to bring some over before curfew.'

The beadle was looking brighter now. 'Was there something in particular you wanted, brother?'

'No no, I only came to offer my apologies.' I started to leave. 'Unless...' I came back into the room. 'There is one slight matter you might be able to help me with. Yesterday was a normal trading day in the market?'

He nodded. 'It was.'

'And the usual order obtained? Normal hours were kept?'

'We stick strictly to our ordinances brother; you've no need to worry on that score.' He put up a reassuring hand.

'So that means the market square was cleared by when? - three of the after noon?'

'Earlier. This time of the year the light begins to fade quickly. Many traders, especially those who have come a distance, don't like to travel the roads in the dark. Cutthroats and footpads, you see? But this is not really my province. You should be talking to the market reeve.'

'Bear with me,' I smiled. 'My question is about the area of the market where that girl's body was found. It is near where the blacksmiths have their forges, I believe?'

'What's your point?'

'Just this: If the town blacksmiths are anything like ours at the abbey then they like to carry on working right up to the curfew bell, being reluctant to dowse their fires earlier than absolutely necessary.'

The beadle drew himself up. 'Not with my sanction they don't.'

'Nevertheless it happens, am I right? I'm not condemning, I merely want to confirm that the area where the girl's body was found was occupied right up to the end of the day.'

'Oh, I get it,' he nodded. 'You want to know what time the body was dumped. Well I can help you there. The crier and I were by the market cross right up to curfew bell. As a matter of fact I rang it myself last night. And I can confidently say that no-one came along with a dead body on my watch.'

'Good,' I smiled. 'That is what I was hoping you'd say. Now while I'm here perhaps I could see the body. I take it she's in there.' I took a step toward the door at the far end of the room.

The beadle put out a halting hand. 'Sorry brother. Out of the question.'

'It will take but a moment.'

'Aye, a moment's view for you and a day in the stocks for me.'

He shook his head vehemently. 'It's more than my job's worth.'

'Very well. In that case I suppose I shall have to make a formal application to the coroner to see the body. A pity,' I sighed. 'I didn't want to have to mention the bribe.'

The beadle sat up. 'Ay? Bribe? What bribe?'

'Why, my apple wine of course. Naturally, I'd have to declare it. Of course, if I happened to see the body *informally*...'

The beadle stood at the door to the street and looked out anxiously.

'I do wish you'd hasten, brother. The Sheriff's men are due at any time to take the body away. If they should see you...'

'They won't even know I've been,' I said peering with a lighted candle in the darkened room. 'I see there are marks around her neck. Is that how she died, do you think? Strangulation?'

'So I believe. Had the breath wrung from her, poor cat.' He glanced up the street then back at me. 'You are hurrying aren't you brother?'

'Ah, now that's interesting.'

'What?' he said coming back inside. 'What's interesting?'

'She has two hands.'

The beadle looked at me as though I were soft in the head. 'How many should she have?'

'One,' I replied. 'The pig ate the other – at least, I thought she did.'

I realised then what had bothered me when I saw the body earlier in the marketplace. The thumb on the severed hand had been the wrong way round – that is to say, the hand I saw was a *right* hand, not a left as I'd thought. Now I could see why. Effie still had both her hands intact. The pig certainly had someone's hand in its mouth, but not Effie's. The question was, whose?

The beadle was starting to look agitated again. 'Look, are you finished yet, brother? The Sheriff's men are due at any time.'

'Just one more thing before I go. I don't suppose a priest has seen her today?'

The beadle shrugged, so I placed my hand on Effie's cold brow and closed my eyes in silent prayer.

'No time for that, brother. I can see the tops of their pikes coming up the street.'

I opened my eyes again and glared at the man. 'Amen.'

'Amen,' echoed the beadle. 'Now brother, if you wouldn't mind…'

*

From the beadle's office I went to the tavern where Onethumb and I had been the previous evening. In daylight I could see that it sported the sign of The Hanged Man - an unfortunate omen if ever there was one. I hadn't noticed then but I could see now it was in a street known for its taverns and its whorehouses, although by day it was an ordinary thoroughfare. But still it wasn't wise to be seen lingering there for too long in case anyone got the wrong idea. Which placed me in a quandary: Should I hang about outside and make people suspect my purpose, or should I venture inside and confirm them? In the end I decided to wait and hope that anyone who saw me might think I was there on a mission to dissuade the fallen from their sinful ways. From the looks I was getting from passers-by I don't think anyone was fooled - which made me wonder how many other monks from the abbey had been here.

A couple of vagabonds seated on the ground by the entrance were taking an unwelcome interest in my presence although I was doing my best to ignore them. One looked to be a leper with a filthy bandage covering one arm while his companion kept sniggering and sniffing as though he had a permanent rheum. Much as our Saviour values every creature on His good earth I could not help feeling that even He might baulk at these two. I could smell them from several feet distance. The one with the bandage fixed me with his stare and which I tried to avoid with difficulty. But he was determined to catch my eye and when at last he succeeded he shot to his feet, raised his unbandaged hand and in the most portentous tones delivered to me this stern warning:

'Beware the whoremongers! Beware the seductress who flatters with words and forgets the covenant of God! Beware the immoral woman dripping with honey, her mouth smoother than oil and - '

'Shut up Hervey!'

Blessed holy saints and patriarchs, it was the girl who Raoul had been draped around the previous evening who now emerged from the tavern door. At her words the vagabond preacher instantly ceased his blathering and squatted back on the ground again next to his companion where he crouched as quiet as a mouse. I was impressed and regarded the girl. She blinked back at me and then up at the threatening sky before pulling her shawl around her and starting on up the hill. I hastened after her.

'Young woman - a moment of your time if you please.'

She stopped and looked me up and down. 'You're not one of my regulars.'

'Madam,' I said indignantly, 'I assure you -'

She shrugged. 'Suit yourself,' and set off again up the hill.

'B-but you do have something I require,' I stuttered trotting to keep up with her. 'Information.'

She snorted without slackening her pace. 'That's a new word for it.'

'For which I am happy to pay.'

She looked me up and down sceptically. 'I don't think so.'

'Go on, Netta,' yelled a passing young man. 'Charge the monk double. The old hypocrite!'

She looked me up and down again. 'How much?'

I fumbled in my belt pouch and held out a coin.

She remembered Raoul all right. Last night was the second time he'd been in. It seems he'd taken a particular fancy to her among all the whores and sought her out. The first time had been fine but last night he made a bit of a nuisance of himself.

'Anyway, you were there,' she said. 'I remember you and that cripple. You must have seen him.'

'Indeed,' I replied, 'but last night, wasn't there some kind of a...disagreement?'

She folded her arms across her chest. 'Oh, so that's what this is about, is it? You tell him he pays for the hour. If he can't get it up that's his problem.'

'No no,' I said frowning at her candour. 'That's not why I'm here. I just want to hear from you that he was in the tavern for most of the evening.'

She regarded me with curiosity. 'Not till he pays.'

I fumbled in my pouch again and took out another coin.

'Why'd you want to know?'

It seems Raoul was there all right, all evening. Netta hadn't been able to shift him, he was too big. He just slept on the edge of her bed like a baby.

'While you…entertained…other gentlemen?'

She shrugged. 'He didn't notice and they didn't care.' She smiled slyly. 'Like to hear that sort of thing, do you?'

I could feel my face glowing bright red. 'No, I er… Thank you. Thank you very much.' I fumbled in my robes and brought out another penny.

She stared at the lonely scrap of silver lying in the palm of her hand. I fumbled again and gave her another penny then shrugged to indicate it was all I had left. With a snort of contempt she snapped her hand shut and turned up the road again, muttering.

Well, I thought as I watched her go, at least she confirmed what I had hoped, that Raoul was in the tavern before the curfew bell was rung. Not that Netta or anyone else would likely testify to the fact. I doubted whether anyone could be found who would admit to being in the tavern last night - I certainly wouldn't. But what I found baffling was why a personable young man like Raoul de Gray with a beautiful young wife and a family reputation to uphold would feel the need to seek out such as Netta – delightful and charming as I was sure she was…in the right environment. Raoul's behaviour was mystifying. I sighed. Not for the first time I found the human condition perplexing.

Now that Netta had gone, the vagabond she called Hervey started up again: 'If your right eye causes you to sin, brother, tear it out! If your right hand causes you to sin, cut it off!'

I squatted down next to him in the dust. 'And is that what happened to you, my friend?' I asked him indicating his bandaged arm.

His companion who was squatted next to him sniggered and I had to breathe shallowly for the odour of his breath was so foul that I would have coughed to breathe normally. From Hervey's vacant eyes I could see the poor man was not fully sensible, though clearly he must have had had some learning from all the quoting he was doing from scripture. I wondered how and where he came by it. I wasn't at all sure I was going to learn the source from his lips which were never still but conveyed little sense. I could only lament the distance he must have fallen to have arrived now in his shredded rags and stinking like a bale of rotting fish. Whatever was going on behind those mobile eyes and was struggling so painfully to get out I was never going to learn.

I could see now that he wasn't a leper after all but his injury was recently inflicted for there was freshly-dried blood on his rags. I gently eased the bandage off and grimaced at what I found beneath: A stump where the hand had once been now blackened with pitch to stop the bleeding - perhaps by his rheumy friend. I felt my stomach leap. Another lost hand. There seemed to be an epidemic of lost hands. The skin around the stump of this one looked red and angry and I did not want to touch it for fear of causing man even more discomfort, but I had no doubt from the smell and colour of it that the fire that was growing in it would soon spread to the heart. There was nothing I could do for him except pray that his parting this life should be quick and, if God is compassionate, insensible.

I gently replaced the bandage and addressed his companion. 'Who did this to him? Do you know?'

But Hervey just sniggered. I felt once again deeply inside my pouch and found one last penny and held it up to tempt them.

'Now, what can you tell me about last night?'

It took a while but eventually I got the tale. The two of them had been outside the tavern when Raoul was being ejected as I suspected they might. In the struggle Raoul's cap had fallen. Hervey had quickly picked it up and scuttled off with it. Rarely did anything as valuable as a cap ever come his way. But he did not keep it for long. Into the blackness of a nearby alley someone had followed him. There was a brief struggle which was only going to end one way. The stranger could not prise the cap from Hervey's hand so determined was he to keep it, so with the flash of a knife he took both cap and hand. That, doubtless, was what I had seen in the pig's mouth this morning in the marketplace. Whoever the stranger was he had been as determined to have Raoul's cap as Hervey had been to hang on to it, and I'm afraid the price for Hervey was going to be his short and troubled life.

And then he said something that made no sense at all – or rather, it made more sense than most of what he said, but still it lacked reason. When I asked him again who had done this terrible thing to him he repeated what his friend said - that it was an angel, but then added something else. I was so shocked that I wasn't sure I'd heard right and asked him to repeat it again.

'An angel, brother, a beautiful white angel.'

Chapter Eleven

OF DEVILS AND ANGELS

An angel had cut off Hervey's hand? A devil more like. Normally I'd dismiss such nonsense as the ravings of a confused mind, but Hervey's injury was real enough, as was the severed hand that I'd seen grasping Raoul's cap – I still shuddered at the memory of it. Was it Hervey's hand? If so how did it get to be next to Effie's body? Was this the real murderer? I was unable to get any more sense out of Hervey or his odorous companion, and from the increasingly threatening looks I'd been getting from the locals it was clear I had plainly outstayed my welcome; it seemed the presence of a monk was not conducive to good business in that part of town. What was clear was that whoever was doing this was trying to implicate Raoul in Effie's murder - and no heavenly angel but someone much closer to earth. I had my own suspicions who that someone might be.

Netta's account of Raoul's behaviour also cast doubt on his supposed drunkenness, for if the ale he drank was anything like the watered-down stuff Onethumb and I had been served then he would have had to consume an enormous quantity to have passed out on her bed and again later on my floor. That suggested one thing to me: He had been drugged, and once again the purpose seemed to be to incapacitate the boy so that he could not account for his movements at the time of the murder. It was sheer good fortune that Onethumb and I happened to be on hand to vouch for him.

So Raoul was not Effie's murderer. Then who was? And why? What possible threat could a young maid, a child, pose that called for the ultimate sacrifice? Perhaps the simplest, the most obvious answer was the right one: that Effie had been ravaged against her will and her death was the necessary price of her silence; she would not be the first young girl to suffer that fate. But that wouldn't account for her troubled state of mind which had been so evident in the chamber and on the stairwell. That message she mouthed to me - *Ee-ma-mum-ma* - she desperately wanted me to know and was apparently so important that she risked a beating in order to tell me. It was the key to everything yet it remained as much a riddle as ever it did. I wondered, now that she was gone if I should never know the answer.

Returning to the abbey I went straight to the lavatorium to wash away the taint of my morning's plunge beneath the murkier waters of Bury life. As I finished drying my face and hands I noticed Eusebius reading on the opposite side of the cloister garth and remembered I was supposed to be his mentor. According to the prior he had asked for me specifically. I wasn't entirely sure I believed that. More likely Herbert suggested my name and Eusebius went along with it. Still, I had an obligation to give him my time having been promised. It wasn't his fault he was a pawn in one of Herbert's silly games.

So engrossed was the boy in his book that he didn't notice my approach.

'Good day to you, my son – no, don't get up.' I patted his bony shoulder. 'What's this you're reading?' I took the book from him. 'William of Saint Thierry. Dry stuff indeed - but commendable reading.'

He blushed as I handed him back the weighty tome. 'I got it out of the abbey library. I like to read. I find much comfort in the wisdom of others. Saint Hugh of Lincoln said that books are food for the soul.'

'A wise and holy man, Hugh. And Brother William too. What has he taught you?' I said sitting next to him.

'That when we go to bed at night we should take with us thoughts that will help us to fall asleep peacefully.'

'He should know. Personally I have always found his writings a most useful inducement to sleep.'

Eusebius squinted at me. 'Are you mocking me again, master?'

'Not at all. But I do hope you are getting enough sleep yourself. You are looking a little drawn. Try not to read too late into the night.'

'Saint Bernard of Clairvaux thought sleep a waste of time.'

'Yes, but he suffered from headaches - also from colic, as I recall. Which reminds me, how are you finding your new diet? Any more nosebleeds?'

He frowned. 'No, master. I'm fine now.'

'Good. But I think we'll leave you on it for a few more days yet, see how things go. And if you are having trouble sleeping then don't suffer in silence. There are potions I can give you.'

'It is true sometimes my thoughts will not quieten at night,' he admitted. 'I find it helps to meditate on the Holy Mother. Do you not agree, master?' He looked up reverentially at what I saw now was a statue of the Virgin on the pillar above our heads.

'Ah yes, the Queen of heaven has charms to soothe many a troubled mind.' I smiled up at the pink plaster face.

Eusebius gazed adoringly at the statue. 'Saint Bernard himself was a great devotee. You know the legend of him receiving the Virgin's milk as a sign of Her great love for him?'

'Indeed - expressed direct from nipple to lip,' I chuckled. 'She must have been a good shot.'

He frowned and turned sharply from me. 'You really shouldn't be so flippant about these things, master.'

His sudden outburst startled me a little. I kept forgetting just how deeply Euphorics felt their faith.

'You are right,' I nodded. 'I am well rebuked. I will try to remember in future. Well, if there's nothing else I can help you with right now, I'll get on.'

I got up to leave, but the boy put his hand on my arm. 'Master, will you pray with me?'

I looked about us along the cloister arms. On every side were many of my brother monks all engaged silently in their daily duties of copying, reading, darning, painting. 'What, now? Here?'

He nodded. 'Saint Bernard's own prayer to the Virgin - the *Memorare*?'

'Will we not disturb our brothers at their work?' I said hopefully.

Eusebius seemed unconcerned. '*Please*, master. It will take but a minute.'

I looked at his imploring face. It reminded me that I have had similar moments - yes, even I - when the need for prayer becomes urgent, although in my case it has usually occurred when I have been alone or in church and not in a crowded cloister range. But it was part of my function as his chaplain to indulge the boy in his spiritual needs whenever the moment arose, however inconvenient the timing.

'Oh very well,' I agreed with reluctance. 'But quietly - we don't wish to disturb our brothers'

We went down on our knees before the statue and I composed my mind for prayer. Eusebius shut his eyes but instead of putting his own hands together he took hold of mine and held it tight to his breast as he began to recite:

'Remember, O most gracious Virgin Mary, that never was it known that anyone who fled to thy protection, implored thy help, or sought thy intercession was left unaided. Inspired with this confidence I fly to thee, O Virgin of virgins, my Mother. To thee do I come. Before thee I stand sinful and sorrowful. O Mother of the Word Incarnate despise not my petitions but in thy mercy hear and answer me. Amen.'

'Amen,' I echoed, and started to rise, but he pulled me sharply back down again. He then he held out his free hand aloft and began intoning again but this time in a much louder voice and more urgently:

'Hear us, oh Heavenly Mother. Oh Blessed Virgin Mary, we offer you our hearts, our lives, our souls. Thou who art the purest temple of the most Holy Trinity, intercede we beg you that we may repent of our sins. Handmaiden and mother, only bridge of Christ to men, the awful loom of the Incarnation. Oh Queen of heaven, full of grace, Holy Virgin Immaculate, grant us thy injunction we beseech you!'

Tears were now rolling down his cheeks as he almost sobbed with the intensity of his emotion. All my brother monks had stopped what they were doing to stare, some with astonishment, some with embarrassment, others with amusement. One or two actually got down on their knees and prayed with us. Watching us, too, was Prior Herbert standing in the open door of the church with a bemused curl to his lip. Well, at least he could not accuse me of avoiding my responsibilities. As for myself, I could feel my cheeks burning like beacons as I at last managed to extricate my hand, stagger to my feet and stumble away.

Damn the boy! And damn Herbert for foisting him on me! Euphoric he may be but I didn't have time to indulge his fits of ecstasy just now. At any moment Raoul de Gray could be carted off to Norfolk where he would be out of my reach for ever. If I was to help him I needed to act quickly and not be diverted by other matters.

When I got back to my laboratorium I found Dominic waiting for me and looking very nervous.

'What's the matter? What's happened now?' I asked him irritably.

'Master, I'm sorry - I didn't know.'

'Didn't know? Didn't know what? Dominic is this another waste of my time? What is it?'

Then I saw the lad's face, filled with fear and apprehension and realised I was being quite unreasonable. What just happened just now in the cloister was hardly his fault.

'It's all right, my son,' I said more gently. 'Just tell me what's happened - but slowly, I beg you.'

'I have been quizzed, master. By Prior Herbert.'

I should have guessed this would happen. 'About our guest last night?'

'Yes, master. He wanted me to confirm that Raoul was here...' he looked at me shyly '...and that you were not.'

'And you confirmed it.'

The boy was practically in tears. 'I couldn't see anything wrong with admitting it. We'd done nothing wrong, had we master? And he put me under oath so I was compelled to speak truthfully. I should have realised when he did that that there was more to his questions. It was only afterwards when I thought about it that I realised you would have told him you were here all night which you would have done to save me. Instead I've betrayed you. I'm sorry, master.' He went down on one knee before me.

'You've nothing to be sorry about, Dominic,' I said raising him up again. 'You did right by telling the truth.'

'But will it not harbour uncertainties for you, master?'

Harbour uncertainties for me? Oh yes, undoubtedly it would do that. Herbert already thought I was concealing things from him; this will simply confirm it. But it wasn't fair to involve Dominic in these games.

I smiled at him. 'Dry your tears, my son. You've nothing to reproach yourself for.'

His face puckered into an angry snarl. 'Sometimes I hate myself for my timidity!'

I had to chuckle at that. 'You are a beacon in a dark world, my son. Thank God for your honesty - and for your timidity. Would there were more like you. Now off you go and think no more about it. All you have done is drawn a little line in the sand. A battle line. From now on Prior Herbert and I will know on which side each of us stands.'

When Dominic had gone I got down to the business I had intended doing before I was distracted by Eusebius.

Normally any waste from my laboratorium gets removed promptly by the abbey servants but there are some days when they are lax in their duties and, God be praised, this was one of them. The bucket containing Raoul's vomit which I had mopped up from my floor was still outside the door. I quickly heated some of the filth in a bowl with a little water and force-fed the resulting soup to one of my laboratory rats. Within minutes the animal's breathing had become laboured and shortly after that it was dead confirming that Raoul had indeed been drugged. And then I remembered something else. That's what must have happened to the cat that Dominic discovered in the bushes the night we brought Raoul back. I was guessing Raoul must have been sick there too and the cat ate it and died. That didn't surprise me for even as the mess was warming I could smell the distinctive odour of henbane rising from the bowl. Henbane is a very potent poison and is not at all easy to get hold of. I kept a small stock of it carefully secured in a stoppered jar - a jar which I now saw had been tampered with. And from the amount that had been taken I was forced to revise my earlier assumption. Someone had drugged Raoul's drink all right, but not just in order to deny him an alibi for the time of the murder. Enough had been taken to kill him. It was only that he'd vomited up most of it that his killer hadn't succeeded.

This altered matters completely. Raoul himself was in danger.

Even Herbert must see now that someone was trying to harm him. I had to act quickly before they succeeded and warn him to be on his guard. But any advantage this might have given the boy was about to be thrown away by what he did next.

Chapter Twelve
ESCAPE

𝓕𝑜𝑟 more than fifty years the abbey gaol has been located at the top of Abbot Anselm's tower which is also the bell tower to Saint James's church as well as one of the main abbey gates. It is thus a highly useful and versatile structure as well as being a rather fine building - a fact that I am sure would have delighted the good Anselm. Personally I have mixed feelings about the place having once been a reluctant guest there myself — a circumstance that was also, coincidentally, at the instigation of the dread Geoffrey de Saye. I owed my freedom then to the intervention of Abbot Samson who overruled de Saye and had me released. Unfortunately no such champion was going to ride to the rescue of Raoul de Gray - certainly not Prior Herbert - and Abbot-elect Hugh was still far away in France. Being thirty feet above the ground, the gaol is ideally suited to its purpose. Isolated, sheer and built of good solid Barnack stone, it is virtually impossible to escape from or to gain access to - unless, of course, you have the wherewithal to bribe the gaoler. Unfortunately I was running short of suitable currency with which to barter, the beadle having had my stock of apple wine and Netta my spare coin. As it turned out I needed neither for when he made his bid for freedom Raoul needed no assistance from me.

It was shortly after vespers when the light was beginning to fade that I began my ascent of the stone flight up the outside of Anselm's monument. I was barely half way up when I heard a commotion at the top. It was not much more than a muffled cry but loud enough to be heard in the gatekeeper's lodge below. I glanced down expecting to see the man emerge in response - but he didn't. And when I thought of it, he hadn't stirred when I approached either which was unusual. Only later did I find out that like the gaoler he, too, had been knocked unconscious. And that looked like being my fate next as before I got any higher a figure suddenly darted out of the gaol-room and flew down the steps past me nearly knocking me from my narrow perch in the process. My immediate thought was that it must be Raoul and had I been quicker-witted I might have made a grab for him. What stopped me was the realisation that the figure clearly wasn't Raoul - or any other male for that matter, but female. There was no doubt in my mind the figure was Adelle de Gray - I recognised her long blonde hair. But by the time I'd registered the fact and got over the shock she had already made it to the ground below and was out of the gate and into the town where she disappeared, robe and flying hair notwithstanding. There was then further disturbance from above and as I looked up I saw that this time it really was Raoul who emerged through the gaol door. When he saw me barring his way he hesitated.

'Don't try to stop me, brother. I don't want to hurt you but I will if I have to.'

'Raoul - stop,' I said quickly. 'Don't be a fool. Come with me to Prior Herbert. We can make him understand.'

He shook his head. 'You don't understand. They'll hang me anyway.' He took a step nearer but I barred his way with my hand.

'No they won't,' I implored him. 'Think about it. At the moment you are merely accused but if you run you will be as good as admitting guilt. I can prove you didn't kill Effie.'

Behind him I could hear the gaoler coming back to life. At any moment he would raise the hue and cry and all would be lost. I could tell Raoul was not going to wait for that.

'It's too late, brother. Stand aside,' he barked in desperation. 'Please!'

I stood my ground but he was thirty years my junior and far stronger than I as he demonstrated on the bedchamber floor. I had no hope of stopping him. He ran at me and I braced myself for the blow. But instead of pushing me off he steps as I feared he somehow leapt over and past me down the stairs and in a moment was away across the square in the same direction as Adelle had gone. All I could do was close my eyes and pray to a merciful God that neither of them should come to any harm.

*

'Aow! Careful brother, that stuff stings.'

The gaoler was making the most of his injury as I dabbed at the wound on the side of his head.

'It's only a graze,' I told him. 'You'll have a proud lump to show your children in the morning.'

'What about me?' said the gatekeeper. 'My bump is on the

top of my head. Will the prior recompense me, too?'

'You'll both stink of vinegar by the time I've finished,' I reassured the pair of them. 'Don't worry. No-one will doubt your heroism.'

The three of us were down in the gatekeeper's lodge. The shouts of men, hallooing of horns and bark of dogs in the distance told me that the hue and cry was already well underway. Fortunately it was a cloudy night and so, God willing, Raoul and Adelle should be able to evade capture – at least for tonight.

As soon as Raoul had gone I'd run up the remaining steps to check on the gaoler. Raoul needn't have panicked. The man was still sitting on the floor holding his head and wondering what had happened to him. There was plenty of blood but then even a superficial head wound can bleed profusely. It looked worse than it was. Having satisfied myself that the gaoler's injury was more to his pride than to his body, I led him downstairs to be with his friend the gatekeeper who was suffering in a similar vein - after all, no man likes to think he has been outwitted by a woman.

'It was the boy who hit me,' insisted the gatekeeper.

'And I'm the King of Scots!' said the gaoler. 'Sorry brother, but the boy was still in his cage when he got thumped.'

'Well who else did it, then?' the gatekeeper retorted. 'No girl can knock out a grown man in his prime.'

'You haven't met his wife,' muttered the gaoler behind his hand. 'You just don't want to admit you was caught with your pants down, that's all.'

'And you weren't, I suppose?'

'I was just being polite, treating a lady with respect.'

'You spoke to her?' I said, rinsing out the cloth in my bowl.

'The Lady Adelle?'

'Prrf! That was no lady,' snorted the gaoler. 'She was a right little prick-tease – begging your pardon, brother.'

'And you'd know all about one of them, wouldn't you?' mocked his friend. 'Pretty girl smiles at you and you just hand over the keys like a puppy.'

'I didn't just *hand* them over, pea-brain. She *took* them - after she whacked me over the head with her hammer.'

'Ha! Whacked you with her perfume, more like - eh brother?' The gatekeeper laughed at his own quip.

This didn't sound at all like the Lady Adelle I knew. A flirt - and no lady? But I suppose any wife who fears for her husband's life might stoop to such depths to secure his freedom, even one of such noble birth as the Lady Adelle's. Or maybe these two were simply embellishing the tale in order to cover for their own negligence.

Whatever the truth of it, I wasn't going to find out more as the door was suddenly thrown open and both men instantly leapt to attention. I turned in dismay to see Geoffrey de Saye standing on the threshold.

He snapped his fingers at the two men. 'You two – out!'

They didn't need telling twice. My two brave warriors darted out with amazingly renewed agility, all thoughts of injury now gone.

De Saye quietly closed the door after them and for the first time in fifteen years we were alone together. Suddenly the room seemed very small indeed.

'Well well bone-breaker, here you are again. I can call you that, can I? Bone-breaker?' He cupped his ear facetiously. 'I hear no-one laughing now.'

'I merely go where I am needed, my lord,' I said holding up the vinegar bowl with its bloodied rags for him to see. I was annoyed to see that the hand that was holding the bowl was shaking very slightly.

He glanced briefly at the bowl and then back at me. 'Except that this time you were here before your skills were called for - before the boy escaped.'

'If your spies told you that, my lord, they will also have told you that I tried to persuade him *not* to run.'

He cupped his chin in his hand and nodded thoughtfully. 'You still think he's innocent?'

'I'm sure of it.'

I debated whether to tell him about the poison - but was there any point? His next utterance convinced me there was not.

'The evidence says otherwise.'

'No court in England will convict him on it.'

He smiled wryly. 'No court in Suffolk, maybe.'

He was right, of course. If he managed to get Raoul out of Bury and back to Norfolk he could pack a court with his own men and get whatever verdict he wanted - assuming he'd even bother getting him that far and not have him killed en route. Raoul wouldn't be the first prisoner to be shot while trying to escape.

'In any event it's all academic at the moment, wouldn't you say? The bird has flown.'

De Saye shook his head. 'He won't remain so for long.'

'Well, he seems to have successfully eluded your lordship so far.'

'Meaning?'

There was only the two of us. Why not tell him what I really thought?

'I know about the meeting in Stamford,' I said. 'I'm guessing Raoul de Gray is the real reason you are here.'

At that his smile evaporated confirming at the very least that Onethumb's theory about the two London merchants had been correct.

'Why would I be interested in the fate of a bishop's nephew?'

'I don't know, my lord, but you seem very keen to have him convicted for this murder.'

'That's because he did it.'

I smiled crookedly. 'We will have to disagree on that.'

He took a step closer to me - too close for comfort. The memory of the last time we were alone together still haunted me. Fifteen years older he may be, but I still found his presence intimidating.

'Whether you agree or not, bone-breaker, is of little consequence.'

'It's curious though isn't it, my lord, that you should arrive in Bury now just as there has been another murder in the town? Just like last time.'

He stepped even closer so that now I could feel his breath on my face. It was all I could do not to cringe.

'What are you suggesting?'

'It was merely an observation.'

'You think I killed the girl?'

'I don't know who killed her.'

'But you have a theory.' He nodded. 'Very well. We're alone, there's no-one to hear. Tell me what you think happened.'

I took a deep breath. 'I think we both know Raoul de Gray

didn't kill his wife's maid. I think you know who did and the reason why. I think she knew something, or discovered something that so terrified her that she needed to tell someone about it. She did try to tell me but failed and then she was killed before she could tell anyone else. I think you want Raoul de Gray blamed for the murder so that you can take him into custody and have him convicted though for what reason I don't know. There are a great many other things I don't yet know. But I will and when I do…'

I got no further before he had his hand on my throat and me pressed up against the wall. I cried out mostly in shock but also in some pain as his fingers dug into my neck so I could hardly breathe.

'Now you listen to me,' he growled. 'You've been warned once by the prior. Now I'm warning you. Stop this meddling in matters that don't concern you and go back to being a monk or by Christ and all His saints the de Gray boy won't be the only one to feel the hangman's noose.'

As he said it he tightened his grip on my neck until I could hardly breathe at all. I was starting to panic from lack of air.

'Is this wise, my lord?' I choked trying to prise his hand from my neck and failing. 'There are witnesses. Those two men are abbey men. They will attest that they left us alone together. If my body is found here even you will find it difficult to explain away. We are not in the forest now.'

My words seemed to strike some kind of a chord with him. I don't think he realised quite how close he was to throttling me. His eyes seemed to have a mist behind them that took a minute to clear. It was that reference to the last time he attacked me that did it, I think. He momentarily increased his grip before relaxing his hold and letting me go. I gasped holding my throat. I cannot describe the relief it was to be able to breathe again.

'We have unfinished business, you and I,' he breathed. 'Don't imagine anything on that score has changed. And when all this is over, rest assured we will speak again.' With that he turned smartly and marched out of the room letting the door bang shut after him.

I have never been so relieved to see the back of anyone. After a moment I fell gratefully to my knees with the room swimming around me and looking down I was amazed to see broken pottery on the floor and realised it was the vinegar bowl I had been holding.

'Well,' I coughed to the empty room. 'It is always pleasant to renew old acquaintances.'

I dragged myself onto the gatekeeper's stool with my legs still unsteady beneath me and my bowels loosening. My throat felt as though a hammer had hit it but with each swallow it was getting easier so there was probably no permanent damage done. I didn't really think he'd kill me - not then at any rate. But what did amaze me was that he hadn't arrested me. It was surely an ideal opportunity given the circumstances. The old Geoffrey de Saye would have done so without a moment's hesitation. But like a great many unanswered questions that day it would be a while before I learned the reason why.

PART TWO
The Chase Begins

Chapter Thirteen

A CHAPTER OF LIES

The next morning the abbey was rife with rumour about Raoul's dramatic escape from Anselm's tower. All had heard the hue and cry which had gone on for most of the night and many of my brothers approached me for details. having heard of my part in the affair – or what they thought was my part in it. It was curious how much each man's version of events differed from the next, and so far from the truth that in the end I was unclear myself as to exactly what happened. I had been hoping my two friends, the gaoler and the gatekeeper, might be able to shed more light but when I looked for them I learned to my distress that they had both been put in the town stocks. This seemed excessive punishment simply for losing a prisoner but entirely in keeping with Lord de Saye's vindictive nature. As soon as I was able, I hurried to the marketplace where I did indeed find them shackled by their ankles and wrists and to my further dismay saw that de Saye had also silenced them with gags so they could not tell what had really happened. But

I could at least examine their wounds and to reassure their questioning eyes that nothing worse would befall them. In this I spoke more in hope than conviction since nothing was certain where de Saye was concerned.

I returned to the abbey in time for Chapter where I was disturbed to find de Saye already seated at the front next to the prior. Now what? More games? Seeing him here at least gave me hope that our meeting in the gatekeeper's lodge might have worried him more than he pretended and that I was therefore onto something. But what I saw beside him now made my heart sink. A table had been erected upon which was prominently displayed Raoul's bloodied cap and next to it, mercifully hidden by a clean linen cloth, was what I guessed from the shape must be the remains of poor Effie. I could see that we were in for some of de Saye's theatricals.

Prior Herbert opened the Chapter with the usual prayer of supplication:

'The Peace of the Lord be with you and may He give His blessing on these our solemn deliberations - Amen.'

The response was more muted than usual, in deference, I presumed, to the dead person in our midst, and there was no reading today from the Rule. Instead, Prior Herbert waited until every last shuffle and cough had died away before rising again slowly and beginning his address which he did in a voice that was barely audible:

'Brothers, you have all heard the news I know. Yesterday morning the body of a young girl was found in the marketplace which has since been identified as being that of the maid to the Lady Adelle de Gray and her husband, Raoul.'

This was greeted with gasps of anguish. It was indeed dreadful news, not just because of the death but because of who the victim was. Along with her master and mistress Effie was a guest of the abbey and therefore under Saint Edmund's personal protection. It is thus a great dishonour to him and to the abbey that any harm should have come to her whilst in our care.

'How did she die?' came a voice from the back of the room.

'Strangled,' Herbert replied glancing at de Saye for confirmation. 'Yes, I believe she was strangled.'

It was just as I feared: Herbert was allowing himself to be manipulated by de Saye – something Abbot Samson would never have permitted and possibly not Hugh Northwold either. Where was Hugh now when we needed him?

More agonized murmurings now from my brother monks. 'Is there a suspect?' asked one. 'Do we have a name?'

'We do not know for certain,' Herbert admitted, 'but evidence points to the girl's master as her likely murderer. My lord de Saye here, acting with my full authority, arrested Raoul de Gray shortly after the discovery of the body and placed him in the abbey lockup. However, late yesterday afternoon he managed to escape and is currently at large.'

Louder groans of distress came from my brothers.

'He had help, of course,' Herbert continued. 'He could not have managed it alone. The question is, help from whom?'

He looked meaningfully around the room and while he did not look directly at me everyone in the room knew I'd been there when Raoul escaped. I squirmed uncomfortably in my seat.

'It has been suggested,' Herbert went on after a suitable

pause, 'that the Lady Adelle was somehow complicit. But we have to ask ourselves if a mere female, especially one of such gentle and noble birth and so recently weakened by the efforts of giving birth, would have had the strength to free her husband from a secure cell, or how she could have achieved it?'

Ask the gatekeeper, I felt like saying, he will tell you how – with guile and cunning. The voice at the back of the room piped up again:

'You mentioned evidence, Brother Prior?'

Herbert nodded. 'Thank you brother, I was just coming to that. But first we have to ask ourselves why? Why did he run? After all, is this the action of an innocent man? Why did he not remain to defend himself? And why did the Lady Adelle not try to dissuade him?'

More murmurings of disquiet from my brothers, but that voice at the back spoke up again:

'Any fox will run when he sees the flash of the farmer's knife. It does not prove he stole the chicken.'

A chuckle or two at this eased the tension a little. I looked round to see if I could identify the owner of the voice but could not. But Herbert was not to be thrown so easily. He conferred quickly with de Saye before turning abruptly to the table beside him and lifting from it Raoul's battered cap - using the same little stick, I noticed, that I had used in the marketplace the previous day. The cap looked much as it had then except that the blood had congealed into an even stickier mess. A gasp of revulsion went up as brothers recoiled from it.

'This was found beside the body of the murdered girl,' Herbert announced waving the wretched thing around dramatically.

'What is it?' whispered one agitated voice.

'A cap,' answered his neighbour.

'Indeed it is,' said Herbert. 'A man's cap. And I can confirm that it has been irrefutably identified as belonging to Raoul de Gray.'

More moans from the room. I was growing more and more uneasy as the drama unfolded. This was turning into a trial with Herbert as prosecution counsel. But where was the defence? Or, for that matter, the judge? But Herbert was unrelenting:

'Some of you may have heard the rumours about this boy. What we know for sure is that at the very moment his wife was giving birth to their first child and most in need of her husband's support, Raoul de Gray was in the town cavorting with prostitutes and drunkards. And when he returns at last the worse for ale and doubtless still filled with unsated lust, what does he do? His wife, nobly modest before her newborn infant, naturally declines his attentions, so he turns instead to the one person unable to resist his advances: His wife's maid. We can only guess where those excesses may have taken him.'

This was outrageous. Herbert could not possibly have known what had gone on in the privacy of the de Gray's bedchamber. But his graphic description had the effect he wanted. Heads were beginning to shake in disgust and I even saw one or two fists being shaken. It was no good, I could remain silent no longer.

'Just one moment, Brother Prior,' I said rising to my feet.

'Ah,' smiled Herbert. 'Master Walter - the fugitive's friend.'

All heads turned to look at me. Now I was being accused too by association. There was no passing this cup from my lips. I had to reply:

'Not his friend, Brother Prior, merely one who wishes to

see justice done. The accused man is not here to answer for himself so I must. What you say is mere supposition. There is no evidence that Raoul harmed the girl.'

'You do not deny he behaved aggressively towards her? You told me as much yourself - in the presence of a witness.' He indicated de Saye.

'What I said was he may have *disciplined* her,' I said, 'as is the right and duty of any good master. And that is a long way from murder.'

'Who can say how far he went?' returned Herbert. 'Drunkards are rarely in command of their actions. Maybe that's what happened. Maybe that's all of it. If so then he should return here and own to his mistake. If not we can only suppose his reasons for running away.'

'But he wasn't drunk,' I countered. 'At least, not on the night of the murder. He was drugged.'

Gasps all round at this and Herbert's eye twinkled. 'I take it you have proof for this bizarre claim?'

I was about to say I did, but then I remembered I'd already thrown the vomit away careful this time not leave the poison lying around. I hadn't thought I'd need it again. No doubt Herbert's spies had told him all this as well. No wonder he was looking so smug.

'Well?' prompted Herbert when I didn't reply.

'A quantity of henbane went missing from my shelves. I believe the thief may have used it to taint Raoul's drink.'

'You *believe*,' snorted Herbert.

'No - more than that: I *know* his ale couldn't have incapacitated him,' I insisted. 'It was virtually water.'

Even before my words were fully out I knew the mistake I'd

made.

Herbert paused to allow my gaffe to resonate fully. 'Was it, indeed? And how could you possibly know that, brother - unless you were drinking it yourself?'

There was no point denying it. Groans of disapproval now from my brothers, even from those who might have been sympathetic. I'd made a complete hash of it. I glanced at de Saye who was gazing levelly back at me in triumph. Herbert, too, was looking pleased with himself - and why should he not? Like any well-prepared advocate he was only asking the questions to which he already knew the answers. Was there anything his spies had not told him?

'Master Walter,' he continued in leaden tones, 'your litany of indiscretions astounds even me. If you're not visiting young ladies alone in their private rooms you are drinking in taverns with their husbands. We have to wonder what sort of degenerate we been harbouring in our midst.'

I snorted at the absurdity of that remark. 'Oh, this is ridiculous. We are getting away from the plain fact which is that Raoul de Gray could not have strangled this maid.'

'Oh? Why?'

'For the simple reason that at the time of the murder he was -'

I stopped. My brother monks stared silently agog to hear my next revelation. But I didn't have to. Herbert finished it for me:

'For the simple reason that he was asleep on your *floor*.'

I looked round at my brother monks. Not one of them could meet my gaze. This was far worse than visiting Adelle in her chamber or drinking with her husband in The Hanged Man — worse, possibly, even than murder. A drunken man asleep on cloistered ground and in the cell of a senior obedientiary - it was an outrage. Even those who had previously been on my side were now shaking their heads in dismay.

Herbert was conferring once again with de Saye. 'If this is true,' he said rising, 'it is yet another woeful admission. But even so we have only your word for it. You may simply be inventing more lies.'

'No, this time I have a witness,' I blustered on.

Herbert smiled. 'Then produce him.'

I'd meant Dominic. He would be able to confirm that we had nursed Raoul on my floor of my cell while the murder was being committed. Indeed, it was he who had done the nursing while I went back to my own cot. And conveniently, here he was seated right next to me. I turned to him now but as I did so I saw the look of horror on his face at being dragged into the fray — and I simply couldn't do it, not to save Raoul's neck, not even to salvage my own reputation. It would be the end of his life in the abbey. I stood staring at him unable to go on or to think of a way out. The silence became oppressive. Finally with a dismissive wave of his hand Herbert sat down whereupon the room erupted.

But I needed one last chance:

'The cap!' I yelled above the rumpus.

Herbert looked up wearily. 'What about it?'

'*That* is my witness, the cap,' I said pointing to the thing on the table. 'When it was found there was a hand holding it.'

'Indeed,' nodded Herbert. 'The maid's hand — lost in the struggle with her murderer.'

'No, it was a man's hand.'

'What?'

'I was the one who found it. I can attest to it being a man's hand.'

Herbert snorted. '*How* can you attest it?'

'Witnessed by at least a dozen people,' I persisted remembering the crowd in the marketplace.

I seemed at last to have caught Herbert unprepared. He looked fleetingly at de Saye who gave the slightest shrug of his shoulders.

'You'll need more than that.'

'I have more,' I said confidently. 'I can produce the owner...'

Here I felt a slight tug on my sleeve.

'...a vagabond preacher...'

'Master -'

'...who can be brought here before this house...'

'Master please -'

'...where I have no doubt he will confirm...'

'Master!'

'What Dominic?' I said turning irritably to the boy and pulling my sleeve from his grasp.

'Hervey died last night.'

At that moment a cock crowed somewhere in the far distance cutting through the silence in the room. I looked round at my brother monks many of whom were shaking their heads in dismay while others were smiling with satisfaction. I noticed in the pause that having stepped forward from my seat to deliver my peroration like a Roman senator of old, I had inadvertently stepped onto Abbot Samson's recently-interred grave. In my mind's eye I could see him now beneath my foot, shaking his head and tutting.

However, the thought of him lying there gave me renewed

strength of purpose and what I did next broke ever more of Herbert's precious rules. I marched boldly down to the front of the chapterhouse and threw back the linen cloth that was covering poor Effie exposing her bloated and naked body for all to see. Cries of shock and outrage rang out as my brother monks covered their eyes or looked away. But I didn't care. I knew I was about to vindicated.

Except that I wasn't. Geoffrey de Saye was one step ahead of me. I'd expected to see lying beneath the cloth what I had seen in the beadle's office – Effie's body with both hands attached. Of course they weren't. Only one hand was attached. The right had been sawn off – and I mean sawn not chewed by any pig. To make it clear to everyone that the hand was detached from the body, it had been placed deliberately the wrong way up next to the stump of poor Effie's mutilated arm. I gasped at the outrage and glared at Geoffrey de Saye whose smug face told me everything I needed to know. I had fallen headlong into his trap. Not that my pointing this out would have helped. Was there now a soul left in that room that did not believe Raoul de Gray to be the murderer of his wife's maid and that I was his accomplice? It was clear now why de Saye had not arrested me the previous day – it was in order to inflict this crushing blow. But it was not too late. He could arrest me now before the entire assembled monastery and make my humiliation complete – and who would have blamed him if he had?

The Chapter broke up in disarray and without the customary *Verba mea*, although I muttered it under my breath with a deeper conviction than I have felt it before: Dear Lord, hear my prayer and let my cry come unto thee!

*

I felt utterly deflated. I could not believe what had just occurred. A dreadful, dreadful distortion of the truth. Manipulating evidence was one thing, but de Saye had gone one stage further to actually manufacture false evidence. It was a low I would not have anticipated even he would stoop to. It begged the question of why he should wish to do such a thing? Surely there could be only one answer to that: He had to be the murderer.

As the brethren dispersed I sought out Dominic. The boy was full of apology:

'I'm sorry, master, I could not -'

'Yes yes, never mind,' I waved him down. 'It's not your fault. Just tell me, where did you hear that about Hervey?'

'His friend came to the almonry this morning with the news.'

'He sought you out? Why?'

'I don't know, master. I was to tell the news to you personally – he was quite specific about that. But you had already gone in to Chapter.'

'Yes I see, yes,' I said thoughtfully.

It was one more tactic of de Saye's and I could not help a wry smile for it was nicely choreographed. I was to be told of Hervey's death but only when it was too late to prevent me making a fool of myself. The timing had been perfect.

'How did he die?'

The boy shrugged. 'I don't know, master. But I believe he was half way to God's bosom already.'

I nodded. 'He was indeed very ill, poor man. Thank God that his suffering now is over at last.'

'Amen,' said Dominic, and smiled wanly. 'At least he went in the company of his angel.'

I took hold of his arm. 'What did you just say?'

He shrugged. 'That's what his friend said to tell you: That Hervey's angel came for him. He said you would understand. I thought it a charming conceit.'

More of a conceit than he could know. 'Thank you, Dominic.'

Perhaps it was Hervey's time to go to God – or perhaps someone had hastened him there prematurely. This mysterious angel again. What did it mean? I should have liked to see Hervey's body and perhaps brought it to the chapterhouse to prove I was right about his missing hand. But even if I could have found it, was there any point now? My brother monks already considered my exposure of Effie's body a profanity. Two corpses would be more than they could tolerate. I would have to find another way.

Chapter Fourteen
A PLAN HATCHES

I spent the rest of the day expecting guards to burst in at any moment and haul me off either to the gaol-room or, more likely, to join my two friends in the pillory. In the event neither happened for far weightier matters were afoot about which as yet I knew nothing. But I am getting ahead of myself. For now I was free to pursue my normal duties and to observe the offices of the day, albeit keeping as low a profile as I could. After the fiasco in the chapterhouse I was shunned by a good many of my brothers although others did offer me their sympathy - most notably my dear old friend Jocelin. Perhaps he was remembering the last time something like this happened in the long distant past when we were both caught up in a similar struggle against a similar adversary. Fortunately the liturgical day was becoming progressively shorter the nearer we approached the year's end which left me more time to ponder the fate of the little de Gray family.

They appeared to have vanished into thin air. Edmundstown

is no mean vill having as it does some four thousand or so souls within its walls, but even here it should not be possible for a family of three to disappear completely, especially with a warrant out for their arrest and everybody looking for them. They were strangers in the town and as far as I was aware they knew nobody. So where had they gone? The only place I could think might hold a clue was their former lodgings in the abbot's palace and so that was where I decided to look first.

I waited until the sun had started its descent below the western horizon before making my move. It is a quiet period of the day when most of my brother monks are busy with work or study and hopefully would not notice me slip into the guest lodgings in the twilight. I took with me an oil lamp whose wick I had trimmed so that it did not burn too brightly. In this I was too successful for I stubbed my toe twice trying to negotiate the unfamiliar surroundings in the little light that I had left myself. I thought I heard someone breathing in the shadows, but when I looked it was just a grey rat that scuttled away at my approach. At last I managed to find the right staircase, the one where I'd had my last encounter with Effie, and climbed to the level the family had occupied twelve hours earlier.

In the bedchamber the shutters were closed and I opened one of them to let in some of the light of the moon that was already rising - the Hunter's Moon. I looked round. I didn't really know what I was looking for – anything that might indicate where the family may have gone. There was very little to be seen. All appeared to be as it was the last time I was here although there were signs of a hasty departure: The bed where the Lady Adelle had lain nursing her baby was still there; the two settle beds, one for the husband and the other, the murdered girl's bed.

I was wasting my time. There was nothing here for me. I turned to leave. But as I did so something caught my eye. The breeze coming in from the open shutter had fanned the embers in the brazier and they started to glow, very slightly, red. I put my hand over the top of the frame and felt heat coming up. Someone had been here recently, certainly more recently than twelve hours ago. And even as I had the thought, I heard them – or rather the baby, just the tiniest whimper. I turned and the little hairs on the back of my neck tingled as I saw the outline of the family silhouetted against the far wall where they had been all along silently watching me: Raoul, Adelle and nestling in Adelle's arms, little baby Alix.

'We tried to leave the town, brother, but could not find a way through,' replied Raoul to my query.

'After your violent escape from gaol, you mean?' I said pointedly. 'And the pain and injury you caused the gaoler and the gatekeeper. Not to mention the poor fellows' punishment in the stocks. My humiliation. Any moral advantage you might have had thrown away.'

'I'm sorry about all that. Please don't blame Adelle. She was only acting in my defence.' He looked like a cornered creature at the end of his tether.

'Yes, well,' I said somewhat mollified. 'In the light of what happened today you were probably right to run. You would have received no quarter from the prior or my lord de Saye. They are determined to have you. But why are you still here? You should be miles away by now.'

'Every road out of Bury is being watched. It is impossible to get further than a mile or two. In the end we had no choice but to come back here.'

'What every road?' I asked in astonishment.

He nodded, the weariness evident on his face even in the gloom. 'Besides, we had to return because of Alix,' he said indicating baby.

'Why?' I asked, stepping forward. 'Is she ill?'

'No, just hungry,' said Raoul. 'You have to understand, Effie...' he flinched slightly at the mention of her name, '... was suckling her.'

'Effie?' This was an astonishing revelation. 'Effie was to be the baby's wet-nurse?'

While I would be the first to admit that I knew little of the art of child rearing, one thing I did know was that a wet-nurse was just that: A sow brim-full of milk and usually a mother herself with a child of her own recently weaned. Effie had been none of these things. Indeed, she was more than a child herself. Hardly a fitting choice.

'What have you been feeding her on since...?'

'Since Effie was murdered?' said Raoul defiantly. He shook his head. 'All we had was a little cow's milk. But that has run out now. I will have to steal some from the abbey kitchen.'

'I wouldn't do that,' I warned him. 'Don't add theft to your other crimes - *alleged* crimes.'

He looked at me shyly. 'Does that mean you do not believe I killed Effie?'

Did I? I still wasn't certain. I brushed the question aside. 'What I think hardly matters now. You have powerful enemies in the prior and Geoffrey de Saye. If they catch you, you will be returned to Norfolk to stand trial.'

'No,' he said backing away from me. 'That must not happen.'

I could see he was in genuine distress. 'Calm yourself, my son. We are a long way from that yet. But you must be careful.'

I described the scene in the chapterhouse that morning and how between them the prior and Geoffrey de Saye had managed to damn him. He listened in silence. When I got to the bit about his cap he nodded.

'I wondered what happened to that. I knew I had it when I went to the tavern. Whose hand did you say had hold of it?'

'A vagabond called Hervey.'

Raoul frowned thinking hard. 'No, I'm sure I know nothing of him. But to be truthful there's not much I do remember after I stepped into the tavern until I left your cell the following morning. I know I got very drunk - but I don't know how. I had very little ale.' He rubbed his brow as though trying to uncover some hidden secret lodged there. 'Did I...kill this vagabond?'

I shook my head. 'No. He died in God's good time not mans'. Nor did you mutilate him – unless you managed to sneak out of the lockup and back again without being seen. Once again the timing is all wrong.'

'Once again,' repeated Raoul.

'Yes, once again. But that won't help you, I'm afraid. No-one is listening to logic anymore. They only hear the message - which is that you murdered Effie. And since there is no other candidate...'

Raoul shook his head in exasperation. 'My head is thick. All is confusion.'

'I'm not surprised,' I said. 'I'm pretty sure someone drugged your ale.'

He looked genuinely shocked at that. 'Who?'

A PLAN HATCHES

I shrugged. 'The girl in the tavern?'

But Raoul just shook his head. 'No, not Netta.'

'Oh, you remember her all right,' I said glancing pointedly at Adelle. But the lady didn't seem to notice. She was too concerned with the baby who, right on cue, woke up and began wailing. Adelle did her best to quieten the tiny thing but with little success. I was concerned someone might hear her and closed the shutters again. The cry of a baby would surely give them away instantly.

'It is time I went,' I said. 'I will be missed if I am not back at my place soon and I have created enough suspicion for one day.'

'And I must go out and find milk,' said Raoul.

'No,' I cautioned. 'It's too dangerous.' Then I resigned myself to the inevitable. 'I'll get it.'

'No, brother, you've done enough. I can't ask you to involve yourself anymore.'

'I'm touched by your concern, my son, but is there any other choice? However difficult it will be for me to find food it will be easier than for you. ' I looked about the darkened room. 'You are fortunate the abbot's quarters are empty and that you have been absent these last few hours. If I thought to look here others will have done too. I am sure the prior's men have been here while you were gone and checked which probably means they won't be back and you are safe to remain. I will go now and return in a little while with some milk for the baby and anything else I can think of. But I fear it won't be enough. She needs proper sustenance - for that matter you all do. In the meantime, show no lights and keep the shutters closed. And don't for goodness sake light that brazier again. Better you shiver in the dark than hang in the light. I will bring blankets when I come.'

I took one last look round and started for the door. But before I could get there Raoul caught hold of my sleeve.

'Why are you doing this? Why not hand me over to the prior? It would exonerate you.'

I looked at his hand on my arm. 'Who's to say I won't?'

Until that moment I still was not certain about him. Had he truly been the murderer this would be his opportunity to silence me before I could betray him. But he released me and I was able to take my hand from the knife I had at the ready beneath my robe in case he should not.

I opened the door and checking that the coast was clear, stepped outside. 'Do not despair,' I smiled encouragingly. 'I will be back before you know it. God be with you all.'

'Can we trust you brother?' asked Raoul as one last shot.

'You have no choice,' I replied and quietly closed the door.

Chapter Fifteen

ROSABEL

Plans were rapidly forming in my head as I hurried out once again through Anselm's gate. The old gatekeeper had been replaced and this new one was unknown to me. I had to assume he was one of de Saye's men and so took a circuitous route through the town to reach my destination. Once I was certain I had not been followed, I came back down through the town to the marshlands - a remote area to the south of the town, low-lying and damp. Here Onethumb and Rosabel had a room in her parents' house in a street that ran down to the Linnet River. It had to be remote because of the type of industry that was carried on here. Rosabel's father worked in the tanning trade curing leather hides which is a notoriously noisome and evil-smelling activity. Neighbours tended to shun them as a result which suited my purpose. The process also required a constant supply of urine, the more acrid the better, which Rosabel's father stored in earthenware jars in the back yard and could get very ripe indeed, especially in summer. Crucially, they also had a cow.

It was Onethumb who answered the door to my knock. They were in the middle of eating their evening meal and he invited me to join them. But I was too agitated to eat. We went instead out into the back yard where we could talk in private.

Before I revealed the de Gray family's whereabouts I needed to be sure Onethumb was as convinced as I was of Raoul's innocence for only then would he be likely to help me with the rest of my plan. I asked him first if he remembered the curfew bell the night I met him on the street. He answered that the bell was still sounding when we met - in fact it had been the signal for him to stop work and start for home. So far so good. Next I asked him about the blacksmiths in the market. He signed that he knew the blacksmiths from his days as a street urchin when he would hang around their fires for warmth and companionship. He corroborated what the beadle had told me that the smithies were nearly always the last to pack up usually well after the curfew bell sounded.

'So do you see the point I'm getting to?' I urged him. 'Effie's body couldn't have been dumped in the market before the curfew bell or the blacksmiths would have seen it. And since Raoul was in the tavern at the time and with us thereafter, he had no time to deposit the body. *Ipso facto* he couldn't have been the murderer.'

Onethumb screwed up his face.

'What?' I asked him impatiently. 'Tell me, what have I missed?'

Onethumb signed that Raoul could have killed the girl before we saw him, hidden the body somewhere and put it in the market square some time later.

I shook my head. 'He was never out of sight again until the

next morning.'

Onethumb still looked unconvinced. *Are you sure he was never left alone even for a short while?*

'Positive,' I affirmed. 'Dominic was with him all night – well, except for a few minutes around midnight when he answered a call of nature. But he would have seen if Raoul had left the laboratorium.'

And Dominic didn't fall asleep? Or leave the room even for another few minutes?

'He assures me not. Oh God, now you're putting doubts into my head again.' I scratched my naked pate in thought. 'No,' I said resolutely. 'I'm sure he wouldn't have had the time. He'd have had to kill Effie then gone off to the tavern to see Netta and someone else would have had to dump the body. It's all too elaborate. And another thing, he was drugged – I found enough henbane in his vomit to kill a horse. He wouldn't have done that to himself,' I grimaced. 'Would he? To throw us off the scent?'

Onethumb walked away thinking while I nervously bit my nails waiting for his decision. Eventually he came back nodding. To my enormous relief he seemed as convinced as I was of Raoul's innocence. I was about to tell him the rest of my news when he started signing again. Watching him, I couldn't help but smile.

'Nothing gets past you does it, my friend? Yes, you are right, I do know where they are.'

I took a deep breath and told him. He listened with a serious face. When I'd finished he signed that they would need milk for the baby. Being a father himself of a young child, he'd know all about that.

But that's why you're here, isn't it?

'Naturally I'll pay you,' I said. 'But first there's something else I have to ask. Something of a delicate nature…'

'No, absolutely not. Don't bother asking again because the answer will still be no! No, no and again I say no. No!'

Ah, sweet Rosabel. If I were twenty years younger and not already betrothed to Christ and His church, I could easily lose my heart to this beauty. Full and rounded and voluptuously feminine, she was my ideal of a true woman - none of these skinny, boyish girls with flat chests that seem to be the fashion these days. She combined the face of Helen, the form of Aphrodite, the complexion of a rosebud - and the temper of Tisiphone, the fiercest of the Furies. Her parents must have had a premonition of how their daughter would turn out for no-one could have been more aptly named: Rosabel, *Bella Rosa* - a beautiful rose indeed, but every rose has its thorns and none sharper than Rosabel's. Many's the time Onethumb has threatened her with the cucking-stool for a scold, and many's the time he has come home to a burnt supper as a result - or no supper at all. How he managed to win her in the first place has long been a source of wonderment to me. Not uncomely of face himself nor unmanly of form, Onethumb nevertheless did not strut with his fellows or excel with the longbow as they did. And try as we might, we cannot ignore his natural handicaps which surely must put off many a would-be suitor. I once asked her what she saw in him, and Rosabel simply smiled secretively and winked. He clearly has attributes that appeal to woman but evade the eye of the casual male observer. I put it down to the same spirit that won him the pennies I'd thrown in the air when we first met on the street fifteen years ago. Competing with other fully-limbed lads, Onethumb had managed to collect more of the trophies than they did despite having no tongue and only half their complement of fingers. But that was typical of Onethumb. Once he had determined upon a quest, little could deter him. And he had been determined upon his Rosabel.

They made a fine couple and all the finer when their son, Hal, arrived to bless their relationship six months ago. For all their apparent discord in public, clearly in private they harmonised well – Hal was the living proof of that. Five years younger than Onethumb, Rosabel was quite a buxom wench made all the more so by her recent pregnancy - which was the reason I risked venturing into the tigress's den tonight. But it was clear from her initial response to my suggestion that we were going to have difficulties persuading her. Arms akimbo and brow exquisitely furrowed, she tapped her toe impatiently upon the garden path.

'In case you haven't noticed,' she sneered, 'I have a child of my own. I don't need another.'

Onethumb smiled at me and shrugged as if to say "I told you so".

But I wasn't about to give up just yet. 'Madam,' I said to her in my sternest patrician's voice. 'Your husband commands you. It is your duty to obey him.'

That was the cause of the first pot of urine to be tipped over. Onethumb angrily rebuked her for her wastefulness and threatened to beat her for her obstinacy - and that was the cause of the second pot going over and for good measure this time she picked up the ladle brandishing it threateningly at her husband. Like cowards before this great Bathsheba we both cringed in a corner. She was magnificent! Onethumb winced at the mess in the yard and glanced anxiously back at the house where his father-in-law must have heard the crash and known what it was. Since he did not come out he evidently guessed who had caused the damage and thought better of challenging his daughter.

Threats having got us nowhere, Onethumb tried a different tack. He explained in some of the most exquisite choreography I have ever seen him execute the plight of the lady Adelle and poor little starving Alix. The hunger pangs, the mother's tears, the despair. His performance certainly convinced me. I thought I saw Rosabel mellowing after his efforts and sought to press home the advantage:

'Madam, there is no disgrace in being a wet-nurse,' I ventured. 'King Richard had one and she greatly prospered from the association achieving wealth and status after the king's death.'

'And will I prosper too from your proposal?' she asked haughtily.

I squirmed. 'God will reward you in heaven I am sure.'

'Ha!' Rosabel nodded knowingly. 'I thought not.'

I looked imploringly at Onethumb who insisted that it was because Rosabel was such a wonderful mother - a caring, loving mother - that we ask her. He also pointed out, delicately, that although Hal was weaned she still retained plenty of milk on the tit and so could easily cope with the needs of a young baby girl.

She frowned suspiciously. 'Why do you need me? Why not a proper wet-nurse? A proper *paid* one.'

'It is a delicate matter,' I said. 'We have to keep this arrangement *private*.'

'Why? What have they done?'

'Nothing,' I replied rather too quickly. 'At least, nothing

proved.'

Then light dawned in her eyes. 'It's that dead girl, isn't it?' she said quietly. 'The maid. The child's father's the one accused of murdering her. And this is the household you want your wife to enter?' She turned angrily on her husband and smacked the ladle hard against Onethumb's thigh. It is the only time I have ever heard Onethumb utter any kind of a sound – a sort of strangled animal whimper.

'He didn't do it,' I insisted.

'Well, that's easy to say,' she said whacking me now and making me yelp in surprise. 'You're not the one he'll murder next.'

Onethumb guffawed as it to say "He wouldn't dare!"

That got him the second slap making him hop about in pain.

'I suppose when I'm butchered and lying on a dunghill somewhere, you'll be able to look after your son, will you?' she snarled at him.

Right on cue, Rosabel's mother appeared at the back door with little Hal in her arms. From his grizzling he'd evidently been woken up from his sleep by the noise in the yard and looked about him wide-eyed and fearful. When he saw Rosabel he started to bawl and put out his arms.

She nodded with satisfaction. 'There's your answer. Your son needs his mother. Here, chick, mummy's not leaving you. She's going nowhere, don't worry.'

She went to take the child from her own mother's arms, but as she approached, Hal's bawling grew worse and as Rosabel went to take him he screamed, pushing out past her towards his father. Onethumb took his son from his mother-in-law's arms and Hal's bawling instantly stopped as he grizzled contentedly in his father's arms. Mouth open in astonishment, Rosabel threw her ladle down in the dirt in disgust.

'Men!'

It has always intrigued me that in a world rightly dominated by men it is often the female that turns out to be the most useful - and not just among humankind but right across the animal kingdom. It was a cow, after all, that provided the milk that will give life-giving sustenance to little Alix. The herdsmen on my mother's estate will very often kill off or sell any young male-cattle for meat while heifers are nurtured to full maturity with many productive years ahead of them. Likewise chickens provide eggs while the cock merely crows and struts. How odd that God should arrange things so.

Men, of course, are the more capable of the two sexes – that is self-evident and the reasons why are simple to explain. Men's brains are bigger than women's for a start, which is a scientific fact established by Aristotle. And we mustn't forget that it was a female, Eve, who brought sin into the world without which Adam would still be enjoying the innocent delights of the Garden of Eden, as God originally intended. I suppose the real answer is that men are stronger in body and spirit and are thus better equipped to order society. I shudder to think what a mess the world would be in if ever a woman was put in charge. So I suppose the correct balance between the sexes has been struck - at least in terms of human society if not that of animals.

But I digress. With a bundle of food and some warm clothing together with a pannikin of warm cow's milk, I hastened back to the abbey where I stayed just long enough to deposit my cargo and then rushed back to take my place in the abbey church in time for vespers praying that no-one watching had guessed what I was up to. The cow's milk, I knew, was only a temporary solution to the problem. What the baby needed was not my ministrations but Rosabel's unique *feminine* attributes – and soon. And with this in mind I arranged to meet up with Rosabel later that evening by the south gate of the abbey, the least guarded of the abbey's five gates, and smuggle her into the abbey grounds.

She came wearing a disguise of a pair of her husband's breeches and hood to cover her long red hair. Heaven knows what sport Prior Herbert would have made of this had he ever found out. Bringing a woman inside the abbey walls after sunset violated a whole array of his precious rules. One dressed as a man would have condemned us all for sure. But it was far too late to worry about such trifling matters. And I think we managed to get away with it, smuggling Rosabel over to the abbot's lodgings without drawing curious attention. I barely had time to deposit her with the family before having to rush back again to sing compline.

With all this rushing from here to there, when at last it was time to retire I collapsed, exhausted, onto my cot. Subterfuge is a young man's sport not for the likes of a man of my mature years. But at least I could rest easy in the knowledge that the de Grays were no longer in danger of discovery. The abbot's palace had been virtually abandoned since Abbot Samson's death with only the rats and mice and bats now in residence, and until the new abbot was appointed it would remain so. I felt I was able to relax at last. It was Friday 31st October – All Saints Eve. In pagan times this was the night when the souls of the dead return to earth to inhabit the bodies of the living. Heathen nonsense, of course, for what could possibly happen to disturb the peace and tranquillity of the abbey on this of all blessed nights?

Chapter Sixteen

THE FAMILY VANISHES

I awoke next morning with a start. The bell for prime was sounding but that's not what stirred me. Muffled voices were coming in through my cell window that I couldn't quite hear properly but something about them worried me even in my half-wakefulness. I opened the shutter and peered bleary-eyed across the Great Court towards the abbot's palace where I could just make out three men with axes and hammers standing outside the entrance exactly where the de Grays and Rosabel were holed up.

Barely stopping to heave on my boots, I rushed over just as one of the men was raising his axe to the barricading. 'Stop! Stop!' I cried. 'What are you doing? The palace is sealed, no-one may enter except the new abbot!'

'Aye,' the man agreed, lowering his tool. 'The new abbot – or the king.'

'The king? He's not coming. He's in France!'

'Well I don't know about that, brother,' said the man. 'I

just been told to get on and free these doors because the king commands it. Whether it's France or Indi-land that's what he wants and that's what I do. Now, stand aside brother if you please lest you get hit by flying splinters.' He nodded to his companions and again raised his axe above his head.

'No! Wait! ' I said putting my hand on his arm. 'You can't – you mustn't!'

The man faltered nearly dropping his axe. He looked at me sternly. 'Brother please, don't do that. You'll hurt yourself. If you have a complaint, see Brother Peter. I have my instructions. Now I'm asking you politely - step away.'

There was nothing more I could do. I stood back as the three man spat in the palms of their hands, raised their axes above their heads and brought them crashing down into the boarding. I flinched. The sound of splitting wood and tearing nails sounded to me like an animal's death throes. I looked up at the building. Heaven alone knew what the family inside was going through. They must be terrified. What worried me most was that Raoul must be thinking I had somehow betrayed him. In that frame of mind there's no saying what he might do.

I went quickly over to the cellarer's range in search of Brother Peter to try to grapple with him. But he simply shrugged impotently. It appeared that during the night Hugh Northwold had finally arrived back from France bringing with him the news that King John himself was coming to the abbey in three days time.

'*Three days*, Walter,' tutted the beleaguered cellarer. 'That's all the notice they've given me. I don't know how it's all to be done in the time. But that's how it is now with the king keeping his movements a secret until the last possible moment.' He shook his head despondently. 'It's a sad day when the King of England cannot trust even his own household for fear of being betrayed.' He went off still shaking his head.

I too was reeling from the news. The king's timing could not have been worse. For the family it was a disaster. No-one had set foot in the palace since Abbot Samson's death and in the fifteen years of his reign King John had stayed there only twice. And now half the abbey was trying to get inside. What mischievous sprite had prompted him to choose this of all moments? And it's not just the king, of course. Wherever he goes he takes with him the Government of England, which means all his officers of state, their stewards, secretaries, clerks, scribes, chaplains, ushers, huntsmen, men-at-arms, body-guards, archers, chamberlains, servants and attendants all needing food and accommodation. No wonder Peter was looking despondent. And in the middle of it all was my little family.

I stood in the courtyard biting my lip and watching with mounting anxiety as boards were ripped off, doors flung open and an army of servants marched in with brushes, cloths, buckets all intent upon cleaning the place from top to bottom. At any moment I was expecting a cry to go up and the family to be discovered. A cry did indeed go up and I spun round to see one of the servants being boxed about the ears for dropping a wine urn on the cobbles and losing a gallon of the precious liquid.

With my nerve close to snapping, I rushed round to the rear of the building to see if I could catch a glimpse of the window behind which I imagined the family to be cowering in terror. God be thanked, it remained closed. But even as I watched one of the shutters opened and I waited with baited

THE FAMILY VANISHES

breath for the shouts of discovery. But then an anonymous hand appeared through the window and vigorously flapped a cloth sending a cloud of dust into the weak morning sunshine before disappearing back inside again. Then another shutter opened - and another. Still no alarm. I couldn't understand it. Why had they not been detected? Surely catastrophe was but moments away.

I hurried back to the front of the building again and made my way up the stairs past the noise and bustle to peer through the open door of the bedchamber. I saw the brazier from the previous night and the beds stripped and upturned on their sides. But of the family there was no sign. The room was completely empty – except for yet another party of servants being supervised by a fastidious little fat monk called, I think, Maurice.

'Can I help you, master?' he said wiping the perspiration from his brow.

'No no,' I smiled. 'I was just checking.'

His eyes widened to saucers. 'Checking?'

'Yes checking, of course *checking*,' I bluffed. 'I am abbey physician and this is the king we are preparing for. His health is our prime concern, is it not? We cannot be too thorough.' I squinted up at the rafters and ran a critical finger along a ledge. 'Hm-hm, aha. All seems very clean, very...erm...hygienic. Good. Carry on.'

Maurice muttered something inaudible under his breath and bent ever more vigorously to his task.

Where had they gone? Vanished with the dust and the cobwebs. Raoul was adept at disappearing but this was little short of miraculous. My one faltering hope was that Onethumb might somehow have got wind of the king's arrival and spirited them away in the night. He was the only person apart from me who knew they had been there. I prayed with all my strength that it was so for the alternative was unthinkable: That they had been discovered already and were even now languishing in one of Geoffrey de Saye's dungeons.

*

I found Onethumb at his workplace behind Joseph's shop in Heathenman's Street. As soon as I saw him my hopes were dashed for I could tell he knew nothing. Indeed, the look of expectation on his face evaporated the instant he saw the concern on mine.

What's happened? he signed.

'I'm not sure.'

Rosabel?

All I could do was shrug. Thankfully Joseph appeared just then having closed up the shop to join us and both now they both listened while I recounted everything that had happened since the discovery of Effie's body in the marketplace, through Raoul's escape from the gaol, the farcical meeting in the chapterhouse and ending with the latest news of the king's impending visit to the abbey in three days time.

As I spoke Joseph's scowl grew blacker and blacker. 'I wish you had come to me earlier,' he said when I'd finished.

'Why? What would you have had me do? Abandon the boy?'

'Yes,' he said forcefully. 'That is exactly what I would have done. He is dangerous.'

Inevitably, my jaw dropped open. 'You of all people say that? You who suffered so much from prejudice and injustice yourself? My conscience would baulk at it – and so should yours being an outsider yourself.'

'It is because I am an outsider that I make it my business to understand these things. It is the only way my kind can survive. And you, my brother, are not thinking clearly. You allow your prejudices to govern you.'

I stopped myself saying more. He looked hurt. No, not hurt – *righteous*. Damn his eyes, he'd provoked me deliberately. I dare not look at Onethumb. How could I explain to him that this is how Joseph and I were with each other, how we had been since childhood? Our vitriol meant nothing. It was just our way.

Joseph sat down heavily on one of his infuriatingly uncomfortable cushions and sighed. It was the signal that we were about to receive one of his lectures, though no doubt imbued with much insightful wisdom and high moral rectitude. I growled under my breath but I had no option but to hear him out.

'Let us look at the facts,' he began. 'Since you already know that Bishop John is one of the king's most trusted and devoted servants you must also know he was King John's choice as Archbishop of Canterbury. Indeed, he was so appointed until the pope annulled the appointment and replaced him with Cardinal Langton. It is said to have been the spark that ignited all the king's present woes.'

I snorted petulantly. 'What present woes? The king has settled his argument with the pope.'

'With the pope, yes, but not with his barons.' He looked askance at us. 'No doubt you've heard about their recent meeting in Stamford?'

My jaw dropped open in astonishment and I looked accusingly at Onethumb. 'How did you...?' I began but stopped for Joseph was smiling in that infuriating way he has of letting you know he knows something you don't.

'It is at the heart of all that has passed since,' he intoned grandly. 'You have to remember who King John is. He is an Angevin, like his father before him. And Anjou is a little county. Their counts did not inherit their titles, they married them. King John's grandfather married the Empress Maud while his own father married that other great lady, Eleanor of Aquitaine. Those two alliances gave them all of England and half of France and made them the most powerful family in Europe. Many of John's barons, on the other hand, trace their titles back to the Conqueror. They regard the Angevins as upstarts. That was all right while England held great territories, but now John has lost them and the King of England is a mere count once more. Many of the barons don't like that – among them your friend Geoffrey de Saye.'

'So the barons are unhappy,' I shrugged. 'What has that to do with my little family?'

He put up his hand for patience. 'Throughout the king's quarrel with the pope Bishop John de Gray remained his staunchest ally - so much so that despite the pope's reconciliation with King John His Holiness has so far refused to forgive the good bishop who remains excommunicate. That is where he is now, in Rome seeking absolution. But that only solves half the king's problems. His barons are still not happy - hence their meeting in Stamford. That's as much as I have been able to ascertain. I haven't yet found out what they discussed at their meeting. But somewhere in the middle of all this is your "little family", as you call them. Find out where and you will be able to answer all your questions – including, no doubt, the reason for the

THE FAMILY VANISHES

maid's murder.'

Onethumb had been listening to all this without interruption. To be truthful I'd forgotten he was there, so engrossed had I been with Joseph. But now he decided to make his presence felt and began to sign aggressively. He was clearly angry. He didn't want to hear about kings and popes; he wanted to know what we going to do about Rosabel who, he reminded us, had disappeared and may be in grave danger. If he'd known beforehand what she was getting into, he signed, he would never have permitted her to go with the de Grays. We should be concentrating on finding her not worrying about barons.

Joseph and I both looked stupidly at him neither of us able to offer him any comfort. He nodded as though to say "I thought as much". More angry and frustrated than I had ever seen before, he stormed out of the shop. I called after him but Joseph put his hand on my shoulder.

'No, let him go.'

'But he might do something stupid.'

Joseph shook his head. 'What can he do? He doesn't know where the family is any more than we do. But wherever they are I am sure they are safe – for the present.'

'How can you be so sure?'

'Because nothing is going to happen while the king is in Bury. De Saye or anybody else will want to let matters rest for now.' He stroked his beard thoughtfully. 'Yes, John's presence here may well be your best card. Play it wisely, my brother.'

He drew me into an embrace and I hugged him for the fifty years of our friendship.

'The king,' I said releasing him. 'Why is he coming – do you know?'

'He wants to know who is to be the next Abbot of Saint Edmunds.'

I snorted. 'He's already had his answer to that.'

'He wants another. He's already had his choice of archbishop quashed by the pope, and now you monks are trying to do the same with this new abbot. Kings don't like to be told "no" too often. It makes them look weak - and that is the last thing John needs at the moment.'

I snorted. 'King John isn't weak. He's just unlucky.'

'Kings make their own luck,' sighed Joseph. 'And I'm very much afraid John's is beginning to run out.'

Chapter Seventeen
THE LETTER

I wish now that I had paid closer attention to what Joseph was trying to tell me but then hindsight is always perfect, isn't it? Much more difficult is to anticipate events before they happen, for only God has the all-seeing eye - for all that diviners and soothsayers may claim. But my very dear and cherished half-brother did offer one ray of hope: If the purpose of the king's visit was indeed to resolve the impasse over the choice of new abbot then it was indeed good news. If nothing else it would mean an end to Prior Herbert's stultifying dominion over us. Similarly, Joseph's comment about de Saye not wishing to cause a stir while the king was here was also encouraging. It might mean I'd retain my liberty for long enough to trace the whereabouts of my little family - though what I would do with them when I found them I really had no idea.

One thing I thought I might do in the meantime was try to see Hugh Northwold now that he was back in the abbey for a while. If I could convince him of Raoul's innocence then his support might be just the counterbalance to Prior Herbert and Geoffrey de Saye I needed. I gathered from Peter the Cellarer that both Hugh and the king had arrived from France a fortnight earlier though on different vessels, Hugh landing at Dover and John at Dartmouth. Hugh had come straight on to Bury to prepare the way while John had gone off to Corfe Castle for a few days' respite. Before the king arrived, therefore, I thought I'd try to ingratiate myself with our erstwhile subcellarer, and by happy chance my mother may just have given me the vehicle with which to do it: Her letter. I still had it secreted in my laboratorium. Hugh and the Lady Isabel were old friends and I proposed to use that fact and her letter in order to speak to him during the course of which I would bring up the case of the murdered girl and tell him of all that had been going on here in his absence. A glimmer of hope at last, perhaps? I should have realised it was a false dawn.

Hugh was a busy and important man these days. Since he allowed his name to be put forward for abbot he seemed to be in virtual permanent conference with his supporters and advisors. But I finally managed to beard him in the cellarer's range where he was holding unofficial court. He was courteous enough to ask after my mother's health before accepting the letter of whose contents I still had no notion. He glanced at the seal but unlike me was undaunted by its grand embossment. Smiling graciously, he handed it to a subordinate to open.

Remembering my mother's exhortations to me, I put my hand out to stop him. 'Erm, I believe, Brother Sub-cellarer, the contents are intended for your eyes only,' I smiled obsequiously.

Hugh shrugged and took back the letter slipping a practiced finger under the wax seal and separated the two halves in one movement. He unfolded the document and having glanced briefly at contents, his eyebrows shot up to the top of his head. Aha! I thought. The note must indeed contain something of some import to illicit such a reaction and I was at last about to discover what it was.

But then Hugh's face changed. First his eyebrows came back down and knitted hard together. Then he looked confused. Then he chortled to himself. I was becoming increasingly uncomfortable sensing that things were not quite right. Hugh held the note out for his colleagues to read. They too seemed baffled by what they saw. By now the back of my neck had begun to prickle. What was written on that sheet that so amused them all? Finally Hugh held the document out to me and there I saw that it contained...nothing. The page was completely blank.

'This is a joke, Brother Physician?' he asked. 'If so, I am not laughing. I have important matters to occupy my time and precious little to waste on jests.'

He dropped the document on the floor and I scooped it up and stared disconsolately at it. My head was swimming. I felt sick but I had just enough presence of mind to reply:

'Brother, I-I am merely my mother's messenger,' I stammered.

'Then you will require an answer to take back to her from me. Tell your mother my answer is...'

He leaned towards me and very carefully, very precisely - stuck out his tongue. He looked exactly like one of the gargoyles on the outside of the abbey parapet. It was funny. Everybody laughed. Even I laughed. But if my mother had been in the room at that moment I would happily have rammed the letter down her gullet.

*

Back in my laboratorium I tried everything I could think of to tease a message from the letter, but nothing seemed to be written on it that naked flame or acid could expose. There was no secret writing. No writing of any kind. It was indeed a completely blank sheet of parchment.

I threw the thing away from me in disgust. What was my mother playing at? If she was trying to make a fool of me she'd succeeded admirably. I had expected the note to bear a message of profound significance to do with the abbot's election or the king's visit or some other great matter. But it was just a cruel joke and one that wrecked any chance I might have had of gaining credibility with Hugh who must now think me a complete buffoon. What possible reason could my mother have for playing such a cruel trick on me? I was baffled.

It was while I was still fuming over this that a knock came on my door.

I felt a sharp intake of breath. Was this the knock I had been waiting for? The one that signified my being carted off to God-knows what hell-hole with no-one left to befriend me? And if it was, how cruel to have come now just as I had lost my last hope of any help from Hugh. Tentatively, I opened the door a crack and peeped out into the gloom.

But instead of a group of soldiers in hauberks and chain-mail, I saw standing before me a young man dressed in the white robes of a novice.

I recognized him immediately as Timothy, a gentle youth who I had been ministering to on and off for the past year. His mother had died young and his father, broken-hearted, drowned soon after, probably by his own hand and leaving ten-year-old Timothy to look after his four younger brothers and three sisters. To his eternal credit and as practically his final act on earth, Abbot Samson had of charity taken Timothy into the cloister and made provision out of his own will for the care of his siblings. It was a kind thing to do and one typical of Abbot Samson who for all his faults was never anything less than generous to those who he thought deserved it. As it was I who nursed his mother during her final illness, Timothy has always regarded me as a sort of second father figure and frequently asks my advice even though I am not his chaplain or his novice master. From the worried expression on his face I imagined that was his purpose this night. I must have startled him as much as he startled me for he took a step back.

'Master. I am sorry. I can see you are busy. I will come back some other time.' He turned to go.

'No, it's all right, Timothy,' I said with relief. 'You startled me that's all. Erm - come in.' I quickly cleared away the remnants of the destroyed letter. 'What can I do for you?'

Once I'd recovered my presence of mind I could see that he was distracted and unhappy. It pained me to see one of such a normally sunny disposition looking so despondent and I wondered if perhaps he was ill again – he was frequently depressed and worried about his siblings who were in the care of a distant aunt. Timothy was not naturally drawn to the cloister but was here by force of circumstance. As I said before, many find it difficult to adjust to the life. It takes time and perseverance. The younger men in particular very often bear suffering with fortitude seeing it as a weakness to complain. Often it is something as simple as belly ache or some equally minor disorder that is easily remedied. It is surprising what a little oil of peppermint can do to ease the constitution and lift the spirit.

He came fully into the room and stood in the glow of my oil lamp looking rather nervous. 'Forgive the intrusion, master. I...I have not been sleeping well lately.'

I smiled cheerfully. 'Another one. Well I can give you something for that.' I went to my shelf of concoctions.

'Another one, master?'

'The new man from Shouldham, Eusebius, was having similar problems.'

I noticed he flinched at my words, and waited.

'It's not a potion I need, master,' he said at last.

'No?' I stopped fumbling around my shelves and waited, but he seemed hesitant to speak. 'Timothy, there is no need to be shy. Whatever you say to me here will go no further, you know that. And I have been a doctor for many more years than you have been alive. Whatever it is that is troubling you I am sure to have come across it before and will not shock me.'

His frown deepened distorting that clear brow of his. It pained me to see God's perfection so deformed. They all had it - the mother, the daughters, the sons - an unusual beauty of countenance that is rare and precious that lifted the heart whenever I saw one of them. I waited, smiling affably, until he was ready to speak.

'Master, do you believe that on the Day of Judgement we will atone for our sins here on earth?'

'That is what Christ taught us,' I nodded. 'But you are a young man with many years ahead of you before you have to worry on that score. Plenty of time to correct any misdeeds you may, or may imagine you have, committed.'

His frown deepened. '*Mis-thoughts* as well as mis-deeds?'

'Those too,' I nodded wondering where this was going.

He looked at me shyly. 'What about *unnatural* thoughts, master?'

Ah. That I hadn't anticipated. But then, with Timothy's particular physical attributes it is not hard to see the opportunities to stray are more plentiful than for most.

'What does your novice master say?' I prompted gently.

'Brother Solomon counsels patience.'

I nodded. 'Solomon is a wise man. Timothy, we are all God's children, all of us human with human feelings and failings. Perhaps you should simply try to avoid situations where you might be tempted -'

'No, you do not understand, master,' he said, his cheeks colouring. 'It is not I who is tempted.'

I brightened at his words. 'Oh well, in that case, you need not worry. Just be sure to keep company at all times and not be alone. Strength is in the many.'

'That is not always easy when one is lying...so close.'

'You mean it is someone in your own dormitory? In the novices' hall?'

He lowered his head. 'At night he whispers, telling me things I do not wish to hear. I try to stop my ears and sleep but he wakes me again with more words.' He looked at me in anguish. 'Oh master, such *words*.'

I cupped my chin thoughtfully. I knew, of course, that such things went on in the cloister and that the young, because of their innocence or curiosity, were especially vulnerable. And if it is an older man then he can be hard to resist. Friendship can be mistaken for something more intimate. The problem is always present in a community such as ours, devoid as it is entirely of female contact. That is the very reason the novices have their own dormitory - so that a closer eye can be kept on them. But they cannot be watched every minute of the day and night. My duty, however, was clear: To preserve this child's innocence if I possibly could - if it wasn't already too late.

'Listen to me Timothy, you must tell me of whom you speak. I promise it will go no further but if I am to help you I have to know the source of the problem.' I forced a laugh. 'After all, you wouldn't want me to chop off your left foot if the wart is on the right, would you?'

He smiled briefly at my poor attempt at humour, but then frowned again. 'I do not wish to get anyone into trouble, master.'

'You are a good and generous young man. What possible trouble could you cause?'

He lowered his eyes. 'It is the one you mentioned earlier, master. The new one.'

'Eusebius?' I nodded. Of course. Why did I not guess this earlier? It made sense. His obsession with Our Lady; his lack of sleep - even his nose-bleeds were all symptomatic of a troubled mind. It seemed from what Timothy was saying that Eusebius's problems were more than just religious.

'I will speak to your novice master. Do not worry, I will be discreet. I will not mention our conversation, merely introduce the subject as if it were from my own observations.' I smiled encouragingly. 'Rest assured you will not be bothered again.'

'Did I do wrong in telling you, master?'

'No Timothy, you did not do wrong. You did exactly right. You have saved your own soul and possibly that of your brother, too.'

He smiled with relief. 'That was what I was hoping you'd say, master.'

I made the sign of the cross above his head. 'Go in peace, my son, in the knowledge that all will be well.'

Anyone other than Timothy I might have delayed helping, but the child had had enough tragedy in his life and deserved a little of my time. And Eusebius was also my responsibility, however reluctantly. I could spare a little time to sort out what was surely just a matter of separating the two young men in their dormitory. I therefore sought out his novice master first thing the next morning

Solomon was a kindly soul who had been doing the job of novice master for as long as I could remember. Wise by name and wise by nature, he was an old man now but his patience and understanding of the young far exceeded that of anyone younger, or indeed older. I found him in the herb garden engaged in his other great passion, horticulture - another pastime requiring patience and understanding. When he saw me he stopped hoeing and wiped his pate with a rag.

'The garden is looking beautiful, brother, if a little bare,' I told him. 'You achieve miracles, brother, when the ground is so hard and offers such little promise.'

'Autumn is the time of consolidation, brother. The trees shed their leaves and draw in their sap in readiness for the next season of growth. The little plants sleep in the soil ready to awaken when the time is ripe and they can achieve God's design for them to fill the world with fruitfulness and joy. These things cannot be rushed.'

We walked a little to the furthest side of his garden. I had forgotten just how reinvigorating can be a stroll in a quiet garden, refreshingly so after so much that had been going on lately.

'Good habits are not achieved with blows,' said Solomon. 'The weak need gentleness from others, kindness, compassion and loving forbearance – or so thought Saint Anselm of Canterbury.'

'And you agree with him?'

'We are all vulnerable to doubts and temptations, brother, the young especially who are often restless and fearful. It is what the Devil hopes to exploit. In this place he sometimes shows us the delights that we once enjoyed or have yet to enjoy and tries to tempt us.' He smiled. 'I know why you are here, brother. I saw young Timothy returning to the dormitory last evening.'

'And are we right to give in to those temptations? Or should we cut them out like a canker?'

He considered for a moment. 'The question is, I suppose, how deep should we cut? Is your eye so keen that you know when to stay the knife? Too little and the canker returns. Too deep you kill the plant.' He stopped and looked at me. 'You were never one of my novices, Walter, but even you were young and innocent once yourself. Can you remember asking me if God watches us every minute of the day, even when we are sitting on the latrine?'

'I asked you that?' I said, amazed.

'You did. You were always a very literal child.'

I laughed. 'Hardly a child. My childhood was squandered in too many medical schools.'

'You were still a child to me, twenty years my junior. But

since you can't remember asking the question you won't remember my answer.'

'Yes I can. You told me that God loves us for our faults as well as our virtues. He does not look away when we blush.'

We walked on. 'But the Devil is subtler than that. He sours the air by suggesting that sins committed within these walls are natural and inevitable in the young and would be cancelled out merely by virtue of their monastic vows. Defeating him is not achieved by mutilating the soul but by showing compassion and forgiveness.'

'There are some here who may not agree with you.'

'Then they must take charge. But while these delicates are in my hands they will not be choked or cut down before their tender shoots have had a chance to reach the light.' He bent down, picked up a small pot of apparently bare earth and held it out to me. 'It's Meadowsweet. Put it on your shelf, nurture it and next year you will be rewarded with a pretty yellow flower. The stem and leaves are also useful medicine.'

I took the pot from him gratefully.

'I thought young Timothy was looking a bit peaky when he returned last night. You are the doctor but I prescribed a little more air for his lungs. That is why I moved him from his usual place in the dormitory to the other side of the room by a window where the air is more plentiful. I'm sure he will sleep more soundly there.'

I smiled. 'You are a good and wise man, Dom Solomon.'

'We can only follow where Christ leads, Master Walter.'

I next sought out Eusebius. I was still his mentor and it was my duty to correct any errors. I found him seated in his usual place beneath the statue of Our Lady. Today he had another huge volume on his lap and was engrossed reading it. I slowed my pace uncertain how to make the correct approach on so delicate a subject. I did not want to be too direct and embarrass the boy but nor did I want to be so circumspect as to be obscure. Striking the right balance was not going to be easy. I wasn't sure that I was equal to the task.

I put on my most avuncular smile. 'Good day to you, my son,' I said glancing at the tome he had on his lap. 'What are you reading today? Ah - the letters of Saint Anselm of Canterbury. Very apt. Anselm was much influenced by the founder of your own rule, Saint Augustine of Hippo.'

He was looking at me expectantly. There was nothing for it but to plunge straight in:

'Eusebius, I -'

'Master, do you believe that the Devil wishes to capture all men for himself and that he particularly wishes to seduce us monks who by our lives are vulnerable to his jaws?'

I drew back. 'Erm, well yes I suppose so. Feelings of restlessness and discontent are natural in the young. Is that… how you feel, my son?' Maybe this was going to be easier than I thought.

He frowned. 'I do think sometimes the Evil One is trying to tempt me. Sometimes he puts thoughts into my head that I wish were not there. Thoughts that are…unworthy.' He lowered his eyes.

Bless the boy - he really was trying to confess. My heart was filled. I determined to ease his burden if I possibly could:

'Brother, I have to tell you that I know of your affliction.'

He didn't look up. 'Do you master?'

I nodded. 'Indeed I do. And I understand. Well no - I sympathize at least. I wish to put your mind at rest that we are all here to help you. It is not unknown for a young man to have thoughts such as yours. Your solution is in prayer. But in addition to prayer there must be...forbearance.'

'Forbearance?'

'Yes,' I nodded. 'Forbearance - or perhaps *restraint* is a better word. A good word - yes- very apt under the erm...'

I was not finding this at all easy. But once again Eusebius eased my burden, blessed boy. He looked at me shyly.

'You are speaking of Timothy. Is that why his bed has been moved?'

'That was not my doing – but I approve. And it will help you both.' I sighed with relief. 'You must see you are being unfair to Timothy.'

He nodded. 'I have been keeping him awake at night.'

'Have you?' I squirmed uncomfortably on the bench. 'Eusebius, I have spoken to Dom Solomon - a good and knowledgeable man. He is far more experienced on the subject than I am. He is your best guide. Consult with him. And in the meantime you have my blessing. Yes indeed.' I tapped him perfunctorily on the shoulder. 'Good. Excellent. Well, I'm glad we've had this chat. Go in peace, brother.'

I made the sign of the cross over his head just as I had over Timothy's and rose to leave feeling I had done my duty. If he knew there were people there to support him he might find the strength to help himself. But I could at least satisfy myself that I had a better understanding of the boy now. What I had thought was a purely *religious* fervour I could see it was something far more down to earth. Rather more *human*. I must say that the revelation came as something of a relief. Now that I saw the true nature of his problem, while he was not out of the woods, at least it was manageable given the right precautions and he would have no gentler and understanding a manager than old Solomon. I hurried away feeling rather pleased with myself at a good job well done.

Chapter Eighteen
KING JOHN

With Eusebius' problem resolved I could hope at last to have time to concentrate fully on the de Grays. But it was not to be. Suddenly there was no more time for anything for all at once the king was upon us. Carts and people and animals had begun arriving at the abbey ahead of King John himself. There was the usual vast baggage train of court personnel and paraphernalia – clerks, scribes, chaplains, ushers, cofferers, cooks, saddlers, armourers, smiths, carpenters, wheelwrights, leather-workers, yeomen, tent-makers, fletchers, minstrels, heralds together with those essential items of personal comfort that John could not do without: His bed, his tapestries, his windows, even his latrine seat and, I was amused to note, his bath. All this vast panoply of goods and people accompanied the king wherever he went, be it on pilgrimage or to war. In my mind's eye I can still see them now. It seemed at the time as though an occupying army had suddenly invaded our peaceful community - as, indeed, it had.

Even so, it wasn't as bad as the first time he visited the abbey. Then it had been a great pageant with the newly enthroned King John looking young and splendid and eager to win his subjects' approval. It had also been a gloriously sunny day in June then, not this dull November morn, and he had cantered in on a splendid steed at the head of an army and supported by all the great men of church and state. This time a tired, middle-aged and portly John limped into town escorted by just a few of the lesser magnates. Among them, I was dismayed to note, was Geoffrey de Saye, who must have ridden out specially to meet him. But what drew my attention most was his personal escort for it consisted almost entirely of foreign mercenaries — Flemings, Bergundians, Genoans. It seemed Peter the cellarer had been right and the king could no longer trust his own people to protect him.

He did, however, have one enthusiastic supporter waiting for him. Obsequious as ever, Prior Herbert was waiting at the south gate to greet his monarch and make his supplication on bended knee. No-one was ever quite sure where Herbert's true loyalties lay but rather like the reeds in the River Lark they were forever bending this way and that with the prevailing political current. Mine wasn't the only lip that day that curled with contempt.

Once within the abbey walls the royal party was quickly escorted to the freshly-scrubbed and appointed abbot's palace. But there was no great banquet of welcome this time or a triumphant address to the burgesses of the town. Instead a diminished and subdued King John ate with us quietly in the monks' refectory. I sat with my old friend Jocelin, still alive then though in his seventh decade and going blind. I wondered if he remembered the last occasion we broke bread with our sovereign. Poor Jocelin; he could no longer see well enough to write, which was a great pity for writing was his joy so cruelly snatched away from him. Nor would Herbert allow him an amanuensis for all our scribes were busy on far more important work than the vain scribblings of one aging monk – or so he said. What observations Jocelin may have had after he finished his famous Chronicle would have, alas, to remain locked within his wise old head.

'What do you think?' I muttered to him as I leaned across the table for a jug of cider.

Jocelin squinted at the dais. 'He's l-looking tired.'

Indeed he was, tired and old beyond his years. For a man not yet fifty John could easily pass for a decade more with grey lacing his beard and that once lustrous auburn hair thinning. That's what comes of having to be constantly on the move never spending more than a day or two in one place. His father, good King Henry, had become bow-legged in old age and suffering, it was rumoured, from an anal fistula – none of which surprised me for all are symptomatic of too many hours spent in the saddle. As to the reason the king was here at all, it soon became clear that Joseph had been right and he let it be known he wished to settle the question of who was to be our next abbot. To this end John's herald announced his desire to enter the chapterhouse the following day and address the assembled brothers.

Now why, you may ask, should the election of an abbot so much matter to the monarch that he should bring his entire court half way across England in order to personally oversee it? The answer is that abbots and bishops are more than just clerics but also politicians, businessmen and administrators. As Baron of the Liberty of Saint Edmund, our abbot sits on the King's Council and personally holds sway over half the county of Suffolk, the richest and most populous shire in the land. The man who holds this post is very powerful indeed, custodian of that great office though he may only be. And while in theory it is for the monks of Bury to choose their pastor, no king since the Conqueror has permitted the position to be filled without his approval. The secret is to divine the king's preferred candidate beforehand and to make sure this name is included on the shortlist from which the king can make his final decision. Or if he has no favourite at least make sure there is none that is abhorrent to him – that, I believe, is how Abbot Samson was chosen.

However, the process this time had been complicated by the elevation of Cardinal Langton to the archiepiscopal throne of Saint Augustine. Langton was the choice of neither the king nor the monks of Canterbury but a direct appointee of Pope Innocent. The whole question of clerical elections therefore had become a trial of strength between the pope and the king. Sensing an advantage, the monks of Bury have thus far resisted the king's interference while for his part King John has deliberately equivocated over our choice which was why Hugh Northwold has been chasing the king half way round France trying to obtain his approval – so far without success. And that was how matters stood this November morning as John entered the chapterhouse preceded only by the earl of Winchester, Saer de Quency, and Philip de Ulecotes who carried before him the Sword of State.

John's speech was long and rambling and at times a little bitter.

It was a cold day and the vapour from his breath iced his words. He spoke a lot about loyalty and duty and I got the impression that he had others in mind than the seventy shivering monks who were listening in respectful silence. Not much of what he said was relevant to us, but he did eventually come to the point:

'My brothers, I have detained you for long enough. All I ask is that you proceed according to custom and not infringe upon my historical rights as your king. If you do this I will be happy to accept whoever you choose as abbot, either him who calls himself abbot-elect,' here he graciously acknowledged Hugh Northwold who was sitting alongside, 'or anyone else you desire.'

But then he finished with a stark warning:

'But let me caution you, if you choose to ignore my advice then you risk incurring the wrath of your ruler. That may not be a wise position to hold.' He looked sternly around the assembled faces before smiling graciously. 'I leave it now to you to ponder my words.' And so he sat down.

Personally I thought it was a good speech. It seemed to give everyone what they wanted. We could choose who our abbot should be and John would not contest our choice provided we agreed to abide by his decision – which would be to confirm that choice. As a piece of face-saving fudgery it was masterly and equal to anything his wily father could have devised. I could not see how anyone could object to his offer and I confidently looked forward to Hugh being confirmed as our next abbot.

A brief discussion followed. Then Hugh stood up and bowed low to the king. He thanked his grace for his words and answered that the house would divide on the issue. Those in favour of the king's proposal should move to the left of the room, those against to the right.

Now, this wasn't the first time this had happened. Back in May a similar division had been conducted under the auspices that time of William Marshal, the earl of Pembroke, when the split had been more or less even – half for the king and half against. This time, however, those in favour of the king were overwhelmingly outnumbered by those against. It was a deliberate slap in the face for the king and frankly I was astonished. It seemed to me an act of gross ingratitude considering how far the king had moved to accommodate us.

What had happened since May to so harden their faces against the king? Well what happened, of course, was that John had lost the war in France. It was as Joseph had predicted. In the eyes of the world he had been fatally weakened and sensing it, the brothers had become obstinate. Understandably furious at the result, John stormed out of the chapterhouse threatening all manner of retribution. Thus instead of achieving harmony and reconciliation we had prolonged acrimony and recrimination.

*

It was probably not the best moment to pick for what I did next but I felt I had no choice. For all I knew John would have one of his famous sulks and leave town forthwith before I had the chance to put my case to him. Having failed so dismally to win Hugh Northwold to my side I was determined not to make the same mistake with John. Uppermost in my mind was Joseph's advice to play the royal suit as possibly my only trump card. I just hoped it did not turn out to be another Joker.

With this in mind, I rushed from the chapterhouse arriving at the abbot's palace just ahead of the bodyguard that was escorting the king to his chambers. In the middle of the party the king was talking animatedly with his advisors including among them once again Geoffrey de Saye. Seeing my great adversary so cosy with the king I was tempted to withdraw but I knew I owed it to Raoul, Adelle, Rosabel, Onethumb and to Effie at least to try. Summoning all my courage, therefore, I stepped out directly into the path of the king.

'Sire, may I -?'

I got no further before one of the guards pushed his pike into my face cutting my lip and sending me sprawling on the floor. He was a great lump of a German and in another moment he would have skewered me to the floor if the king had not intervened.

'Whoa there, monk!' he said putting out his hand to stay the guard's hand. 'Don't you know it is impertinent to address the king uninvited? Men have been garrotted for less - assuming this brute hasn't decapitated you first.' He gave the guard an amiable shove in the shoulder.

Seeing me, de Saye immediately stepped between us. 'Sire, I know this man. He's a trouble maker. Let us continue.'

He placed his hand on the king's arm - a fatal mistake for one thing I did know about King John is that he has a strong dislike for being hoodwinked. John removed de Saye's hand from his arm and gently but firmly eased him out of the way.

'Well monk,' said John glancing down at me still flat on my back. 'Have you come to apologise on behalf of your brothers, or gloat at your king's humiliation?'

'Neither, your grace,' I said in as clear a voice as I could muster. 'I have come to give you a message.'

John rolled his eyes to heaven. 'Oh God's teeth, another soothsayer. I warn you, I hanged the last one. What is it this time? Is my kingdom doomed? Am I to eat less meat? Take fewer baths? Go on pilgrimage to the Holy Land?' Then he squinted at me. 'I know you. We've met before.'

'Indeed sire,' I said scrambling to my feet. 'I am -'

'No, don't tell me,' he said waving me silent. 'I have an excellent memory for faces.' He tapped a beringed finger on his lips but eventually had to shrug and give up. 'No, it's gone. But you were in the chapterhouse earlier, I think.'

'We all were, sire.'

'Indeed. So tell me, which way did you vote?'

I swallowed hard. 'The…fairest way, your grace.'

His smile evaporated. 'Fifty against nine. Do you call that "fair"?'

'Sire, I…' I started, but he interrupted:

'Fair to gainsay your royal liege? Fair to sew controversy where none need be? To set king against pope?'

For a dreadful moment I thought my efforts had been in vain and he was going to go into one of his famous rants. But as suddenly his smile returned and he snapped his fingers.

'I've remembered who you are. You're the bone-breaker. You cured my bellyache.' He grinned round at his companions who to a man laughed appreciatively at the joke.

'Sire,' I bowed.

'Well well well,' he continued to chuckle. 'The bone-breaker. But I can't keep calling you that. Only a fool would call you that – wouldn't you say my lord? A foolish phrase, *n'est-ce pas?* Bone-breaker?' he said pointedly to de Saye who blushed a fine shade of scarlet, much to my delight. It seemed John was not quite the fool his courtiers took him for.

'I am Walter de Ixworth, sire. My mother is the Lady Isabel

de Ixworth of Ixworth Hall and -'

'Yes yes yes, I know who you are,' he said impatiently waving me silent. He snapped his fingers again. 'I know what I'll call you: *Bumble*, because you're for ever poking your nose into things you shouldn't ought. Eh? Eh?' He grinned round at his courtiers again. 'Do you like that, my lords? Bumble? Like the busy bee? Buzz-buzz?'

They liked it very much. In fact, judging by their reaction, it must have been the funniest thing they'd heard all year.

'Sire,' said de Saye trying again, 'we should move on.'

'In a minute,' frowned John irritably. 'Well go on then,' he said to me.

'Sire?'

'A message you said. Let's hear it. I haven't got all day.'

It was what I had come for. It was now or never. I took a deep breath.

'Sire, there is a boy – Raoul de Gray by name. You may have heard of him. He is the nephew of Bishop John de Gray of Norwich.'

'What of him?'

'He has been wrongfully accused of murdering his wife's maid - by Prior Herbert and my lord de Saye, here.' I nodded to Lord Geoffrey.

John looked round at him inquiringly.

De Saye looked furious. 'Sire,' he said confidentially, 'it is as I said. This man is a trouble maker. Nothing he says can be relied upon.'

'Well, if he is indeed malicious I will have his tongue pulled out and his nose split.' John smiled brightly at me. 'You have proof of what you say?'

'I do, my liege.'

Again the king looked expectantly at de Saye.

De Saye exploded. 'This is preposterous!'

But John would not be fobbed off. He waited, eyebrows raised.

'The evidence condemns the boy,' growled de Saye reluctantly. 'This monk alone denies it.'

'The *evidence*,' I insisted raising my chin defiantly, 'such as it is, exonerates Raoul.'

'Isn't that for the courts to decide?' said John. 'I presume my justices have been informed?'

'No, sire,' I put in quickly before de Saye, 'they have not.'

John raised his eyebrows again at de Saye who was getting redder and redder by the minute.

'Sire,' he growled, 'the boy has absconded and is now a fugitive. By his own actions he condemns himself.'

'That makes sense,' nodded John to me. 'If he is innocent why would he run?'

'I don't believe he has run,' I replied. 'I believe my lord de Saye has him under guard.'

At this de Saye almost exploded.

'Really?' John cut across him. 'To what purpose?'

'I don't know. Only my lord de Saye has the answer to that, so maybe you should ask him.'

I caught the look of annoyance on John's face at that but by now I could not stop myself:

'Raoul de Gray and his entire family vanished overnight. They could not have done so without Lord de Saye's knowledge. His troops were everywhere. Surely you must have noticed on the road?'

I thought Geoffrey de Saye was about to jump me, but John said quietly:

'You know, come to think of it, I do remember you now. Something about some money being owed to a Jew. Wasn't it at the beginning of our reign? Yes, and there was a murder that time, too, I think.' He looked rather pleased with himself. 'Bumble, we shall be here for a day or two yet. Maybe we will find time to speak again. Right - on!'

And with that he moved off leaving me standing alone unsure whether I had achieved anything or whether it had all been for nothing. Prior Herbert had no such doubts. As the king's party disappeared I saw him lurking in their wake where he had been watching the little drama unfold with a look on his face somewhere between amusement and incredulity. He waited until the others were gone before coming over.

'Well now Walter, that was quite a performance.' He wiped a small trickle of blood from my chin with his thumb. 'I do believe you may just have signed your own death warrant.'

Chapter Nineteen

THE PRICE OF LOYALTY

I didn't know whether I was doing right by challenging de Saye so openly in front of the king or whether I had, as Herbert so graphically put it, "signed my own death warrant". It was a gamble. But it certainly felt good. Just the look of pain on de Saye's face was reward enough for the pain he inflicted on me in the gatekeeper's lodge. I was, however, under no illusion that John would take my side against one of his leading nobles whatever the rights or wrongs in the matter. Abbot Samson once said to me that the great families of England stick together "like dog-shit sticks to fur"; and he was surely right because ultimately whatever threatens one threatens them all. What gave me hope this time, however, was the sense I got that my lord de Saye did not entirely enjoy the king's confidence. Whatever else John was he was nobody's fool. He knew exactly the worth of Geoffrey de Saye. So Joseph may also be right when he said de Saye was unlikely to do anything to antagonize the king while he was in Bury. That surely boded well for Rosabel and the de Grays.

Meanwhile John let it be known that he would remain in the town for a few more days during which time he expected the decision taken in the chapterhouse over the new abbot to be reversed. Fat chance there was of that happening. My brother monks were cock-a-hoop over what happened believing they had twisted the lion's tail. But the lion can bite back, and John needed to do little in order to draw blood. He could simply leave the abbacy vacant and continue to reap the income for himself, and all the while the abbey's wealth and prestige would slowly ebb away. We needed a resolution to the question of the new abbot even more than he did. But John was a capricious man and could change his plans at any minute. It wouldn't surprise me to wake the next morning to find the whole abbey turned upside down again with the king gone and his entourage hastily packing up ready to leave. But while John remained he gave me time to find out where de Saye was holding the de Gray family – if indeed he was holding them - and in this I had help from an unexpected quarter. King John had a well-known penchant for entertainment and to this end our customary Christmas celebrations were hastily brought forward under the able direction of Brother Kevin, the sub-novice master. John would surely stay for that.

I have long been an admirer of Brother Kevin's talents despite his flamboyant mannerisms which some of my more staid brothers find distasteful. He inspires all with his enthusiasm and energy and on this occasion rose magnificently to the challenge of amusing the king, beginning with a Feast of Fools. This was enacted by some of the novices and students from the abbey school who were in effect given licence for one day to mock their elders and betters and generally to say under the anonymity of the mime what they were constrained from saying openly the rest of the year. Not that anybody was fooled by the disguise; we all recognised the identities of players beneath the masks. But the fiction of secrecy was maintained thus enabling the targets to learn some home truths that would otherwise not be voiced, and possibly amend them. And it is all done in a spirit of good humour, albeit humour with a sting. We had a Pope of Unreason, a Boy Bishop, and even someone got up as the Abbot of Fools – or should that have been the *Prior* of Fools for the lad playing him got Herbert's whining voice off to a T. Herbert laughed along with the rest of us though I suspect he was enjoying more the prospect of my impending demise than his own lampooning. The king certainly enjoyed himself going blue in the face with laughter and nearly falling off his chair. His was the one character that was not mocked, however – there was no *King* of Fools, probably wisely under the circumstances.

After this there was a cock fight followed by jugglers, clowns and acrobats from the town, all splendidly professional and exciting. Finally as the sun began to sink a series of tableaux of scenes from the Bible were acted out. Adam and Eve in the Garden of Eden - a moment of unintentional hilarity here when the novice playing Adam bit into the apple only to find it rotten inside and immediately spat it out again. Jocelin who was sitting next to me whispered gleefully that had the real Adam done the same it might have altered entirely the subsequent history of the world.

Next came Jonah and the Whale. With so much water being flung about to represent the waves, the "whale" slipped on the wooden boards, broke in half and regurgitated a somewhat surprised Jonah prematurely onto the shore who had to be hastily reinserted back into the whale's belly by Brother Kevin. Noah and the Flood fared hardly better although there was so much water left over from the previous tableau that there was little need to imagine the deluge – the "animals" in the ark looked as though they were already half-drowned before the waters had even begun to rise.

The grand finale was the Christmas story itself with a sombre representation of the Stable in Bethlehem: The three Wise Men; the shepherds; Mary gazing tenderly at a rather grotesque and oversized dummy of the Christ-child, Joseph looking suitably contemplative and aloof - all played by the older novices. The Holy Mother was convincingly portrayed by young Timothy, I noted, whose angelic face charmed all, while the angel was played by a stoical Brother Eusebius garbed in his odd Gilbertine robes. As he appeared the audience gasped for he seemed to rise unaided above the stable and remained there suspended by invisible cords, his robe flapping like wings in the breeze. Once the initial shock was over we all burst into spontaneous applause as we realised the trick Kevin had played on us with ropes and pulleys. It was a fine end to the entertainment but seeing both Eusebius and Timothy on stage together gave me a slight feeling of uneasiness.

As the performers took their final bows and we all applauded with heart-felt enthusiasm, I felt a tap on my shoulder. Turning, I saw it was one of the royal servants in his dark blue livery. It seemed the king was now ready to receive me.

*

'Ah, there you are, Bumble. Come in, come in. You've met the queen?'

I entered upon an unexpected and charming scene of a happy family at their ease, albeit the grandest family in the land. King John was standing with his back to the fire while seated before him upon a cushioned chair was a beautiful young woman in her mid-twenties together with three attending ladies-in-waiting all chattering in French. From her magnificent raiment of silk and shot gold there could be little doubt that this was the fabled Queen Isabelle of Angoulême, King John's second wife. I had no idea she was even in the town; she must have arrived quietly while the entertainment was underway. She was playing with a child of about seven or eight years of age who I assumed be one of her children. The little boy's wide eyes took me in as I fell to my knees before his mother and bowed my head low.

'My lady.'

I have to admit to goose pimples prickling my flesh as she deigned to permit her eye to fall upon me. All Europe had heard of this lady's beauty which was rumoured to have so captivated the king from the moment he first saw her at the tender age of twelve that he stole her from her betrothed in the very hour of their wedding. I had seen her only once before and that at a distance when John had shown her off to her new subjects in a progress around the country shortly after her coronation. Then she had been a beautiful young girl who had stolen the heart of every Englishman who saw her. Seeing her now a dozen years later I could see she had lost none of her magic.

'We have met before?' she asked me in her thick French accent.

'Unfortunately not, my lady,' I replied - and then added: 'But I have long cherished the name Isabel for it is also my mother's name.'

THE PRICE OF LOYALTY

'*Non*,' she replied wagging an imperious finger. 'You are wrong, *mon frère*. Your mother has *my* name, not I hers.' So saying, she stood up and with a sigh took the small boy by the hand. 'Come Henri. We must leave your father to his business.'

As the door miraculously opened by itself and she passed through followed by the three ladies, I heard the little boy ask, 'Who was that funny man, *maman*?'

'*Juste un vieux moine, petit. Pas quelqu'un important*,' she replied. Just an old monk. Nobody important.

As soon as they had gone the guard stepped forward to frisk me, but John put up his hand. 'There's no need. Brother Bumble and I are old friends, and old friends don't stick knives in each other, do we Bumble?' he smiled.

'I hope not, sire.'

The guard looked a little perplexed and stepped back but kept his hand poised on his sword hilt just in case.

John giggled. 'Go on,' he said pushing the man gently. 'You can go too. Bumble and I have things to discuss that are not for your ears. Go and get a tankard of ale. I'll call if I need you.'

Reluctantly, the guard went out leaving me alone in the room for only the second time in my life with the most powerful man in England who shivered as he pushed a stray log back into the fire sending sparks flying to the roof and rubbed his backside against the flames.

'Christ in heaven, it's cold here. How you monks put up with no heating is beyond me. You must have ice in your veins.'

'We have a fire, sir,' I replied. 'In the warming room.'

He grunted. 'One fire for seventy. God help the littlest, I say. Well now, Bumble. What shall we talk about?'

I had hoped we'd be discussing the murder and Raoul de

Gray. It was what I thought I had been summoned to discuss.

'Sire…' I began.

'So you think he's the right man for the job?'

I stopped. 'Raoul de Gray?'

He frowned. 'No no no. Hugh Northwold. A Norfolk man - like the last abbot.'

I had to quickly refocus my thoughts. 'I, er, think he could make a fine abbot.'

John nodded gravely. 'So do I. But it wouldn't do to let that lot know it.' He nodded to the door as though the entire brethren of Saint Edmunds were standing outside. 'Makes me look weak, see?' He smiled.

'Would it not make your highness look statesmanlike to graciously accede to what was so overwhelmingly a joyful choice of his brother monks?' I ventured hesitantly.

His smile vanished. 'No, it would not. Not with half my baronage threatening rebellion at any moment.'

My jaw started to drop open but I managed to stop it in time. I was at a loss to know how to respond.

John grinned and rubbed his hands together. 'Tell me, what did you think of my entertainment? Good wasn't it?'

Another jolt. 'I, er… enjoyed it very much, sire.'

He giggled delightedly. 'So did I. Nearly pissed myself when that goat shat on the stage.' He sniggered like a naughty schoolboy.

'Sire, I…'

'It's what they're planning,' he cut across me. 'Rebellion against their lawful king. That's treason, you know?'

'Surely not, sire.'

'No? You think not? They've done it before. To my father

when he was king as well as to my brother. But Richard was never here. That was the thing, see? Ten years as king and less than six months of it in the country. He wanted to go off and fight Saracens and they were happy to let him - so long as he left them alone to run the firm their way. But I won't, see? And that's what they can't stand.'

I could see he was working himself up into one of his rants and I was beginning to think my hopes for Raoul de Gray had been entirely foolhardy.

'But surely, sire, the barons are your most loyal subjects?' I said naively.

He snorted. 'Loyalty! You fancy this manor? Fifty marks and it's yours. A bishopric? A thousand marks. A county? Ten thousand. Only you never pay, see? And I never ask for payment. That puts you in my debt. That's how a king keeps control. Loyalty comes at a price. It's a sad reflection, Bumble. A sad reflection,' he said poking the fire again.

I didn't know what to say, so I said nothing and waited listening to the wood crackling in the flames. Eventually he refocused on me again, his expression dark.

'Now that I've told you all this I suppose I shall have to silence you, too. Can't have you blabbing my strategies to all and sundry, can I?'

He took out a gold-handled dagger from beneath his jerkin and flashed it in the air.

'So what do you suggest? Should I slit your throat? Or just cut your tongue out? And since you are a fine, literate fellow, I suppose I should cut your hand off as well. Tell me, which would you prefer to lose, the right or the left?' He pointed to each in turn with the tip of the dagger.

Then he chortled gleefully. 'You should see your face. Don't worry, Bumblehead, I'm not going to harm you. Not because I don't think you'd tell – although funnily enough I think you of all people probably wouldn't. It's because it doesn't matter any more whether you tell or not. It's too late, see? It was already too late back in July when that idiot nephew of mine, Otto - may God shrivel the ugly little toad's balls to peas - lost me my empire.' He growled. 'Do you know what that fool did? Refused to fight on a Sunday. Can you believe that? Wouldn't break the Sabbath for fear of damning his immortal soul. I know you're a man of the cloth, but dash it all, can you credit him? As a consequence he lost the battle and me the war.' He snorted with disgust and threw his dagger on the table, to my intense relief. 'Well, he'll never be emperor now, I'll make sure of that. And at least I'll keep my English kingdom.' He smiled ruefully. 'For the present at least.'

'Oh but surely England is safe, sire. Your subjects love you,' I said cringing inwardly at my own sycophancy.

'Safe? From this lot?' He snorted contemptuously. 'They're a pack of rabid dogs.'

He scrubbed the underside of his chin with his hand seemingly lost for a minute in his own thoughts, then looked me up and down.

'Anyway, enough of that. That's not why I brought you here. It's about this murder. Oh don't look so surprised, Bumble. You think I don't know what's going on in my own realm? You said it yourself, Raoul de Gray is the nephew of the Bishop of Norwich, one of the more loyal of my servants.' He snorted. 'Oh yes, I know Raoul de Gray well. He was one of my wards of court - did you know that?'

I frowned. 'No I -'

'Bit of a foo-foo. Too fond of religion.' He chortled. 'Unlike his uncle the bishop.'

I tried to reconcile this image of Raoul with the one who threatens young girls and gropes tavern whores. He must have changed since he was the king's ward, I guessed. Or maybe John didn't know him as well as he thought he did.

'When you say Raoul is keen on his religion, sire, you surely don't mean he intends to take the cowl?'

John considered the question. 'My late mother, Queen Eleanor, became a nun in her final years. That's after having eleven children, two husbands and God alone knows how many lovers including her own uncle and my grandfather. The old hypocrite even promised me to the church as a child – can you believe that? Five years I spent freezing my bollocks off in a God-forsaken place just like this one. So I suppose anything's possible. Monk, yes - but murderer?' He shook his head. 'The boy wouldn't be capable. He'd bungle it.'

'My lord de Saye thinks he did it.'

John scowled dangerously. 'I've already given you my opinion of my barons.'

I suddenly saw my opportunity to frustrate de Saye's plans and perhaps gain an ally in the king.

'Lord de Saye intends to pursue him – to take him to Norfolk for trial.'

'Then you must stop him, Bumble. The boy's uncle is in Rome at present grovelling to the Holy Father. When he gets back there are things here I need him to do. I don't want him distracted with tales of murdered maids. So find the boy, Bumble. Prove him innocent or bring him to justice – I don't much care which. Do this and you will have earned your sovereign's gratitude.'

*

I am often asked my opinion of King John especially by my fellow monks who had never met him or did not know him even as well as I did. Much of the history of those times has been written by churchmen with whom John was never popular and who have consequently given him a bad write-up. The question I am most frequently asked is, "What was he really like?" to which I always give the same reply: King John was promiscuous, intelligent, extravagant, suspicious, greedy, self-indulgent, irreligious, mean, vicious, generous, amusing, and sarcastic. He was also given to bouts of tremendous energy when he achieved at least as much as his more esteemed older brother, Richard, coupled with equal spells of lethargy and indolence when he did nothing at all. A vain man, certainly, with his taste for fine clothes and jewellery, and fastidious to the point of excess – four baths in six months is, in my opinion, taking personal hygiene to extremes. He also hated war but could on occasion be a great military strategist. A capable administrator and reasonable to deal with but he was also prone to occasional acts of crass stupidity and cruelty that alienated those who would otherwise wish to be his friends. As an example of this I cite the moment of his departure from Bury, and then I will say no more about him:

The morning began with a commotion at the abbey gate as dozens of irate townsfolk suddenly appeared trying to petition the abbey authorities. Many of us monks rushed out into the square to see what the problem was and there we were confronted by a scene of utter chaos and misery. Dozens of wailing children and their baggage were being loaded onto carts by soldiers with pikes and swords with their anguished parents looking on unable to stop them. These children were the sons and daughters of local dignitaries whom the king had decided to take with him as hostages in order to ensure the town's good behaviour. This may be normal practice in times of war, but the country was still nominally at peace and Bury folk were, by and large, docile and supportive of the government. It was meant, I think, as a warning to another, more powerful audience who may have been thinking of opposing his regime and not really aimed at Bury folk at all.

As it turned out it was all bluff for in a great show of magnanimity the queen suddenly appeared in the square and dramatically begged her husband to relent which he did, swiftly and graciously and released all the children back into the relieved arms of their waiting parents. John never had any real intention of taking cart-loads of juveniles all the way to Winchester especially at this time of the year when the weather was so unpredictable and the roads so treacherous. It was just a piece of theatre designed to make a point, but as an act of political ineptitude it was unsurpassed. At a stroke he managed to turn a sympathetic population into bitter enemies and ensured that any future acts of opposition would go unreported - as indeed it exactly turned out.

Chapter Twenty
AN OLD MEDICINE WOMAN

With the king's endorsement ringing in my ears I was spurred on in my quest to find the de Grays while there was still time to do so. But where to begin? Once again they seemed to have vanished into the good clean air of Suffolk. This time, however, I was to get some help - and from a quite unexpected quarter...

The last place I would have expected to find any clues was in the inner sanctuary of my own abbey church. But had I ears to hear and eyes to see I would have realised that the blessed Edmund had been prompting me to do this all along, for one chill morning the great Saxon king and martyr spoke to me - and happily this time I heard him.

I happened to be passing through the chancel of the church as I often did between the high altar and the shrine when I

AN OLD MEDICINE WOMAN

noticed a large bundle of old sacking that had apparently been dumped on the tiles. As usual the area was packed with the sick and crippled all vying with each other to get as close as possible to the saint's body in hope of a cure; but however much they crawled over each other like cockroaches over a carcass, they seemed to leave a wide berth around this bundle. Genuflecting next to the thing, I quickly realised why: There was a most dreadful smell coming from it.

I stopped a young monk whose name I think was Ambrose as he hurried by with a lighted taper. 'Excuse me, brother – what is that?'

He gave the bundle a disdainful snort. 'An old medicine woman from the town.'

I looked again and could see now that the bundle was indeed human since it was moving ever so slightly as it breathed. On closer inspection the shape seemed familiar – or rather the *odour* did - and took me back to a time in the distant past.

'Mother Han?'

A grimy claw slowly emerged from within the bundle and pulled aside the hood that was hiding her face. Mother Han squinted sideways at me and made a grunting noise that I took to be a greeting – or at any rate, recognition. She didn't get up. She appeared to be licking the floor.

'What's she doing?' I asked Ambrose.

'She was caught stealing from the blessed Edmund who is duly punishing her,' he sneered.

'Caught stealing? How?'

Ambrose sighed deeply. 'As I'm sure you are aware, master, as well as placing offerings in the collection boxes located strategically around the church and in every chapel, pilgrims are encouraged to throw money at the foot of the shrine in anticipation of a personal blessing directly from the saint himself. For some time we have suspected this money was being stolen but we did not know how or by whom.' He tapped the side of his nose with his forefinger. 'But the blessed Edmund knew. This foul hag has been coming to the shrine and in a great show of reverence goes down on all fours to kiss the floor. Only she wasn't kissing the floor; she was licking up the coins she found lying there. As reward for this abomination the saint has fixed her tongue to the tiles.' His lip curled with satisfaction. 'A most fitting punishment under the circumstances, don't you think?'

I took a closer look. Mother Han did indeed have her tongue pressed firmly on the tiles, but it wasn't so much the saint's fingers that were holding it there as Jack Frost's. Ice had formed around her tongue and lips gluing her mouth to the floor and made worse by her breath that was freezing on the cold surface at every expiration.

'It is the saint who holds her,' insisted Ambrose when I pointed this out to him. 'It matters not how he chooses to do it.'

I nodded with resignation. 'How long has she been there?'

'Two days.'

'*Two days!*'

Ambrose seemed unconcerned. 'And there she will remain until the saint decides to release her. Now if you will excuse me, master, it is I who must be released. I have my duties to attend to.' And with that, he bowed and went off still nursing his dwindling taper.

Two days! I'd known Mother Han for nearly two decades. She was ancient when I first met her; she must be well over seventy by now. If she stayed here in these freezing conditions another night I was certain she'd be dead by the morning.

'You foolish old woman,' I whispered harshly in her ear. She grunted back something incoherent. 'Wait here,' I said, as if she had any choice in the matter, and went off to my laboratorium. Ten minutes later I was back with a pale of warm water.

'Aow!' she whined as I slopped the steaming liquid over her mouth and the tiles. 'That's hot!'

'Good!' I said. 'Let that be your reward for your thievery.'

But the remedy worked for the blessed Edmund in his mercy released his hold on the old reprobate who slumped back on her hind quarters and covered her mouth with her hand.

'Give!' I said holding out my own hand to her.

She moaned and shook her head as if in pain.

I leaned closer. 'Mother Han, give it back right now or so help me I'll hold you down myself until the water freezes and you'll never get up again.'

'You would, too,' she said reluctantly spitting out a silver penny, slimy with her saliva, into my palm. I put the revolting object into my belt pouch meaning to drop it in the poor box later.

'You didn't have to make it so hot,' she complained indicating the empty bucket. 'You burnt my tongue.'

'Payment for all the lies it has uttered over the years.'

'Oh, don't worry, I won't be trying that one again,' she said rubbing her thighs. 'I haven't the knees for bending anymore.'

I looked at her with exasperation. 'Why are you stealing from the church? Does your husband not provide for you anymore?'

'He's dead,' she sniffed.

I checked myself. 'Oh, I didn't know. I'm sorry. When did he die?'

'A while back.' She blew her nose on her sleeve. 'The pain eases with time.'

'I'm sure it does,' I commiserated sincerely. 'Even so, it must be difficult. The pair of you being so…close.'

I was thinking of the night some years previously when I'd witnessed Mother Han and the then abbey gaoler - her "husband" - engaged in energetic and noisy coition outside the cell in which I had been unjustly incarcerated. No two people could have been closer, or an exhibition less edifying.

'When I say he's "dead",' she said wiping her sleeve on her skirt, 'he was put to swabbing the abbey latrines where no lady may venture.'

'Mother Han!' I growled.

'Well, he might as well be dead for all the use he was to me. I lost my income when he went,' she said scratching herself. 'What would you have me do, starve?'

I pursed my lips. 'One day your blasphemies will catch you out. Heaven's gate will tremble before your litany of deceits.'

'Oh, Saint Peter won't keep me out. He'll have to let me in if only for the sake of those queuing behind.' She cackled heartily at her own joke.

I sighed with despair. 'And what did Brother Ambrose mean when he called you a medicine woman? Since when did you know anything of the physician's art? I warn you,' I wagged a stern finger. 'If I find you've been curing illegally…'

'I - er - oooh!' She suddenly went cross-eyed and grabbed my arm.

'That won't work with me,' I said shaking my head. 'I won't be deterred. I know your tricks.'

'No trick, brother. I…oh-ahhh!' She held her chest, blew out her cheeks and her face was turning pale.

'What is it?' I said suddenly concerned. 'What is happening? Are you flushing? What do you need?'

'I need…' she gasped holding my arm.

'Yes?' I urged.

'I need…'

'I'm listening. You need…?'

'…a shit.'

I drew back. 'What?'

She gave me a doleful look. 'Two days, brother. It's too long at my age.' She pulled on my arm as she struggled to rise. 'You'll have to help me. I can't get up by myself.' I hesitated but she looked in earnest. 'Unless you want the mess here on the altar steps.'

The thought was appalling. We headed out as fast as we could through the south transept, Mother Han hobbling painfully on my arm and holding the back of her skirts. We managed to get as far as the Great Cemetery a few yards outside the transept door before she dived behind a bush while I stood guard listening to the unearthly noises coming from within. Not that she needed me to safeguard her dignity. The smell alone was enough to deter the most curious passer-by.

'Oh, that's better,' she said emerging after a few minutes and adjusting her clothing. She jabbed a filthy thumb over her shoulder and sneered. 'I wouldn't go in there for a while if I were you. Give the vapours a chance to circulate.'

'Mother Han, I have no intention of going anywhere near that bush before the Second Coming.'

She squinted sideways at me. 'Snooty as ever, I see. Well, I'll be off.'

She started to pull away from me, but I held on firmly to her arm and pulled her back.

'Not so fast. I want to know why you are masquerading as a medic.'

'Oh *that*.' She flapped a hand in the air.

'Yes that,' I said sternly. 'Do you realise I could have you whipped for personation? Ten years it took me to learn my skills in some of the finest and most expensive medical schools in Europe. It's not something you can pick up as the fancy takes you.'

She guffawed. 'I seen what you physicians do; t'aint nothing special. Oh, you use few more expensive herbs and fancy potions than me mebbe, but it's much the same thing. Anyway, it's mostly water I give 'em with a bit of mint and arrowroot mixed in. There's no harm in it.'

'Sheer quackery! You're taking money from the gullible and the desperate under false pretences.'

'Works though. And I bet I've killed fewer with my potions that than you have with yours.'

'Well that's just plain nonsense!' I blustered. 'You've no qualification, no licence, no *accreditation*. People like you are a scourge to the profession.'

She stuck out her chin towards me. 'I give comfort to them as can't afford your prices. Without me they'd have no minist'ring at all. Some even live to thank me.'

'More by luck than judgement.'

'At least I don't bleed the poor beggars to death. Or make them vomit their arseholes up.'

Now she had gone too far. 'Bloodletting - or *phlebotomy* to give it its scientific name - is an ancient and well-respected art that goes back to Aristotle. And *voiding* purifies the stomach and cleanses the soul.'

'Prrf! Tell that to the stiffs in the graveyard.'

'Oh, I've had enough of this,' I fumed. 'I ought to report you to the church authorities. In fact, I *will* report you - right now,' and I started to march off.

'Go ahead,' she called after me. 'Shan't bother telling you what I know in that case.'

I stopped and came back slowly. 'Tell me what?'

She grinned revealing her three remaining teeth. 'By the way,' she sniffed, 'speaking of maledictions of the body, how's that boy with the crippled hand?'

'You mean Onethumb?'

'I know what his name is,' she said indignantly. 'Wasn't it me who gave it him? I named all my chicks.'

'Your chicks!' I snorted. But then I remembered she'd known Onethumb even longer than I had. In fact, the reason she was known as *Mother* Han was because she looked after the waifs and strays who lived wild on the streets of Bury, as Onethumb himself had once done.

She looked at me slyly. 'He's got himself a pretty wife - ooh, she's a pretty one.'

'Rosabel?' I said suspiciously. 'What do you know of her?'

Mother Han smiled. 'Looking buxom. Bit too big in the tit, though. I'd say she's weaned recently. Plenty of milk in her still for her chick - or somebody else's.'

'Mother Han,' I said suspiciously. 'If you know something you're not telling me, it could mean a man's life. It could mean Rosabel's life.'

'Oh yes,' she snarled. 'It's different when it's someone else's life. My life counts for nothing.'

'Don't be ridiculous. Your life isn't in danger.'

'Huh! Another day kneeling in front of that box of tricks and I'd've been worm casts for sure.'

'Well you're not in front of the shrine now. Saint Edmund has released you for a purpose. So tell me what you know.'

She gurneyed at me. 'I saw her,' she said.

'Rosabel? When?'

'Two nights back. As a matter of fact, she stayed with me.'

My jaw dropped. 'What? You're saying Rosabel was staying with you? Rosabel? Stayed? With *you*?'

Her eyes narrowed. 'Hard to credit isn't it? A family like that seeking sanctuary in my hovel.'

My jaw dropped even further. 'You're saying the entire family stayed with you?'

'Of course, the whole family. You think you're the only one who knows anything?'

So that's where they'd been. Yes, it made sense. Rosabel would have known Mother Han through Onethumb. They would have had to leave the palace lodge in a hurry when the king arrived. It explained how they managed to disappear so suddenly and so totally. What better place to vanish than into Mother Han's world, a world with its own rules and codes of conduct? I had never been to Mother Han's lodging or even knew where it was, but I had no doubt it was in a part of the town where even de Saye's men would not willingly venture. I didn't know whether to cheer or weep.

I looked at her sternly. 'Where are they, Mother Han?'

She shrugged. 'Search me. They stayed one night and were taken next morning.'

'*Taken?* What do you mean "taken"? Taken by who?'

'By your old friend, Geoffrey de Saye,' she sniffed.

I reeled. 'Dear God woman, are you mad? Didn't you even try to stop them?'

She shrugged. 'I'm just a weak old medicine woman. Besides, they seemed happy enough to go.'

I was speechless. 'Don't you realise, Geoffrey de Saye is the boy's mortal enemy? Now he has them all – Raoul, Adelle, baby Alix and Rosabel too. Dear God in heaven, does Onethumb know about this? Pray God he doesn't for I'm sure he'll try to release them.'

'Like I say,' she said nonchalantly, 'they went willingly enough.' She squinted up at the sky. 'And so must I before it rains. I give you good night, brother.' She pulled her shawl up over her shoulders.

'Just a minute,' I called after her. 'Which way did they go? Did you see?'

'No idea.'

'Wait!' I called. 'Don't you want this?'

She stopped and squinted back at me. I held out the penny she'd stolen from the abbey between my forefinger and thumb. Slowly she came back and snatched the silvery disc from my hand.

Squinting closely at it, she sneered. 'Generous to a fault.'

'You're not lying to me, Mother Han, are you?' I said seriously.

'Why would I lie? I didn't have to tell you anything. I did it for them - not you.'

She pocketed the penny and turned to leave hitching up her rags as she went.

'You tell that boy I was asking after him,' she called over her shoulder. 'I did well by him, didn't I? Oh yes, I did well.'

A moment later she was out through Anselm's gate and gone from view.

Chapter Twenty-one
TRAGEDIES AND CLUES

With the king finally gone there was an added urgency to my quest to find the de Grays. Having failed to get the answer he wanted over the election of the new abbot King John had set off in a pique for Royston Priory just south of Cambridge where another meeting was to be held to try to resolve the matter well away from us monks. And that is where Hugh went scurrying after him. Thus in the course of a single morning we were back to where we'd been before the king's visit although it would take us a while longer to get over the trauma.

My chief concern now was Geoffrey de Saye. It was surely only a matter of time before he had me arrested. His guards who had been quietly withdrawn when the king arrived were once again being seen everywhere though happily not yet within the walls of the abbey itself. But soon de Saye would have the town closed down completely and with it any chance of finding the family.

But at least now I had some kind of lead although not quite the one I would have liked. *Willingly*, Mother Han said; Rosabel and the others had gone *willingly*. But how could that be if it was Geoffrey de Saye who had taken them? On past performance Raoul would surely have put up a struggle. Oh, but this is Geoffrey de Saye we are speaking of. He would find ways to coerce them, no doubt, perhaps by threatening the Lady Adelle - or even baby Alix, I wouldn't put anything past him. Two nights ago they had stayed at Mother Han's. *Two nights*. They could be half way to the north Norfolk coast by now.

And Onethumb was causing me further concern. If he had heard about the family's abduction - and he was much closer to Mother Han than I was - it would be just like him to try to find them on his own. I had to try to prevent him from doing anything stupid. But he had disappeared too.

I tried Joseph's shop first in the vain hope he might have returned to work. As I feared, there was no sign of him, nor had there been since he stormed out. I did, however, find Joseph at Onethumb's desk in the workroom at the back of the shop - unusually for him.

'Would I be doing this if he was here?' he replied tetchily as he ground some paste in a pestle and mortar. 'No, I have not seen Onethumb today and it is very inconvenient. As you can see, I have much work to do and am in need of his assistance. I cannot be in the shop and out here at the same time.'

'Didn't you think to look for him?'

'I'm his employer not his guardian.'

I was exasperated. 'Joseph, how can you be so callous? You know what's been happening. He is desperately worried for Rosabel's safety. If he's gone looking for her I fear he may be overwhelmed. For all we know de Saye's men may have him already.'

'He's a capable young man,' said Joseph. 'Perhaps I have more confidence in his abilities than you do - though less in his time-keeping.'

'I have no confidence at all where Geoffrey de Saye is concerned.'

'It's only been three days. Once he's over his sulk he'll be back.'

'And if his body turns up tomorrow in a ditch with his throat cut?'

'Then you will have been proved right - and I will be in need of a new assistant.'

Joseph was impossible to deal with when he was in this mood. I left him to his grumbling and went on to Onethumb's home. But Rosabel's parents were as unconcerned as Joseph had been. Little Hal didn't seem to be missing his father or his mother - on the contrary, he seemed quite happy to be with his doting grandparents. Once again I left empty-handed.

On my way back to the abbey I took a detour through the marketplace to see if any of the street urchins had heard anything – after all, Onethumb had once been one of them, albeit many years ago. These were the little hedgehogs that Mother Han called her 'waifs and strays' whose welfare she took upon herself to look after. It was something I had always grudgingly admired about the woman and which never quite seemed to fit with what I knew of the rest of her nefarious activities – and yet somehow it did. Certainly Onethumb never showed anything but affection for the old rogue whenever her name was mentioned. I suppose to him and countless others like him she was the nearest thing to a mother they had ever known.

I knew I'd find some of the street orphans in the marketplace. There was never any shortage of the bedraggled scamps scurrying about the detritus of trade like rats in a grain store picking up anything others did not want – and sometimes what they did want. Sure enough, I found a troupe of them idly torturing a cockerel in an alley behind the fish market. They had the wretched creature buried up to its neck in the ground so it had no chance whatever to escape or avoid injury and death. I suppose I shouldn't have been surprised by their wanton cruelty since they had never been taught anything better; certainly never had the benefit of a Christian upbringing – or any kind of upbringing.

'Onethumb?' said the oldest boy casually tossing another flint at the creature's bloodied head. 'That's a stupid name. Never heard of him.'

He aimed another missile and this time calmly exploded one of its eyes - to the whoops of his companions.

I cringed in revulsion. 'I just need to speak to him. I can pay.'

I took out a silver penny and held it up to tempt them. But the boy merely put his hand inside his shirt and took out a much bigger handful of coins. Things had changed since the last time I had dealings with them. I couldn't hope to compete with such a bounty. The boy picked up another stone and threw it with particular malice at the animal's head. The stone hit its mark with such a crack that must have half-killed the creature because this time it did not crow but shuddered unnaturally.

It was more than I could bear. Stepping forward, I dug the

animal out of its tomb with my bare hands. Unfortunately the miserable creature's injuries were already too far gone and the kindest thing to do was to wring its neck and end its suffering.

''Ere!' said the boy making a grab at corpse. 'That's mine!'

'Don't test me, boy,' I growled him. 'You can have the carcass but the game is ended.' I held the mangled corpse out for him to take, its silent head swinging limply from my hand.

'What gives you the right?' said the boy angrily.

'It's an animal, a living thing – or it was,' I said glancing down at the bloodied corpse. 'All such creatures are *God's* property, not yours. And I'll thank you to show a little more respect. Do you know who I am?'

Whether or not he knew he didn't seem to care. Encouraged by his bravado, the rest of his troupe was pressing forward. I clearly wasn't going to get much information out of them now. Indeed, I would be lucky to escape some injury of my own judging from their posturing. Despite their belligerence they were only children. Alone, none of them would put up much of a battle but together they might be a problem. I had to admit to felling a little uneasy. We each stood our ground glowering at each other neither really willing to make a move.

But then from among them emerged the littlest of them all: A girl judging by her clothing who slowly and deliberately walked into the space between us. Smiling sweetly up at me, she took the dead cockerel from me and handed it to the boy. Then she slipped her tiny hand in mine and started to lead me away. Behind us I heard the boy throw the dead carcass and it landed a few feet ahead of us.

'He can have it, silly old fart!' said the boy loudly. 'Probably the only cock he's got anyway!'

For the next half hour the girl led me through a Bury I hardly knew existed. We slithered through passages – I could hardly call them streets – between rows of dwellings that looked as though the merest sneeze would topple them. The deeper we ventured the more apprehensive I grew although my little guide never altered her pace, never spoke and never let go of my hand. Eventually when I thought there couldn't be any town left to traverse we came to the bank that marked the edge of the town, high upon which stood Abbot Anselm's wall and alongside it the gulley known as the hounds-ditch. This I knew was the town's sewer at the very edge of the vill and into it went every article of foul-smelling refuse including many dead dogs – hence its name.

The little girl led me towards it, hopping and jumping over things I did not dare put a name to while a cold wind blew down from the north and several times I nearly slipped on the icy puddles fearing for my limbs. I pulled my robes around me as I caught the eye of one old tramp who grinned back at me as though he was possessed of a devil. I shivered, made a hasty sign of the cross and hurried on.

Finally we came to a patch of ground not much bigger than my cell at the abbey upon which was strewn a slough of black bile that looked as though it had issued from the very mouth of Hell. I thought at first it was just another pile of discarded detritus and muck and was about to hop over it when my little guide stopped and pointed.

'You mean this is it?' I asked incredulously. 'This is where you wanted to bring me?'

The girl merely gave me her sweet smile again and nodded.

'But there's nothing here.'

The girl shrugged and started to walk away. I looked around. This was not somewhere Onethumb would have come, surely. To what purpose? There was nothing here, no sign that any human life could exist here among the rats and the cockroaches.

But then something caught my eye — or rather, two things caught it. The first was a shiny object half hidden in the mud. I picked it up and wiped it. It was a silver penny exactly like the one I had given to Mother Han the previous day.

I was suddenly engulfed in a feeling of dread. Surely not. Surely this wasn't where Mother Han lived — or *had* lived, for no-one could live here now?

I looked to the little girl for an answer but she was already gone, dissolved back into the narrow lanes again. I was beginning to wonder if she had really existed at all or was just a trick of my imagination. Yet here I was and I'd seen enough burnt buildings to know one when I saw it. Something had once stood here, probably a shack like the others round about, a collection of flimsy and mean hovels. Whatever it had been it was now no longer but steaming, smoking timbers. Then as I stumbled forward something else appeared out of the rubble. I picked it up. It was a small knife, silver possibly, valuable certainly, surely not something Mother Han would have possessed. Rubbing the muck from it I read the inscription round the edge: *GdeS*.

Geoffrey de Saye.

A surge of anger welled up in me. Why? What harm could an old woman do to him? Was he so vengeful? The thought struck me that he - or more probably one of his spies — must have seen me speaking to Mother Han the previous day and this was her reward. Brushing away the tears of anguish, I thrust the little dagger into my belt pouch. But now I was even more confused. I had asked the little girl to take me to where she'd last seen Onethumb and she'd brought me unswervingly here. That Onethumb would have come to seek out Rosabel was understandable. But Mother Han insisted that Rosabel had left this place *willingly*. Did this look like willingness? To me it looked like force. I stayed a while longer picking my way through the few remaining items trying to make sense of it all and hoping against hope for any more clues. But I found nothing. All was cinders. One of the scarecrows that passed for humanity in this hell-hole was squatting nearby.

'Did you see who did this?' I demanded of him.

He grinned at me and rung his hands together. I understood the message. Like everyone else he wanted something for his trouble. I gave him my few remaining pennies including the one left by Mother Han.

'It was an angel,' he replied once he'd satisfied himself the coins were genuine. 'A White Angel.'

I caught my breath. A white angel again. Was this the same white angel who had struck off Hervey's hand? Had something of the kind happened to Mother Han too? Was she even still alive?

'What did he look like, this angel? A white angel - a white-haired angel perhaps?'

But the man just giggled before scuttling off.

I felt suddenly very weary. Harm seemed to come to any who came into contact with me in this matter. It was uncanny. All I could think to do was to leave this God-forsaken place and its ghoulish population as quickly as possible before worse descended upon them.

*

I seethed with anger over what had happened to Mother Han and determined to confront de Saye no matter what the consequences for me. But before I had a chance to do that, events took yet another unexpected turn. Returning to the abbey I found the place in turmoil once again. For a moment I thought the king had returned but then I realised these were not the king's men I saw patrolling the streets but De Saye's. They were everywhere, highly visible and behaving as though the town was under siege. All the gates were locked as were the two main gates of the abbey with crowds gathered in front of them and this time not weeping for their children but fearful and confused for their own lives. No-one knew what was going on and no-one would tell them. Normally during daylight hours the abbey gates were open and welcoming so that anyone wishing to enter the abbey grounds could pass freely. But now the only people being allowed in were the choir monks and even they were being vetted and searched first.

I mingled with the noisy crowd in front of the Great Gate wondering whether to risk going through myself when a figure suddenly appeared the other side of the barrier that made me think again: It was Geoffrey de Saye. I ducked before he saw me. Despite my brave intentions to confront him this was clearly not the time. With the place virtually under martial law I'd simply be hauled off and then all my blustering would avail me nothing. What concerned me most was that the abbey appeared to be have been invaded and it's authority in the person of the prior was nowhere to be seen. It was surely an outrage that would never have been permitted in Abbot Samson's day. He would be out here now remonstrating with de Saye and risking his own life in the process. Then another figure appeared who I did recognize pushing his way through the crowd.

'Jocelin, is that you?'

He seemed excited as excited as the crowd. 'W-walter, m-my f-friend. Are you c-coming in?'

'For what reason? What's going on? And where is Herbert?'

He shook his head. 'H-have you n-not h-heard? We have b-been summoned. All of us - th-there are no exceptions. Th-there is to be a m-meeting.'

'What meeting?'

'An important meeting. B-before the H-high Altar. All will be there. You too?' He glanced about unsure whether to utter a name.

'Is it the king?' I asked hopefully. 'Is John to attend?'

'The *king*?' Jocelin snorted. 'N-no, I th-think you can be assured the k-king will be the l-last person to know of it.'

So it had happened: The rebellion that John had been warning of. I wanted to quiz Jocelin further but already we were being separated by two of the guards pushing us roughly apart to create a gap through which two riders quickly cantered. Both were hooded so that their faces could not be seen but I glimpsed the gloved hand of the second man and held my breath. On one of his fingers was a ring that I recognised. Only one person in all Christendom was entitled to wear that ring. Stephen Langton was here.

Jocelin was now twenty feet from me and mouthing something I could not hear above the clamour. I daren't try to get to him for fear of being recognised. Jocelin was being pushed in through the gate by one of the guards and was soon gone from view. Other monks were being shoved unceremoniously through. In a moment it would be my turn. I pulled back. I wanted to be at this meeting, too, to witness the treachery first hand but not with my brother monks. I would see it, but alone. As inconspicuously as I could, I withdrew and made my way round the outside of the abbey walls where there was a little postern gate that few knew about. Just as I hoped, the guards had missed it.

Once inside the grounds I quickly made my way to the back of the church and up through Samson's south tower from where I knew I could get into the loft over the church. The day was dull with plenty of cloud cover. Was it an early Hunter's Moon up there behind the cloud? I wasn't sure anymore, I wasn't sure of anything. It was only much later that I would remember the actual date: Thursday the 20th of November 1214, the Feast of Saint Edmund the King Martyr - the day that England's die was cast.

PART THREE
The Blood Moon

Chapter Twenty-two
A CONSPIRACY OF CUCKOLDS

From my perch high up in the triforium I had a bird's-eye view of the abbey church a hundred feet below and there I watched a truly amazing spectacle unfold. Gone were the usual throngs of pilgrims queuing in hushed tones past the tomb of the blessed Edmund and in their place a quarter of the baronage of England filed in to take their seats in stalls where normally only we monks sat. Some of the figures I knew already, having themselves been to the abbey many times before on pilgrimage - Roger Bigod, Geoffrey de Mandeville and John de Lacy, East Anglian earls all. Others were less familiar to me and I only learned much later: Eustace de Vesci was from Northumberland in the far north, but I also saw Richard de Montfichet and William de Lanvellei whose name I still have difficulty pronouncing; also Henry de Bohun and William Mallet. In all I counted some forty-odd peers whose names would in time become familiar to every Englishman in infamy. And scurrying between them like a rat among lemmings was my lord de Saye. I seethed with anger at the sight of him and I was tempted to lean over the parapet and name him for the murderer I knew him to be. No doubt my moment of defiance would have been quickly ended by a well-aimed bolt from one of his archers who nervously stood guard at the doors, their fingers itching on their triggers, so I kept my peace. Crowding around them all and standing in every possible space were my brother monks, all seventy of them although I was sure many were there under duress. Not so Prior Herbert for there he was seated on the abbot's throne looking proudly smug, the Devil take him. Even from my eyrie I could get a sense of the tension down below with much subdued whispering as they waited for the business to begin. This meeting surely would go down in the annals of perfidy. I was certain once the king got to know of it a great many of the heads raised so arrogantly today would be raised even higher on pikes above the town gates - and well they would look there too.

The last such revolt against a lawful king, I remembered, had taken place some forty years earlier in the time of John's father, good King Harry. That time the conspirators had been the king's own sons Henry and Richard. It had all come to an ignominious end and actually not far from where I was sitting now in the village of Fornham Saint Genevieve a few miles north of Bury when a peasant host armed with little more than sickles and clubs annihilated the rebel army. I was but a child at the time but I can remember hearing the cries of battle and the clash of weapons from nearby Ixworth and later saw the bones of the slaughtered Flemings lying in the field where they remained for years to be bleached by the sun and rain as a warning to others. Clearly that lesson had not yet been learned.

The leader this time seemed to be one Robert Fitzwalter, lord of Dunmow in Essex, who styled himself outrageously as *Marshal of the Army of God*. It was this same Robert Fitzwalter who together with Eustace de Vesci had plotted to murder King John two years earlier but which, by God's good grace, the king had managed to foil and subsequently chased both would-be assassins into exile. A story was later circulated that Fitzwalter's hatred of John was not so much because of his political differences with the king but because John had once made overtures to Fitzwalter's daughter who is then supposed to have killed herself by eating a poisoned egg. Now, I know a little of John's sexual proclivities having witnessed them in the past and I would be the first to agree they left much to be desired, but frankly this story beggared belief. I'd no doubt it was made up simply to justify Fitzwalter's subsequent treasons. And interestingly enough, the other conspirator in that failed murder plot, Eustace de Vesci, is said to have had a similar experience. As a young man John was supposed to have tried to seduce his wife but Eustace managed to smuggle a whore into John's bed in her place. John was so riled when he discovered the deception that he banned the earl from court. So the story went. But again, it sounded more like the invention of some French troubadour in order to discredit our king. No doubt something unsavoury took place but the truth would be altogether more prosaic. In short, this rebellion seemed more like a Conspiracy of the Cuckolded than a movement for genuine political reform. And I might even have been persuaded that it was just that except for the presence among the conspirators of one man

– the Cardinal Archbishop of Canterbury, Stephen Langton seated now next to Prior Herbert. For all that I disagreed with his politics, I could not fault the man's sincerity. He too had suffered humiliation at the hands of King John, although his had been of quite a different hue.

So if it wasn't dehorned husbands or overly-ambitious royal princes, what was the purpose of their lordships' assembly this day? Even archbishops are not permitted within the precincts of St Edmunds abbey without the express invitation of the abbot, and I would have thought with Prior Herbert's liking for rules he would have raised an objection if he could. But that would be to underestimate the persuasive powers of Cardinal Langton. He was no friend of John's, but no lick-spittle either being a man of principle even to the extent of disagreeing with the pope. Clearly something exceptional was taking place here today - and indeed, Langton himself now took the leading role in the proceedings that unfolded beneath the chancel arch.

His voice resonating with all the skill he had honed as a consummate preacher, Langton harangued the assembled nobles for a full two hours exhorting them to demand what he called 'justice and freedom from a cruel and wasteful king'. I won't detail all that Langton had to say but the climax of his performance was the production of a document which he claimed was nothing less than the coronation oath of King John's great-grandfather, King Henry I, and which he said guaranteed the ancient rights of the barons back to Saint Edward the Confessor. Upon this ancient document their lordships now proposed to base a new one: a charter of all the liberties allegedly stolen by John since his coronation and when the time was ripe they pledged themselves to take up arms in defence of those rights. Only now did I fully understand the danger King John and the country were in and what he had meant when he spoke to me of the barons salivating like dogs. They meant to hobble him with legal knots and snares and if he resisted then they would hurl the country into civil war.

I was outraged on the king's behalf certain that he would never accede to such preposterous demands which in effect made him little more than a baron himself. I had no doubt he would throw the document down in the dust where it belonged. I was angry and frustrated in turns and had the greatest difficulty to resist jumping up and denouncing them all. But the final grotesque act had yet to be performed. At the invitation of Cardinal Langton each baron rose in turn to place his hand upon the Holy Book and declare before Christ on His altar - before the holy shrine of the blessed Saint Edmund himself - that if their demands were not met each would take up arms against their lawful king. The whole grotesque scene ended with a shout of support for their leader, Robert Fitzwalter and carried him aloft around the church in gross imitation of a holy procession. It was as much as I could stand and amid the general euphoria I silently withdrew.

*

I managed to get out of the tower without being seen but with so many guards about I dare not to risk the west entrance but doubled round the back of the Great Cemetery. Before I got that far, though, someone stepped out of the shadows.

I jumped back with fright. 'Oh Eusebius! What are you doing here?'

'Master, I have been trying to get in to the church but my way was blocked. Everywhere there seem to be soldiers. I am afraid. What is happening?'

'No, you won't get in,' I replied. 'Only the professed monks are permitted. And it would be better you were not here now. The soldiers are nervous enough and likely to arrest anyone.' I glanced anxiously at the church doors.

'But why?' he asked.

'It would take too long to explain. But I have to go away for a while.'

'You are leaving?'

'It won't be for long. Hush!'

One of the guards was looking in our direction. He must have heard us, his sword already half-drawn at the ready. And here were the two of us crouching like a couple of conspirators. We had only a moment. I turned to Eusebius conscious of my duty to the boy as his chaplain and the fact that this may be my last opportunity to speak to him.

'My son, before I go there is something I want to say to you, and it is this...'

The guard was coming over....

'...we must all try to resist our temptations remembering that however great our sins our loving Father in heaven will always forgive the truly repentant...'

The guard was almost upon us...

'...and we must cut out the offending sin, for which I forgive you in the name of the Father, Son and Holy Ghost.' I quickly made a sign of the cross over him. 'Amen. And now you must forgive me too for what I am about to do.' So saying, I punched the boy smartly on the nose.

It really was only the lightest of taps but it had the effect I wanted. Eusebius yelped - more in surprise, I think, than pain.

But more importantly, blood poured out of him as it had that first day I saw him in the chapterhouse.

'What have we here?' said the guard thrusting his sword in our faces. 'Assassins?'

'Ah, sergeant,' I bluffed. 'You heard my cry for help. Good. We were in the church just now and Brother Eusebius was taken ill – as you can see. I have brought him here to recover but he is still unwell.'

Blood was still pouring through the boy's fingers and dripping everywhere and for that I was truly sorry.

'Dou broge by doze,' mumbled Eusebius his hands covering his face.

'Forgive me, child,' I whispered. 'But there really was no alternative.'

The guard hesitated, his hand still on his sword hilt, frowning with indecision. 'He's bleeding,' he said.

I nodded. 'It's happened before. Spontaneous epistaxis. I'm a doctor, you see. I know about these things.'

The guard still looked doubtful, his sword remaining half-in, half out of its scabbard.

'Well?' I frowned impatiently. 'Are you going to stand there and watch while a servant of Holy Mother Church bleeds to death?'

Eusebius stumbled. The man hesitated a moment more then sheathed his sword as the boy toppled into his arms.

'Oh well caught!' I said to him. 'Now, we need to get him to the infirmary. Can you do that? I will tell my lord de Saye, naturally - he will want to know about this immediately. I follow along afterwards. What did you say your name was?'

'Gerard,' said the man, Eusebius fainting into his arms.

'Right Captain Gerard,' I nodded. 'I'll tell him you were helpful.'

'Very well, sir. But it's only "Gerard", not "captain".'

'I'm sure that's just a matter of time,' I beamed, 'once Lord de Saye gets to hear of this. Now, off with you both to the infirmary. You know where it is? It's that way. Go!'

I waited a moment or two more until the two of them were out of sight then rushed off in the opposite direction to my laboratorium. No doubt Lord de Saye would indeed hear of the incident in the graveyard, and that a physician in a monks' habit had been the cause of it. It would take him but a moment to put two and two together and realise that I had been in the church while the assembly was in progress. And then I would have but very little time before more guards were dispatched this time looking for me. Poor Gerard. I wouldn't have liked to be in his boots when he told him. But it couldn't be helped.

When I got to the laboratorium I found Dominic waiting for me.

'Master, there you are.'

I put up a warning hand. 'Do not delay me, Dominic, I'm in a fearful hurry.' I began filling a leather bag with things I thought I might need: Spare clothing, a water bottle, a few candle stubs - they're always useful - a knife...

'Master, someone has been here looking for you. A brother.'

I grimaced. 'Already? What did he want?' I began hunting for a scrap of linen to write on.

'He didn't say, master.'

One of Herbert's lackeys, no doubt. I would have to be quick. 'Dominic, I want you to do something for me. Do you know my brother's shop in Heathenman's Street?'

'No master – I mean yes master.'

'Go there and tell Joseph to meet me urgently at the market cross. Here's a list of things I need him to bring.' I handed him the scrap of linen. 'He will understand and will not ask questions. Can you do that?'

'Yes master. But where are you going?'

'Better that you don't know. That way you won't need to lie when they ask you. Not that I know myself yet.'

'Who are "they" master?'

I shook my head. 'Never mind. Swear on the Holy Book if you have to that you know nothing of my whereabouts, that way they will know you are telling the truth for it will be so.' I looked at Dominic's wide open, trusting face. 'Yes, they will see you are incapable of lying.' I gave him my benediction. 'Now go – quickly!'

*

I kept my hood up and my face covered while in the crowded marketplace. Fortunately with the weather worsening most people were doing the same thing so I didn't look conspicuous. The place was crawling with soldiers but hopefully not yet looking for me. As I approached the market cross I could see the unmistakable figure of Joseph hovering nearby. Sometimes his magnificent frame was a handicap. He had his head covered, too, but even so he was not difficult to spot. Few men walk as straight or as tall as he and I cursed his Arab pedigree for being so long-limbed. When he saw me he made a gesture for me to follow him. He casually moved off and disappeared behind a stall and in a moment I caught up with him.

'Joseph – thank you for coming.'

'You did not give me much choice. Your boy told me you were leaving. He didn't know where and I didn't ask.'

'Good, because I don't know myself.'

From beneath his voluminous robes he produced a leather satchel. 'This is what you asked for.'

I opened it and looked inside. There was food – enough for a few days – some twine and another bottle of water.

'Thank you.'

He looked about. 'My brother, it is not safe to remain here. We must separate, there are guards everywhere. I wish you God speed. Let us hope the next time we meet it will be in happier circumstances. May the Lord God give you wings and keep you safe.'

'Amen to that,' I said sincerely.

With that he hugged me to his breast and started to move away. But something was wrong. I sensed it. He turned and I saw it on his face, too. He started to say something but was cut short by a blow to the stomach as a guard descended upon him. Then I felt a hand grip my shoulder and I could not move. Two guards now had Joseph and another two had hold of me. We were trapped. There was no escape.

But then something amazing happened. In an instant the world utterly changed. One moment the air had been clear and fresh and the next it was white and choking and impossible to breathe. It took me a second to realise what had happened: From out of the sky a missile had descended and burst upon the ground next to us sending a plume of white powder up into the air covering everything. The explosion momentarily stunned the soldier who released his hold on me. It stunned Joseph too but he was quicker to react than the rest of us. I saw him swing his arm wide winding the soldier nearest him who buckled onto his knees. Then he managed to throw both arms around the soldier holding me and yelled a single word:

'Run!'

I didn't need telling twice. I ran. But which way? The choking powder obscured everything. But as the haze cleared I saw another figure gesturing furiously to me.

It was Onethumb.

Without hesitation I raced towards him - and then there were six of us all running in the same direction towards the Risby Gate: Me, followed by Onethumb, followed by the stall-holder whose sack of flour Onethumb had stolen, followed by three of the soldiers. Onethumb quickly overtook me and launched himself at the gatekeeper who had positioned himself ready to catch us. With a sickening crunch he knocked the man to the ground and we both leapt over him. A moment later we were out through the gate and running as fast as our legs could carry us.

Chapter Twenty-three
IN THE DEPTHS OF THE FOREST

We didn't stop running until we had put a good half mile between us and the town. Only then did I glance over my shoulder and realised our pursuers were not with us. Panting and cursing, I halted and slumped exhausted to my knees.

'I'm too old for this,' I gasped rolling onto my back. 'Leave me to die here by the roadside, it will be a mercy.'

Onethumb grinned down at me, his hands on his knees. He was panting too, I was pleased to see, despite being half my age.

I looked up at him. 'I don't know why you're looking so pleased with yourself. You nearly choked me back there with your antics.'

He nodded enthusiastically, made an arc through the air with his good hand and mimicked the sound of the bag bursting as it hit the ground.

'Yes, very good,' I agreed. 'Now anyone seeking us need only look for "the white monk". Look at me. I'm covered head to foot in flour.' I shook my head sending a cloud of the powdery stuff into the air.

Onethumb peered back the way we had come and signed that he didn't think anyone was following us.

I nodded with relief. 'They must have stopped at the gate, God be thanked.'

I fished out the water bottle from the bag Joseph had given me and took a long draught before pouring some over my head to rid my hair of some of the flour. But Onethumb stopped me and shook his head.

'You're right,' I said putting the stopper back in the bottle's neck. 'We can't afford to waste it. I'm really not very good at this, am I?'

He grinned and nodded enthusiastically.

'This is all a big adventure to you, isn't it?'

He nodded again even more enthusiastically and asked where we were going next. I had to admit I had no idea. It was a question I'd been asking myself. I'd been so concerned with simply getting out of Bury that I still hadn't had time to consider what we were going to do next. And I hadn't bargained on having Onethumb with me. I knew what he wanted us to do: Find Rosabel. Everything else to him was of secondary importance. And I supposed I owed it to him to do just that - after all, I was the one who had put her in danger in the first place. But there was also the matter of the assembly in the abbey church. The king had to know about it and it was surely the duty of every loyal Englishman to tell him. But I also had a duty to Onethumb. The question was where my greatest duty lay: With my king or with my friend?

In the end there was no real choice. We didn't know for certain that de Saye had Rosabel and the family much less where they were. De Saye might well have taken them north as he had threatened, but it could take us days to get to the north Norfolk coast only to find they were not there. They might even still be in Bury. We simply had no way of knowing. On the other hand we knew exactly which way the king had gone, towards London, and that there was a good chance we might catch him up – or at least catch the stragglers from his baggage train who could then hasten our message to the king. And then there was the other matter that still nagged at the back of my mind: That comment Mother Han's about Rosabel going *willingly* with de Saye.

I was about to voice all these concerns to Onethumb when he put up his hand to silence me. I frowned questioningly but then I heard it too, the unmistakable sound of men's voices. We quickly scrambled to the bend in the road and cautiously peered round. What I saw horrified me. Raoul de Gray had said that the roads leading from Bury were picketed with soldiers and I could see now that he was right. There were only three of them but sufficient to deter any would-be travellers, and certainly enough to overpower the two of us. Their presence might also explain why our pursuers hadn't followed us out of the town. If they knew the soldiers were here we could confidently be expected to run into their arms. If we'd gone a few yards further on we would have done.

What are they doing here? Onethumb signed.

I had no answer for him, but every minute we remained here increased our chances of apprehension. We had to get off the road. And with every other road out of Bury as likely as this one to be blocked, there was only one place left to go.

*

The forest is a dangerous place at any time. In its bogs and gulleys a man could easily drown or fall and break a limb, or simply get lost just yards from safety. And there are some fearsome wild animals living in the greenwood - wild boar, feral dogs, even wolves, or so I'd heard. Then there are the wild *human* animals which are even more dangerous; desperate men already beyond the law who would think nothing of dispatching an unwary traveller for the sake of his boots. And of course there is also the *non*-human that are everywhere and nowhere, those malevolent spirits that delight in leading men to their destruction especially at night when the veil between the nether world and our own is thinnest and most penetrable. I shuddered at the thought.

But even if we managed to survive all these there is one other danger that is perhaps the most pernicious of all because it is invisible. I speak, of course, of the hated forestry laws. Common law as it is normally understood in the rest of England does not apply in the forest where life is organised for just one purpose: To ensure the king has good hunting. That means everything else is secondary to its protection. The laws had been around since time unrecorded but had increased drastically since the days of the Conqueror for whom the sport was an obsession. The penalties for killing game now ranged from fining to mutilation and even execution. It is like an iron hand lying upon the land encompassing everything and everyone. Crops cannot be tended or ditches dug or fences maintained if it disturbs the habitat of the deer even if human families starve in the process. A man cannot carry a weapon into the forest or own a dog large enough to worry the smallest doe. And forestry law does not simply apply to woodland or heath. It covers farms, villages, even entire towns. The trouble is that unless you know, it is impossible to tell when you are within its jurisdiction and when you are not for there are no signs, only a vast army of agents whose sole function is to catch transgressors and bring them before the magistrates. Most are ruthless. Many are corrupt.

Such, then, are the multifarious perils facing anyone foolish enough to wander into the forest. The prospect would be daunting for an army of young knights with all their wits and brawn to draw on. What chance an aging Benedictine monk and his one-handed, mute companion? We were about to find out.

Against all the odds we did manage to get through the first freezing night in our makeshift camp, not daring to light a fire for fear of attracting attention. One good thing about having a dumb companion is that only one of us can talk in his sleep. Not that we did much talking despite my desire to quiz him about Mother Han and Rosabel. In the dark he was mute too for I could not see his gestures. All explanation would have to wait until daylight. So we bedded down as best we could in a small hollow as soon as darkness fell, which was earlier and more complete here beneath the thick greenwood canopy than outside. Needless to say I didn't sleep a wink. I spent the night sitting upright with my hands clasped tightly in silent prayer and my knees drawn up close to my chest listening to the cacophony of noises around me. And let no-one say that the forest at night is not alive with monsters and monstrous happenings. I can tell you now with absolute certainty that under cover of darkness trees pull up their roots and walk, dogmen howl and hobgoblins tap you on the shoulder. Urrrgh!

In spite of my fears exhaustion did eventually overcome me and I must have drifted off because I awoke the next morning to daylight and the sound of birdsong and for the briefest moment I fancied I was a child again camping out with my father and Joseph. It took but a moment for the chill November damp of the forest floor to penetrate my robe and for me to realise it was not the sweet twittering of skylarks I could hear but the harsh bark of crows in the bare trees above my head, and then I remembered where I was.

As my groaning announced my re-emergence into the world I saw Onethumb's infuriating grin as he handed me a hunk of bread and a cup of cold beer. His chirpiness was beginning to irritate me.

'What time is it?' I coughed, but I already knew the answer. My growling stomach told me it was long past prime, the third office of the day, after which we monks break our night's fast. The day was dark and made all the more oppressive by the canopy of the forest pressing down upon us and blocking out the sun. How I longed for the ache of a misericord propping up my buttocks in the freezing choir stalls of the abbey church. The thought of it was bliss compared with this damp earthen forest floor. I chewed my bread thanking God with only moderate sincerity for His munificence and looked about me. Everything appeared the same as the previous night and yet different.

Where do you think we are? signed Onethumb.

I could see behind his brave face that really he was as nervous as I, neither of us wanting the other to know how the other felt. I did my best to exude confidence but in truth I wasn't at all sure. At some stage I would have to designate a direction. My heart was for Rosabel but my head was still for the king. I could not put off the final decision for much longer but first had to find out where we were.

When I was a child my father sometimes took Joseph and me on short trips away from Ixworth Hall to show us the skills he learned in the Holy Land. He said it was a good manly pursuit and built character. To my surprise I found I had actually enjoyed it and even learnt a few lessons from his tutoring. And now at last I was able to put it to good use for I recalled that direction can be found from observing the position of the sun. Unfortunately Suffolk has less sun than does Damascus, even in summer, and in November none at all. We needed something else.

'Moss,' I said having another moment of inspiration. 'It grows on the north side of a tree. Find a tree with moss growing on it and that will be north.'

We quickly found a tree with moss growing on it, but it seemed to grow on every side, and on the next tree it grew not at all. We followed one mildewed bark after another getting more and more confused. It was slightly embarrassing because part of this woodland must border onto my mother's estate. I felt sure I should recognise it. However, it was nearly forty years since I last did this sort of thing.

'Aha,' I said after half an hour of wandering. 'I do believe we are getting somewhere at last. Something about this place is familiar to me.' I peered up into the canopy. 'Yes, I have the distinct impression I've been here before.'

We have been here before, signed Onethumb, and pointed to some broken twigs where we had trodden earlier that morning.

We had been going round in circles.

'Perhaps we should pause a moment,' I suggested, 'to offer up a prayer to Saints Christopher, Julian and Raphael. Those three patron saints of travellers must help. And perhaps one extra to Saint Brendan the navigator for his guiding hand to point the way. It can't do any harm.'

Onethumb reluctantly bowed his head while I muttered some hastily assembled words. And they worked! The saints smiled benignly upon us causing the clouds to part just enough to reveal through the trees the sun low in the southern sky. We had our miracle.

'There!' I beamed at him triumphantly. 'It's this way. Follow me,' I said striding off with confidence - and immediately plunged twenty feet into a ravine.

It all happened so fast I didn't have time to react such was my surprise. Once I'd stopped sliding, however, I saw that I had in fact fallen into a deep gulley at the foot of a circular mound of earth. Such mounds are scattered all over this part of Suffolk, nobody knows what they are for. Some say they are the footprints of Gog and Magog, the fabled leaders of an ancient race of giants who lived in these parts. Others claim they are the burial mounds of pagans and that there is treasure buried deep in the middle of them. Whatever the truth of it, this mound was exceptionally high and constructed from the earth which had been excavated, I would hazard, from the hole into which I had tumbled. The hole was certainly deep and filled with brambles, which was why I hadn't seen it till it was too late. It was also extremely steep. I'd managed to slide practically the entire length from top to bottom before finally coming to a halt, and the more I struggled to extricate myself the more entangled I became, not helped by my sodden robe which was never meant for these sorts of surroundings. I looked up in desperation to see Onethumb peering over the rim a few yards above me, and thank God for him for I feared to die alone in this awful place.

But things were about to get worse. As I scrabbled about trying to extricate myself I must have dislodged the soil above me for something dropped out of it and landed with a plop on my shoulder. I shuddered for out of the corner of my eye I could make out a bony white hand and as I slowly turned my head I found to my horror that I was staring at a skull that was grinning back at me, its teeth barred and its eye sockets empty - and that's when I finally I screamed. I admit it, I was stupefied with fear. I was convinced that one of the monsters who lived in the mound had risen up angry at having its final resting place disturbed and was ready to drag me down into whatever heathen hell from where it had just emerged. But by then Onethumb had scrambled nearly down beside me put his fingers to my lips to silence me. We weren't yet safe from our pursuers.

'Which one?' I whispered, my voice trembling. 'Which of them is it?' Please God, I thought, let it not be Rosabel.

With a grimace Onethumb pulled something from the bushes and thrust it up for me to see. It was the shirt that the skeleton had been wearing. I almost fainted with relief. Whoever this was it could not Rosabel or Raoul or Adelle but someone else who must have been there much longer than a mere few days.

Slowly my breathing returned to normal, and at last I summoned the courage to look at the skeleton properly. I could see now that it was in fact old, picked clean by time and the little creatures of the forest. He – for from its clothing it was undoubtedly male - was perched on the seat of a cart which had been pulled by a mule whose own skeleton was still harnessed to the front and bleached as white as the driver's. The entire contraption must have been swallowed up by the ditch and then lost from view as with time the forest grew up and enveloped it. It seemed the driver must have done the same as I had done only he had fallen to his death probably by the jolt as he landed instead of sliding gently as I did. My trembling fingers felt around the back of the neck and confirmed my suspicion: It was broken. At least his death would have been quick. His mule, however, had not been so fortunate. Still manacled to the cart and unable to escape, it must have slowly starved to death over many days struggling hopelessly to free itself while the eyes of the dead driver looked unseeingly on. The cart itself was remarkably intact, its load of hemp rope still secure on the back destined for a delivery that was never to be made. He seemed to me like a harbinger from Hades bringing his load of death into the world and I shuddered at the thought.

And I was still shaking as I scrambled back up the slope aided by Onethumb. It was then I realised I must have lost both my boots in the descent. That would have been bad enough but I had lost hold of my satchel and our own precious cargo of food and water was also at the bottom of the ditch and had now disappeared from view. Short of descending again there was no way we were going to find it. Nor was it wise for us to try for as Onethumb pointed out, we must have made a dreadful racket as we crashed about not helped by my screams. We needed urgently to get away before our pursuers or some other unsavoury opportunist came along. But in this we were already too late. Onethumb tapped me on the shoulder and pointed further down the slope to a distant figure on horseback - a lone rider just standing and watching us, his white tabard and chain mail glinting in the afternoon sunlight. I caught my breath. Was this perhaps the 'angel' mentioned by Hervey's friend and the tramp at Mother Han's? One of de Saye's men? Fortunately he was too far away across the gorge to reach us which was presumably why he didn't try. But he clearly wanted us to see him. It was surely just a question of time before we saw him again.

*

We managed to scuttle further into the forest but the deeper in we went, the denser became the undergrowth, the more disorientated we became and without boots my feet were being torn to shreds. We had to hold up while I ripped my undergarments into strips and with leaves and twigs wrapped them around my bleeding soles – no time for modesty. But linen was no substitute for leather and soon I was having to stop and make more. By now it was getting dark again and a penetrating fog had descended to confuse us even further. We were lost, tired, hungry, cold and with no possible hope of escape. The fog might have worked in our favour for as well as shielding us from view it might mask the smoke from a fire. Whether it did or not and we were discovered by our mysterious white angel surely a swift blade through the brain was more merciful than slowly freezing to death. But along with everything else I had dropped my fire-striker when I fell into the hollow and without it we had no means of making a spark. I was close to despair and was seriously thinking that Onethumb might be better going on without me. Younger and fitter than I, he might just make it out of this maze alive. Better that than we should end up dying alone with only yards separating us.

It was then that they began arriving, dropping silently from the trees above our heads and landing on soft, practised feet. As soon as we knew they were here we were up on our feet and ready to fight but by then it was already too late. Onethumb tried to run but was knocked sprawling to the ground. I didn't even bother to try realising I had no hope of escape. A knife was at my throat and I muttered a silent prayer to a merciful God for a quick death certain our last minutes on earth had arrived.

Chapter Twenty-four
THE MEN OF THE FOREST

'Who are you?' The man's breath was foul against my ear.

'Pilgrims,' I coughed. 'We're pilgrims.'

'Pilgrims my arse!'

There were five of them and they easily overwhelmed us. Having forced us to our knees three then went off somewhere, I guessed to check that we were alone, leaving two to guard us. Did they need any more? We were easy pray and no mistake. But who were they? Not de Saye's men and not the king's either, more's the pity. They looked as though they had been living rough for some time, their clothes were rags and from the smell of them they could have done with a good dowsing. They all wore masks covering their eyes but I took hope from that for if they intended to kill us why bother hiding their faces? My fear was that they would rob us and then leave us tied up here to die of cold and hunger.

'We don't know who you are and we don't care,' I braved hopefully. 'Look I have my eyes closed so I cannot see your faces. You can take all we have, we won't resist.'

It wasn't much of an offer. We hadn't much to begin with and most of what we'd brought was now at the bottom of the ravine.

The foul-breathed man swaggered over to me and stuck his face in mine. '*You* don't tell us. *We* tell *you*.' Then he started pulling at my robe. 'I'll, er, have this for a start.'

I shook my head. 'No.'

He unsheathed his knife and waved it threateningly in front of my nose. 'Did you hear me? I said take it off!'

Still I shook my head. 'Out of the question.'

He grabbed the back of my head and pressed the blade against my windpipe breathing his foul breath into my nostrils and making me flinch. I wasn't sure which I feared the most - the knife or his breath.

'You may slit my throat, but you still wouldn't get my robe.'

'Oh? Why not?'

'Because you've just tied my hands together.' I lifted them up to show him.

For a moment he seemed unsure of what to do next. Fortunately the other man who had been holding onto Onethumb now pulled off his mask, and falling on his knees he clasped his hands together in supplication.

'Oh God, a monk. I knew it! I knew it! Oh God!'

And then to my astonishment he started to moan - in Latin. I looked at him with interest. What sort of cutthroat moans in Latin?

Thankfully this made Foul-breath release his grip on my neck and dance over to the man. 'Stop it,' he growled at him. 'Get up or I'll slit your throat, too!'

'But he's a monk. Don't you see? God will smite us if we harm him.'

Foul-breath snorted and kicked him making him yelp. 'God my arse!'

I relaxed a little. 'He's right,' I said. 'I am indeed a monk. And I'm on important business. For the abbey. You had better listen to your friend.'

Foul-breath danced back to me. 'You said you were pilgrims.'

'Pilgrims of *God*,' I babbled nonsensically. 'It's God's work we are about. So you had better not harm us or God's vengeance will be terrible indeed.'

Foul-breath looked around, his eyeballs rolling. 'Well, *he's* not a monk,' he said pointing his knife at Onethumb. 'He's but a cripple. Maybe I'll slit his throat instead.'

He danced over to Onethumb and twisted his nose making poor Onethumb squirm silently.

'Huh! Mute, too.'

Onethumb snapped at the man's hand making him pull it away.

'Huh! Aggressive little beggar, ain't he?' chortled Foul-breath.

'He's my manservant,' I said quickly. 'And he will desist when I tell him to – won't you Onethumb?' I said forcefully.

'Onethumb!' snorted Foul-breath. 'What sort of daft name is that?'

'No worse than Fitchet.'

We all looked round to see the other three had returned – two men and a youth.

Foul-breath turned angrily to the speaker. 'No names!' he snapped. 'We don't use names.'

The new man now removed his mask.

'Gil, what are you doing?' said the youth.

'It's all right, Lena. They're alone. They're not the warden's men.'

Lena - a girl's name. Yes, I could see it now: The wide hips and narrow shoulders. So - a girl, a buffoon and a moaner in Latin. These were curious cutthroats indeed.

I was beginning to form a measure of our captors. They were not the desperate hard-men I had initially feared. The one called Gil was clearly the leader, a striking-looking man in his early forties. Then there was the girl, Lena, perhaps fifteen summers and a pretty face underneath all that filth. What was she, I wondered – Gil's daughter? Then came Fitchet-foul-breath who kept his mask on covering the top half of his face; and the Latin-speaker who looked and sounded like a defrocked priest. Finally there was the fifth man, the only one who said nothing at all but glared at everyone. I found him the most worrying for as my mother never tired of telling me, it is always the emptiest pots that rattled the loudest - meaning me usually. I wondered what burden this silent man carried around with him that might suddenly burst out and engulf us. I would have to keep a watchful eye on him.

For now, though, it was Fitchet who was concerning me most for he seemed to have taken a fancy to Onethumb. He remained squatting in front of the boy studying him intently. In truth, I was less worried about what Fitchet would do to Onethumb than what Onethumb might do to him. I prayed it wouldn't be enough to get his own throat cut

'I like this one,' said the grinning Fitchet. 'Can I keep him?'

He got his answer to that: Onethumb spat in his face. I

winced, but Fitchet merely wiped the saliva from his cheek leaving behind a smudge of clean pockmarked flesh.

'We are travellers, sir,' I announced boldly to our "host", Gil. 'We wish you no harm merely to resume our journey. If you'll point us in the right direction we'll be on our way and will bother you no further.'

'Travellers, eh? What sort of travellers enter the forest with no food, no weapons and...' he pointed at my bandaged feet. 'No boots.'

I looked down at my bedraggled and bleeding feet. 'I had boots. I lost them.'

Gil nodded. 'And you made enough noise about losing them in that gulley to bring the soldiers down on all of us. We've been watching you ever since you arrived, going round in circles.'

Ah, so that was the reason they attacked us - fear that we would expose them.

'I apologize,' I grimaced. 'We are not used to the ways of the forest.'

'All right,' he nodded. 'So why are you here? Why did you leave the road?'

I shrugged. 'Because of the soldiers. We could not get past.'

'They let the king's men pass.'

At this news my heart leapt, for if the king's men were indeed still in the area we might yet be able to get to them – if only we could get away from these people first.

'Why are the soldiers here?' asked Gil curiously. 'Do you know?'

'No idea,' I said rather too quickly and smiled a little too carelessly.

He smiled too. I could see it was not going to be easy to pull the wool over this man's eyes.

Fitchet, true to his name, was growing agitated with all the chatter. 'I say we slit their throats. Simplest done least said.'

Once again the Latin-speaker, God save the blessed man, came to our rescue: 'No Gil, for pity sake. We are not murderers.'

'No, we won't slit their throats.'

'Thank you, sir,' I said. 'You are making the right decision.'

'At least, not till I've found out what they want.' He nodded to Fitchet. 'Bind them. We'll take them back to camp.'

'No, wait – please!' I implored him. 'It is vital we continue our journey.' I wanted to find the king's men before they finally disappeared.

'Soon as I know why you're here.'

'But I've told you already!' I insisted.

'Funny. I don't believe you.'

He tied a rag round my eyes, stuffed a rag in my mouth and started to push me ahead of him.

'This one won't need a gag,' Fitchet giggled and prodded Onethumb in the ribs with his knife. 'He can't cry out whatever's done to him.'

We walked – or rather, stumbled – blindfolded for an hour or more until I was exhausted and totally disorientated. If they let us go right now we would never find our way again. We could be half way back to Bury for all I knew - or half way to London. But at last we came to a halt, our blindfolds were removed and I looked about us. It was dark by now but when the clouds parted and the moon bathed everything in its eerie glow I could see that we were in a small clearing. It looked pretty much like every other clearing we had traversed that day, empty. Then at a signal from Gil the very ground beneath our feet seemed to come alive: Bushes rose up, earth banks moved and trees buckled over.

'Good heavens!' I exclaimed with delight. 'You live underground!'

'Don't get any ideas about remembering it,' growled Fitchet flashing his knife again.

'Oh, I won't,' I assured him. 'Ask him. I'm hopeless at that sort of thing,' I said pointing at Onethumb.

Gil prodded me through a gap in the undergrowth that had opened up. Once inside this 'door' closed behind us and I found we were in the middle of a small but well-organised stockade. It was still open to the sky but invisible from ground level. Impressive as it was, and comfortable, it was no substitute for a real home. Some might say the life of a monk is harsh but at least when I wake in the morning I am secure in the knowledge that a good stout wall surrounds me and where my next meal will come from. Still, out here in the greenwood they had the freedom of the unfettered with no lord to censure them but God – so long as they remained at liberty, of course.

There was a fire in the middle of the camp and an old woman tending it. I guessed she wasn't the only one for I had the feeling that we were being watched with eyes all around us. I guessed there must be more womenfolk about, and children, but I thought it better not to enquire. It was like an entire secret community here in the greenwood and I have to admit I was impressed. Whatever the old woman was cooking made me realise just how hungry I was. Neither Onethumb nor I had eaten since that morning's hunk of stale bread. They sat us down on the ground and tied our feet together but left our hands free so that he could eat the feast. And what a feast it was made all the tastier for knowing it was the king's venison we were eating.

Over the next few hours I grew more and more to like the look of this man called Gil. He was intelligent and well-versed, not at all the ruffian I first took him to be. I could not begin to imagine what circumstance could have led such a man to his present predicament. But now with our bellies full and a warm fire at our backs we were beginning to relax enough to chatter, and I seemed to be the one doing the chattering. The beer, too, was good and pretty soon I was telling him all about why we were here, our miracle escape, the dreaded de Saye, the meeting in the abbey church, the demands of the barons and the oath to force the king if he refused. He listened to all without comment until I'd finished.

'There'll be no justice in England while there are lords and kings,' Gil said quietly.

I snorted. 'Well that's just plain silly. How can a people be governed except by a king and his council?'

'Your abbey has no monarch until a new abbot is elected.'

'Exactly – and look at the mess we're in.'

'Perhaps you should elect your own abbot.'

'Oh, we've tried that, I said yawning. The king won't have it.'

'Then elect the king as well.'

For some reason I found that the funniest statement of all. 'Elect the king?' I guffawed. 'I've never heard anything so ridiculous.'

I was trying to remember the conversation I'd had with John about how a king governs hoping to impress Gil with my knowledge of the realities of government. But I was finding it difficult to focus my thoughts. I took another swig of the excellent ale hoping it might help and squinted across at Onethumb. But he was preoccupied making Lena laugh with hand shadows in the firelight while Fitchet looked on morosely.

'Anyway,' I drawled. 'That's where we're going – to tell the king all about it.' I winked. 'Only it's a secret.'

'And what do you think he'll do when he knows?' said Gil refilling my cup again with ale.

'That would be telling.' Actually, I hadn't thought that far. But what did it matter? What did anything matter? 'I must say you're very bright for an outlaw, if you don't mind me saying,' I complimented him. 'You don't sound like a commoner. What's your tale, I wonder, or is it a secret?' I grinned inanely.

Gil shook his head. 'No secret. We all have a similar tale to tell. Take Fra William here for instance.' He indicated the Latin-speaker.

'Ah!' I said. 'You see, I knew it. I knew he was some kind of cleric.' I grinned at the man who frowned and shook his head.

'He was part-time parish priest, part-time farmer,' said Gil. 'His crime was to speak out against the injustice of the law.'

'As he should,' I agreed. 'That is his job - as a parish priest, not as a farmer I mean.'

'Try telling that to the warden's men. They took his ox. How many farmers do you know can plough a field without an ox? He was reduced to begging and was half-starved when we found him.'

I frowned. 'Oh that's awful - truly. To lose his ox. Why did they take his ox?'

Gil shrugged. 'Because they could. That's the only reason

they need. That's forest law for you.'

I frowned pointing to Fitchet. 'What about him - Foul-breath? By the way,' I whispered. 'Don't tell him I call him that.'

'Fitchet was a poacher. He took one hare too many.'

'Then I have no sympathy. Poaching is theft. Ask my mother, she'll tell you.'

'Your mother?'

I nodded. 'The Lady Isabel de Ix-worth. She has lands hereabouts - somewhere.' I looked vaguely around. 'Erm, what did they do to him?'

'Cut off his nose.'

I winced. That probably explained why he kept his mask on - and possibly why his breath was so foul. Maybe it also explained his interest in Onethumb, recognising in him a fellow sufferer. I mentally chastised myself for my lack of charity and resolved to be less quick to judgement in future.

'What about this one?' I said pointing surreptitiously to the silent man uncertain if I'd like the answer. 'Not sure about him,' I said *sotto voce*.

'Will Conyer,' sighed Gil. 'He too was a farmer. Last harvest time he was summoned to the manor court.'

'It's every man's duty to come to court when summoned,' I pontificated.

'True enough,' Gil agreed. 'Three days' walk there and three back. With no sons and only daughters the grain would have rotted in the fields by the time he got home. So he was late going and missed the court.'

'And was justly punished for non-attendance?'

Gil nodded. 'The wardens had every right to do so. They burned his crop and his family starved. That's forestry law for you.'

I grimaced again. 'But this is Suffolk,' I protested. 'Forestry law does not run in Suffolk.'

'We are not from Suffolk. We are from Essex County. There the forestry law runs everywhere.'

'And what about you? What law did you fall foul of?'

'My crime was to think my lord was a just man.'

I gave a wry grin. 'If you don't mind my saying my friend, that sounds like the petulance.'

He smiled. 'I was the manager to a great estate.'

'A position of trust and honour.'

'Indeed. Twelve years of loyal service I gave. I was happy to do so. I married well. Life was good. My only sadness was that my wife died giving life to our only daughter.' He looked across at Lena who was laughing at something Onethumb was doing. Fitchet had taken himself off somewhere.

'Pretty girl. Such a shame. And?' I prompted.

'When Lena was fourteen she was raped.'

'Oh. I'm truly sorry for that,' I said sincerely. 'So your complaint was that your lord did not apprehend the rapist?'

'My complaint is that my lord was the rapist - or his son at any rate.'

'You had proof?' I said, genuinely shocked.

'How do you prove a thing like that? They offered her to marry a man forty years her senior. I brought a suit against the family but the magistrates favoured my lord. I was given the choice of accepting the marriage or lose my position.'

'So you lost your position and fled to the forest.'

'I had no choice,' he confirmed, 'once I'd strangled the son and drowned the child.'

That sobered me a little and I sat up. 'Wait a minute. I've heard this story before.' I pointed at him. 'You're Gil of Nayland. All Suffolk has heard of you. It was rumoured you were dead.'

'Well, now you know I am not - which gives me a problem.'

'A problem?' I said sitting up. In my fuddled state I did not immediately catch his meaning. By the time I did it was already too late and they were upon us. Onethumb was quicker than I but Fitchet was even quicker. In a moment we were both on the ground with our hands and feet tied together.

'There's no need for this,' I protested. 'We will not tell.'

'I cannot take the risk,' said Gil. He checked to make sure my bonds were secure and Fitchet nodded to confirm Onethumb's were too. Then Gil stood up. 'It's a pity you had to recognise me, brother. Better you had not.'

This time even the Latin-speaker did not try to intervene but muttered prayers with his eyes tightly shut. As I watched Gil walk away I could feel Onethumb's eyes burning into me. What had I said?

'Nothing,' I whispered. 'I said nothing. I just told him why we were here that's all. And then he told me his story. I recognised him.'

Onethumb rolled his eyes to heaven and I realised my error. For it may not matter what I said to him but it mattered very much what he said to me. Now that we knew who he was and that he was alive the hunt for Gil of Nayland could begin again. And Onethumb and I had the long night ahead of us to reflect on my stupidity – and on our likely fate in the morning.

Chapter Twenty-five
NEMESIS

I awoke the next morning with fifty impish smithies hammering anvils in my head and my throat as dry as a sandpit. Onethumb must have drunk too much too for although already awake he was looking as deathly-white as I felt. We were quite alone. There was no trace of Gil or his companions, no indication that they had ever been there except that lying on the ground next to me were my boots, cleaned and oiled, and my satchel which I had lost down the gully and filled with enough provisions for several days' travel. As I looked around incredulously I recognized things. There was the pile of sticks and leaves I had cut as makeshift footwear lying on the ground where I had left them, and there were the remnants of our last breakfast exactly where we had left them. I realized that despite having marched us around for over an hour the previous evening giving the impression that we were penetrating ever deeper into the darkest recesses of the forest, we had in fact gone precisely... nowhere. We were back exactly where we were when Gil and his friends apprehended us. I looked questioningly at Onethumb but he must have realised the same thing for he shook his head in bewilderment. The irony was that although we recognized where we were, we were no wiser where that was than we were before. But even this Gil must have understood for as the last of the morning mist finally lifted the London Road became visible just a few yards further on. Gil had opened up a gap in a thicket that was not there yesterday revealing the London road just a few yards beyond. We must have been this close to it all along.

'If we hurry,' I said excitedly to Onethumb, 'we might still catch the king's baggage train,' so long as my head didn't explode beforehand, I should have added.

Gathering up our belongings and not even waiting to break our fast, we dashed out through the opening and leapt the final few feet onto the road landing with a joyful crunch. But even as we landed on the gritted surface we were brought up sharp by a sight that struck terror in our hearts and dashed all our hopes in an instant. The white knight who had been following us for two days was barely a hundred yards further along the road sitting quietly astride his charger.

Poor Onethumb. If he could have screamed I believe he would have done so then. He fell to his knees in despair. After all we had gone through to have gotten this close to our goal only to have it snatched away from us. I forced myself to my feet and shook my fist defiantly at the knight.

'Come on then!' I yelled at him. 'What are you waiting for? Here we are! You've got us at last! Do your worst!'

The knight made no reply, his magnificent destrier adding clouds of vapour to the damp morning mist. We were too far away to see the rider's face but we saw him lower his visor and take out his sword from its scabbard.

He was getting ready to charge.

I tried to drag Onethumb up but he seemed incapable of movement, his eyes transfixed with resignation on the white charger.

I pulled at his arm. 'Onethumb, you must get up,' I said hastily. 'If you don't you will die here.'

I tried to lift him but he would not budge - and it was then I had my idea. Some memory of whirling gears, the sound of laughter, surprise, applause. I looked at the figure on the horse. White Angel was he? We would see just how much of an angel he was.

I sat down and quickly started lacing my boots. 'Onethumb,' I barked. 'Listen to me! You remember the gulley? Could you find it again?'

At first he shook his head. But then he slowly nodded.

'Good boy. Go back and fetch some of the hemp rope from that wagon. Do you understand? The rope, Onethumb! Fetch the rope!'

He nodded again and got to his feet. As he ran off I got up to face the knight. He was coming. First a canter and then gradually gathering speed and momentum.

I waited no longer. I turned and ran from him as fast as I could back into the forest the way we had come not daring to look back but hearing the horse's hooves getting nearer and louder behind me. Nothing on God's earth can stop a charging knight at full gallop as I knew full well, but I was gambling that would be my advantage. I might have wished it was not autumn and the foliage thick enough to hide me but it made it easier to get through the thinning undergrowth. This, I thought, is how it must be in a real battle where fleeing foot soldiers are chased by cavalry and hacked to pieces. And this was a real battle with a real knight chasing me but feet away.

Just as he was almost upon me, I managed to leap a fallen tree trunk and I heard his mount rear up nearly unseating its rider. But it would be only a momentary respite for he would quickly regain control, circle to calm the beast and then get ready to give the horse its head. Once clear of the obstacle there would be nothing between me and the knight's sword. I needed Onethumb *now* - but where was he?

And then he was back and slung around his neck was twenty feet of the hemp rope from the buried cart. But there was a problem. The rope was old and rotting from having lain in the open for so long – Onethumb demonstrated by easily tearing it. But we had nothing else. It would have to do. I quickly explained my plan to him. He looked doubtful but there was no time for discussion. We had but a few moments left. He understood and nodded. Once we were ready I took a deep breath, crossed myself and stepped out into the open directly facing the knight.

He looked down at me through his visor. What was going though through his mind? Surprise? Contempt? He had his sword resting at his side but now he raised it again and I could see now exactly why he was the White Angel for even in the dull light of the forest it glinted white-silver. Without haste he drew in his rein making the animal step back to view the terrain, and then began his run. No more choices now, I just prayed my calculations were correct. I waited what seemed like an eternity but can only have been moments as he bore down upon me closer and closer he cleared the fallen tree trunk and leaning over the side of the horse's neck he raised his arm to strike. I waited until the least possible moment then yelled:

'*Now* Onethumb!'

There was a whirling noise, a snap of twigs and then – nothing. The White Angel came on. He was yards away.

'I said "now" Onethumb,' I repeated. 'Now! I really need you nowwwwww!'

Christ and the Angels and all the blessed saints in heaven be merciful, with a jolt I went sailing twenty feet into the air right in front of the horseman's face my legs and arms flailing about like the sails of a windmill. Surprised, the horse reared up in its tracks and then…disaster! Onethumb had been right about the rope. It was indeed rotten. I felt it slip, snag, then snap, and the next thing I was falling crashing down on rider and horse together.

Now all was confusion. The horse stumbled and its rider was shot forward over its head and onto the forest floor. Another moment and I came crashing down on top of him. The horse ran off into the trees and then stopped leaving me lying prostrate across the rider's torso. But he did not move. He was knocked out cold. Quick as lightning Onethumb was there with more rope and soon we had the man tied down so he could not move under all that armour.

'Ha ha!' I yelled hysterically dancing round him. 'Ha ha ha ha! Now I have you my friend! Get up if you can. You brute! You cur! You knave!'

Onethumb, too, danced and somersaulted for joy. If he could speak I am sure he would have been whooping.

But our elation was short-lived. The noise of our antics

had not gone unnoticed in the silence of the forest and other soldiers now appeared from every direction materializing like salt out of brine. We were surrounded. If we'd tried to run we would have been cut down before we made it to the nearest tree. I looked at Onethumb but he too was out of ideas. I tried to think but before I had a chance to do anything the two men in front of me parted and my worst fears were realised.

'No!' I gasped stepping back, for facing me directly was Geoffrey de Saye.

I was too shocked to know what happened next but I believe the noise I heard was me screaming whereupon de Saye stepped smartly forward and removing his glove, placed his hand over my mouth and nose. Panic rose in me as I struggled to breathe but his grip was too strong. I just managed to see out of the corner of my eye one of de Saye's men unsheathe his sword and bring it down smartly towards Onethumb's head before the world swum away from me and everything went black.

Chapter Twenty-six
ANSWERS...

The next time I opened my eyes I was in my own bed in Ixworth Hall. I knew I was dead because I had not been in that bed for thirty-five years. I was clearly in heaven now among my family and loved ones and in the surroundings that I cherished most. But I did not remember seeing Saint Peter at the gate or hearing the last trumpet announcing the end of the world when every soul is resurrected whole and incorrupt.

Then the door opened and in walked Oswald, my mother's servant, looking just as corrupt as ever he did and carrying a tray of spiced ale. I knew then that I was not dead for I abhor spiced ale and wouldn't have it in any heaven of my design.

'Oswald?'

'It is good to see you awake, Master Walter. Lady Isabel is below. She awaits you there if you are feeling better.'

I gawped stupidly at him for a moment before leaping out of bed - too fast, for I staggered and nearly collided with the wall. My head was still woozy though whether from Gil's cider or from suffocation I could not say, but I recovered enough to pull open the door.

'Master Walter, sir!'

I turned back impatiently. 'What is it Oswald?'

'If you are going to see my lady I should first put on my under-drawers. Really sir, I would.'

'Ah, there you are, Walter. Did you sleep well?'

My mother was seated near the fire as I entered and standing behind her were Onethumb and Rosabel. There was a fourth person in the room I did not recognize, a monk judging by his attire, but I hardly noticed him as I dashed towards my friends.

'Onethumb! Rosabel!' I said touching them to make sure I was not dreaming. 'You're alive! You're both alive! Hahahaha!' I laughed deliriously.

'Of course they're alive,' said my mother tapping her stick impatiently on the floor. 'What did you think?'

'But you were killed,' I said to Onethumb. 'I saw you murdered.'

'Clearly not,' sniffed my mother.

'Let me feel your wound.' I felt all over Onethumb's head where I was sure the soldier's sword had struck him. There was a bit of a bump and a break that looked as though it had healed.

I turned to my mother. 'How long have I been here?'

'Three days. Your boy here has a stronger constitution than you.'

'I don't understand,' I frowned. 'How did I get here?'

There was a hesitant pause before my mother answered. 'How else? Geoffrey de Saye brought you.'

I reeled at her words. 'Geoffrey de Saye, that brute brought me?'

'Must you repeat my every word?' she growled. 'Yes, Geoffrey de Saye brought you.'

'But he tried to kill me – to suffocate me. He had his hand over my mouth - thus.' I demonstrated with my hand over my fist.

'Only to shut you up. You were screaming like a demented banshee. Another minute and you'd have brought the king's troops down on top of him.'

I reeled. The king's men. So close and yet so far. 'Would that I had. The man is a murderer, a torturer, a liar...'

'Yes, yes, yes,' she agreed.

'And something else,' I added haughtily. 'He's a traitor. I know. I witnessed his treachery.'

I then began earnestly to describe the meeting in the abbey church and de Saye's part in it. I listed all the nobles I could remember who were present including Cardinal Langton, but my voice trailed away before I finished. She had her hand out for Onethumb to help her up from her seat.

'Come over here,' she said hobbling towards the table at the far end of the room.

On it was a large sheet of parchment that was covered in fine black script. The writing was very neat, very precise.

'What is it?' I asked.

'It's a charter. Drawn up by the barons of England for the king to sign. Those same barons you just named - and me.'

'*You?*'

Was it possible? My own mother a conspirator? But I already knew the answer to that. Yes, of course she was. She had never hidden her disdain for King John. It was all beginning to make sense. How else were de Saye's soldiers able to disappear so easily the day of the king's arrival and reappear so soon after his departure? They must have been using this place as a base-camp. An hour's fast ride from Bury - it was ideally located. And the barons, too - they must have stayed here. And it explained why de Saye hadn't had me arrested – something that had always mystified me. I'd thought it was just in order to humiliate me before my brother monks but I could see now there was more to it than that. Whatever de Saye's personal opinion of me - and I was sure he still harboured a deep hatred for me and my family - he was not such a fool as to harm the son of such a useful ally. That's why I survived. But there were other questions that were not explained.

'Oh don't look so shocked,' said my mother, eyeing me. 'You knew - you must have known.'

I shook my head. 'Not a thing.'

'Then you're an even bigger fool than I took you for. Even Joseph had an inkling.'

'He never said anything to me.'

'Probably because he knew you and that you'd disapprove.' She looked askance at me. 'You do disapprove, don't you?'

Did I? I didn't reply.

'The letter,' I said quietly. 'The one you had me take to Hugh Northwold. The letter that was no letter but a blank sheet of parchment.'

'A necessary precaution,' she sniffed. 'Regrettable - but necessary.'

She looked at me expecting me to understand - but I didn't.

'Hugh is sympathetic to our cause but he would not join us. He would not betray us either. So it was better he was kept completely out of it. If he'd known about the meeting in the abbey he would have felt duty-bound to tell the king, whatever his sympathies, and withdrawn his candidacy for abbot of Saint Edmunds. We couldn't let that happen. We need men like him in high places.'

'And you thought I would go to him with what I knew. So you had to discredit me in his eyes.'

She had the good grace to look ashamed. 'You have to understand - greater things are at stake than any one man's sensibilities.'

'I am not any man, I am your son. Could you not have trusted me?'

'Would you have joined us?' she asked.

My king or my friends?

'No.'

She smiled wryly and nodded.

I looked down at the document on the able. It was quite a thing. I'd witnessed many a charter in my time but never one quite like this. It was written in Latin and in a very fine hand but my eyesight was not what it once was. Realising this, my mother brought out her own reading stone and laid it on top of the document. It magnified the letters four-fold so I could read them. Each line I saw contained a clause, each numbered.

'See that one?' she said pointing half way down the document. 'That's mine.'

'You sponsored it?' I asked.

I *wrote* it,' she said proudly.

Why didn't that surprise me? 'What does it say?'

'Read it yourself. It is to do with the rights of widows to marry who they please and not who the king dictates.'

'But that's absurd! No woman has ever had such a right. The king -'

'The king!' she snorted. 'The king, the king - do you know what that little mongrel wanted me to do? Marry some Limousine low-life. Me, whose forebears came over with the Conqueror when the Angevin counts were still copulating with rabbits.'

'So, it's just an old woman's petulance,' I said dismissing the document with a wave of my hand.

'Don't be impertinent!' she snapped. 'Some of the finest minds in England worked on this.'

'What of the rest of it?'

'Legal matters.'

I nodded. '*Money* you mean.'

She shot me a look of anger. 'No, I'll tell you what it is. It is to do with the rights of every Englishman to live in freedom as his forefathers did. Rights they once had by natural law. Rights stolen from them by greedy and avaricious kings.'

'*Every* Englishman did you say?'

'Every Englishman - and Englishwoman.'

'Even the common folk?'

'Well now, I don't know about that,' she smirked. 'Let's ask them, shall we?' She stepped aside to reveal Onethumb and Rosabel standing meekly behind her.

Throughout our sniping my two friends had remained silent. Once again I'd forgotten they were there. I don't know how seriously my mother would take their opinion, but if by suddenly thrusting them forward she expected to intimidate them, then she didn't know my Rosabel. Onethumb could not speak - so Rosabel did for them both.

For a long moment she said nothing. But finally she did speak, and when she did I thought I could hear the voice of every English-born man and woman, high and low, throughout the world.

'Kings come and kings go,' she mused reflectively. 'But it seems to me little changes when they do. We ordinary folk live and let-live, work and die and pay our dues. Whoever governs over us, it's all one to us.'

She fingered the corner of the document laid out on the table before her.

'I don't know what's written here but whatever it is, will it feed my son? Will it give back the crops stolen from us when armies march across our fields, or rebuild the houses they torch?' She turned to smile at Onethumb and gently stroked his cheek. 'Will it restore my husband's speech or his hand so he can caress me at night? If not, then I don't see what it has to do with me.'

That's my prickly rosebud, I thought. If nothing else she managed to silence my mother - something I've never achieved. But while she was speaking another thought had struck me.

'This project you are building - it is at a critical stage,' I said to my mother. 'One loose word now could pull it down – am I right?'

'You won't get the opportunity.'

'I've done it once. Even your friend Geoffrey de Saye only just managed to stop me. And now that I know the full extent of your treachery I have an even greater incentive to alert the king. Who's to say this time I won't succeed?'

'What do you want, Walter?'

I thought for a minute. 'I want you to include in your charter some easement for those living under the forest law.'

I was thinking, of course, of Gil and his friends. But if I thought I was going to make a contribution to the Great Matter I was sadly mistaken. My mother merely smiled smugly and waved her hand over the document like a conjurer performing a trick.

'Your request is as by magic fulfilled.'

She placed the reading stone over another clause in the document. I leaned over to read it. Like everything else in the charter the clause was written principally to favour the barons who drafted it, but it did appear to offer some relief for those living under this malicious law - too late to help Gil and his friends, alas, for they had by force of circumstance committed too many more "crimes" to be absolved. But it might ease the condition of others that come after them.

'Your friend Geoffrey seems to have thought of everything,' I acknowledged grudgingly. 'But there is one other issue that we still have not addressed. The small matter of a murdered maid.'

My mother shook her head vehemently. 'No, son Walter. He had had nothing to do with that. I have his oath on it.'

'And the word of Geoffrey de Saye is to be believed?'

'No. Brother Clementius's here.'

For the first time I took notice of the anonymous monk who all the while had been standing quietly in the corner listening and saying nothing. I now turned to him with curiosity, and as I did so a memory came to me.

'Dominic mentioned a brother was looking for me. I thought he meant one of Prior Herbert's men, but he meant you didn't he? What did you say your name was again?'

'My name is Clementius,' said the man.

I nodded. 'A Latinized form. Unusual amongst us Benedictines. But then you're not a Benedictine, are you? Your robes - you're a Gilbertine.'

'Clementius came to the abbey to warn you,' said my mother. 'But he was too late. You had already left.'

'Warn me? Warn me of what?'

There was a sudden thump on the floor above our heads.

My mother looked up at the ceiling and drew in her breath. 'Raoul and Adelle!'

I swung round to her. 'You mean they're *here?*'

'Of course they're here,' she snapped. 'Where else did you think they were?'

The door burst open and Oswald appeared in the frame, his face as white as a sheet. 'Oh Master Walter, sir, come quickly! The boy!'

No time for questions, we all raced from the room and up the stairs – me, Oswald, Onethumb, Rosabel and Clementius. But for once I was the first. When I got to the top of the stairs I stopped abruptly as though hitting an invisible wall of stone. There in the middle of the landing was Eusebius. He was standing in much the same attitude as he had been in the cloister before the statue of the Virgin: Arms outstretched in the shape of a cross and dressed in the same robes as Clementius had downstairs but with his white cloak and hood still attached. His face was contorted with…what? Euphoria? Enlightenment?

'Eusebius!' I gasped. 'What have you done?'

'I did it, Master Walter. Look, I have done as you said. I have cut out the offending sin. He cannot despoil again. I am the kindred of the Angels, I am the destroyer of darkness, the refresher. I am the White Angel!'

He held up his hands. Both were dripping blood, the right one clutching a knife, the other clutching...I reeled backwards for there was no mistaking the thing he holding in his left hand. Without thinking, I clasped my own two hands together and brought them down smartly onto Eusebius's forehead knocking him to the ground. Then I ran into the room where Raoul de Gray was crouching in the corner. I dropped to my knees before him and turned him over. But apart from a few smudges of blood on his face and hands he seemed fine.

'I don't understand. I thought -'

'Not me,' Raoul said trembling. 'Him!'

Him? Who was he pointing to? The only other person in the room was Adelle. But then I saw she was lying on top of the bed and drenched in blood. The Lady Adelle - but *not* Adelle.

There was no time for questions or explanations. The life blood was rapidly draining out of her. I ripped off the clothing to expose the wound, the most ghastly butchery I'd ever seen in all my years as a physician. Behind me Onethumb and Rosabel were staring motionless, paralysed and fascinated at the same time.

'Sheets!' I barked. 'Blankets - anything you can find.'

They both continued to stare without moving.

'Onethumb!' I yelled earnestly. 'I need you to concentrate. This wound has to be stopped or he will die.'

Still he did not move.

'*Onethumb!*'

Rosabel was the first to come to her senses. She punched Onethumb on the arm and continued punching him until he shook himself and then they both rushed out of the room together. But the blood continued to pump out of Adelle's body so fast it was going to be impossible to staunch. I could see it was hopeless.

I knew then that I had but moments to act.

'Quickly,' I said to Adelle. 'Do you confess of your sins and acknowledge Christ as your Saviour? – say "I do".'

She moaned something incoherent and I made the sign of the Cross over her.

'Then having come freely of your own will to Christ Jesus, by the power vested in me as priest ordained in the only true living Church I grant you absolution in the name of the Father, the Son and the Holy Spirit.'

I clutched Adelle's body tightly in my arms and rocked backwards and forward and prayed as I had never prayed before:

'Please, please, dear God, for the love of your only son our saviour Jesus Christ grant this child your salvation and accept him to your bosom. I beg you, I beg you - I *beg* you!'

Adelle was dead before Onethumb and Rosabel could return.

Chapter Twenty-seven
…AND EXPLANATIONS

For the sake of their sanity I sent the others out of the room. No-one should have to witness such bestial carnage, least of all an innocent young girl like Rosabel. Eusebius had been bound and quickly bundled off to the stables to be guarded by some of our farm workers, Brother Clementius with them, while I remained with the body until a local priest arrived. When I finally made it downstairs again I was still trembling.

'Here,' said my mother handing me a goblet.

'What is it?'

'Brandywine. It will steady your nerves.'

It was not a drink I knew but I gulped it down just the same coughing at the fumes. When I looked round at the assembled company I got the distinct impression they knew something I didn't.

'I don't understand,' I kept saying. 'I just don't understand.'

'You will,' said my mother patting my shoulder. 'But first, let me introduce you to Thomas.'

I looked at the young man she was indicating. 'But you're Raoul,' I said pointing stupidly at him.

'No,' said my mother. 'That was Raoul, upstairs. This young man is Thomas, Raoul's manservant.'

I pointed up at the ceiling. 'That was Adelle.'

But my mother shook her head impatiently. 'There was no Adelle. Adelle was a fiction. The person you thought of as Adelle de Gray was really *Raoul* de Gray.'

'You mean Adelle isn't... I mean she wasn't...'

'A girl? No, *he* wasn't.'

'But why?'

'Because Raoul had a secret.'

I gave a snort. 'You can say that again.'

'Not *that* sort of secret. Something far graver.'

I shook my head. 'No no no. She had a baby. I saw it - I *delivered* it.'

'No you didn't. You said so yourself - you arrived a few minutes later. Frankly I'm surprised you missed it, great physician that you are.'

Missed it? Yes, I'd missed it all right. But how did I miss it? I'd met Adelle twice — no, *three* times. Ah yes, but always in a darkened room, always modestly veiled, and always from several feet away. And she never spoke, I realised now, not once except to say the baby's name. I had vaguely wondered about that but never thought to question it before. Now I could see why. But I wasn't the only one to be deceived: Prior Herbert, Guest-master Gregor, the gatekeeper and the gaoler — we were all duped. Weren't we?

'You weren't though, were you?' I said to her. 'You knew. Even when I was here last time, you knew and yet you said nothing.'

My mother lowered her eyes. 'I couldn't. You'd have alerted him. I know you, Walter. You could never keep a secret, you haven't the guile. And we had to convince him his disguise was working. If you believed it, the chances were he would too.'

'But why was he even in disguise?' I asked somewhat peeved.

'Because of who he was, of course.'

'Oh, don't start all that again.'

She pursed her lips. 'All right. But you have to understand, he knew about the…the…'

'Rebellion?'

She stiffened. 'Had he been able to warn his uncle, Bishop de Gray would have alerted the king and then everything we have worked for – everything we have been trying to achieve since John came to the throne - would have been for nothing. We couldn't risk that.'

'So you had him arrested.'

'We had no choice.'

'I see. And what were you going to do with him? Kill him?'

'There was never any question of that,' she insisted tapping her stick impatiently on the floor. 'We merely wanted to hold him, prevent him getting to his uncle.'

'But he escaped, and you sent your rat-catcher de Saye to fetch him back.'

Here she gave a wry smile. 'Actually it was Archbishop Langton who asked Geoffrey to find Raoul. The ironic thing is it really didn't matter anymore. Bishop John was already dead. He died a month ago at the Abbey Saint-Jean-d'Angély in Poitou. We only just heard. It seems the journey to Rome proved too much for him.'

'How convenient,' I smirked. 'I suppose it didn't occur to you that the good bishop might be yet another of de Saye's victims?'

'Don't be ridiculous.'

'Oh mother, open your eyes. You know the sort of man de Saye is. Good God, if he can murder a harmless old woman whose only crime was to offer sanctuary to -'

I stopped. I hadn't intended mentioning Mother Han's murder, not until I knew for certain that she was dead. But now the cat was out of the bag. I looked at Onethumb who was gazing back at me with silent horror.

'My friend I'm sorry, I should have told you before. I believe Mother Han is dead, most likely at the hand of Geoffrey de Saye.'

'That is a very serious accusation,' said my mother gravely. 'I hope you can substantiate it.'

I turned on her angrily. 'For once I think I can.' I fumbled in my belt-pouch. 'This,' I said retrieving the little silver knife I'd secreted there, 'I found at Mother Han's hovel – or what was left of it. Proof undeniable of Geoffrey de Saye's murderous activities. It even has his insignia on it – GdeS - Geoffrey de Saye.' I held the knife up triumphantly for all to see.

Brother Clementius, who had quietly come back into the room, now stepped forward. 'May I see the knife?' he asked quietly. I handed it to him. He studied it carefully. 'This is a pen-knife. It is used for trimming the ends of writing quills.'

'Well there you are, then,' scoffed my mother. 'What would a man like Geoffrey de Saye want with a pen-knife? I doubt he can write his own name.'

'Then explain the monogram,' I demanded.

'*GdeS*,' said Clementius thoughtfully. Then he shook his head.

'Not *Geoffrey de Saye. Gilbert de Sempringham*, the founder of our order. This is Eusebius's knife.' He put it down, took out another from where it hung around his neck and placed it alongside the first. They were identical.

My jaw dropped open. 'B-but the knight - the White Angel,' I stammered. 'How -?'

Clementius considered. 'Didn't I hear Eusebius use those words on the stairs just now?'

Of course he had. I'd been too shocked by what had happened to notice, but now I remembered he did say those words: "I am the White Angel." And then I saw again the image of Eusebius wth his arms outstretched before the statue of the Virgin in the cloister. The shape of the cross on his robe – the white cross. That was what people kept seeing, not a knight's sword but Eusebius's robe – the White Angel. At last the truth was becoming clear: It was Eusebius who had killed Mother Han; Eusebius who struck off poor Hervey's hand; and Eusebius who had murdered Effie.

'But why Effie?' I asked.

'Because she was Eusebius's sister,' said Rosabel from the side of the room.

I turned to her in astonishment.

'Thomas and Raoul told me, Master, that first night in the abbey.' She gave a sick laugh. 'I saw straight off that Adelle was not who they said she was. A man might be fooled, but not another woman. As soon as I knew I wanted to leave, but the baby...' She shook her head. 'Raoul and Thomas couldn't look after her, that was plain. I had to stay - for little Alix's sake.'

'Alix!' I said looking around alarmed.

'Oh, she's fine,' said my mother. 'There's no need for you to fuss. She has a proper wet-nurse looking after her now.'

'But then Brother Hugh returned,' Rosabel went on, 'and we all realised the palace lodging was no longer safe. We needed somewhere else to hide and the only person I could think of was Mother Han.' She took Onethumb's good hand in hers. 'She had been kind to us in the past and she was so again. She was a good woman. I'm sorry she's dead. But we were not as clever as we thought. We were seen leaving and the next day Lord de Saye's men arrived and took us away.'

'And then he killed Mother Han to keep the secret and destroyed her home,' I prompted her.

She shook her head. 'No. We left her well and came straight here to Ixworth Hall.'

'Just in the nick of time, too,' said my mother. 'Another day and that mad monk would have found them, too.'

'But he did find them,' I pointed out.

'Yes,' agreed my mother. 'And it's thanks to you that he did.'

'Thanks to *me?*'

'Yes you,' she said tapping her stick again. 'Didn't you notice? He's been following you for days.'

Following me? Yes of course he had. Even outside the abbey church after the baron's meeting. That's how he found Hervey, and Mother Han. I must have led him here, too.

'But why?' I repeated. 'I don't understand.'

My mother sighed wearily. 'You tell him,' she said to Clementius. 'The whole tale, from the beginning. You might as well.'

It began twenty years ago, said Clementius. Two babies born to a Norfolk woman. Brother and sister - twins.

'An unusual event in itself I think you'll agree,' put in my mother wryly.

Clementius smiled before continuing: 'In thanks for this special blessing their mother gave them both to the Gilbertines where in due course the boy became a canon and the girl a lay sister. We named them Eusebius and Euphemia after the fashion of our house. You understand we are a dual house, Brother Walter.'

'Yes yes, I understand the arrangement,' I said impatiently. 'But you said Euphemia - Effie - was a lay-sister?'

He nodded. 'For the mother it seemed the ideal solution. It meant her two children could remain together in the same house while still being dedicated to God. It was her wish that they not be separated.' He shrugged. 'We could see no harm in it. Twins form a special bond, more so than ordinary siblings. It seemed natural to allow them to remain together. Unfortunately we didn't know just how attached Effie and Eusebius were to each other – unnaturally so.'

So that was what young Timothy meant when he spoke of Eusebius's "unnatural thoughts". Not his lust for Timothy as I had thought, but for his own sister. If only I had quizzed Timothy more deeply I might have learned the truth sooner.

I shook myself. 'How does Raoul fit into this?'

Clementius frowned in thought. 'As you know, our house at Shouldham lies within the diocese of Norwich. As the bishop's nephew Raoul de Gray took a keen interest in the priory and was a frequent visitor. Naturally we were delighted. The Grays are a wealthy family and we are a poor order. Endowments followed, gifts, benefactions. Raoul was very generous towards us and took a keen personal interest in the priory visiting us frequently.'

'Which was when Raoul noticed Effie,' I said guessing.

Clementius nodded uncomfortably. 'As a lay-sister she wasn't cloistered like the nuns. She was far more...available. It soon became apparent that Raoul's interest in the girl was more than it should be.'

'Why did you not put a stop to it? Ban Raoul from the priory?'

He sighed. 'Easier said than done. The Grays are a powerful clan. What Raoul wanted he usually got. Besides, when Raoul announced he was going abroad we thought the matter would resolve itself.'

'Which was when?' I asked. 'When Raoul decided to leave for France?'

'I know what you are asking. You are right, it was about the time of the meeting of barons in Stamford.'

'You knew about that?'

Clementius shook his head. 'Not then. But Raoul knew. Already arrests were being made of anyone showing opposition. He was arrested but managed to escape. With both the king and Bishop John abroad he decided his best course was to join them. As you might appreciate, we were not unhappy to see him go. He wanted to take Euphemia with him. Naturally we resisted. But he took her anyway.'

'And how did Eusebius react to his sister being abducted?'

Clementius merely shrugged. 'He wasn't happy.'

'So,' I said, 'Raoul heads south for one of the channel ports disguised as Adelle and passes Thomas off as himself. And since a lady always needs her maid, Effie had her ready-made cover, too. But then Eusebius turns up at the abbey.' I turned back to Clementius. 'Whose idea was that?'

Clementius squirmed uncomfortably. 'I believe it was an arrangement between our Prior…' he paused, '…and Lord de Saye.'

I rounded on my mother. 'There! I knew it! This entire business is down to that man. He arranged for Eusebius to come to Bury no doubt because he knew Eusebius could identify him, disguise or no disguise. He manoeuvred a confrontation - a *fatal* confrontation as it turned out - and now we see the consequences. Two, possibly three people murdered.'

'Geoffrey didn't murder anybody,' snapped back my mother.

'But he must have realised the danger. He cynically used these young people for his own ends.'

'No, not his own ends. Something far higher.'

'Nothing justifies the death of innocents, Mother.'

She didn't reply to that but pursed her lips tight.

'Why did he do it?' asked Rosabel, frowning. 'Kill his sister, I mean. Raoul I can understand, but his own sister?'

'Because he's mad,' pouted my mother.

Clementius had more generous explanation: 'Maybe he didn't mean to. Maybe he tried to persuade Euphemia to return with him to Shouldham and when she refused he lost control. Eusebius can be a very intense young man.'

I could attest to that. I could still feel the bite of his nails in my hand as we knelt together in prayer in the cloister.

Clementius shook his head. 'I've thought long and hard about this - his obsessive devotion to the Holy Virgin; his disgust at the very mention of the sexual act. It's as though his own guilt at his feelings for Euphemia, not as a sibling but as a lover, was too much for him to bear. I believe he lost control when Euphemia refused his entreaties and that's why he strangled her. Then when he realised what he'd done he turned on the one person he really blamed for all this: Raoul de Gray. But there is still one thing puzzling me: How did Lord de Saye know the family would be in Bury? I had to track them across two counties to find them.'

I was able to answer that one: 'It's not so surprising. They had to break the journey somewhere between Shouldham and the coastal ports. Where better than the abbey, a day's ride from both? The irony is they only intended stopping the one night. Unfortunately it was the night baby Alix decided to make her entry into the world.'

'Very neat,' said my mother wryly. 'But aren't you clever men forgetting one thing? Adelle does not exist. "She" was never pregnant.'

'Well I delivered somebody's baby,' I countered, and then in a flash I had it. 'Of course! *Ee-ma-mum-ma.*'

My mother frowned. 'Now what are you gabbling about?'

I turned to Onethumb. 'Onethumb, look at me.' I silently mouthed the phrase to him again. 'What did I just say?'

He shook his head and asked me to repeat it. I did, slowly just as I remembered Effie had done to me that terrible day on the stairs to the abbot's lodging: *Ee-ma-mum-ma*. Onethumb shrugged and then rocked a phantom baby in his arms just as expertly as he had mimed rocking his own son the night I met him with Prior Herbert. There was no misinterpretation this time.

I nodded. 'That's what Effie was trying to tell me. Ee-ma-mum-ma. *It's my baby*. Little Alix is Effie's child – isn't that right, Thomas?'

For answer, Thomas just lowered his eyes.

'But it begs one final question,' I said. 'Who is Alix's real father - Raoul or Eusebius?'

I looked at each of their faces in turn: My mother, Clementius, Rosabel, Thomas and Onethumb. But they all just stared blankly back at me. Only Onethumb made any response, and he merely to shrug.

Epilogue
FULL SPEED TO RUNNYMEDE

Eusebius was never tried for the murders of Effie and Raoul. The newly-enthroned Abbot of Edmundsbury invoked Becket's principle of an independent clergy and took the boy back into his own custody. That's not to say he was allowed to go free. He was eventually handed over to the Prior of Shouldham who, realising the boy could never be allowed out again, made him into an anchorite - a condition Eusebius embraced with enthusiastic, if not to say *euphoric*, zeal. He was thus bricked up in a tiny cell adjoining the priory church where he would remain in solitude for the rest of his life seeing no-one and being fed through a tiny opening in the wall.

Just before his final incarceration, however, I did get leave to visit him. My reasons for doing so were largely selfish: I wanted to atone for my own complicity in the tragedy surrounding the de Gray family – and if possible to find out what really happened to Mother Han. I'd even been back to the site of her hovel in the hope of finding another clue but by then someone else had taken her plot and did not welcome prying questions. I didn't get much more out of Eusebius - indeed, I'm not sure he even knew who I was. He spoke in apocalyptic terms quoting extensively from the many religious tomes he had devoured during his stay with us at the abbey – Anselm of Bec's *Meditations* and *Letters* in particular I recognized - but nothing that made coherent sense. I left him feeling frustrated and none the wiser. But he at least seemed at peace at last and happy in his private world of devotion to the Holy Virgin and daily growing madder and madder.

Meanwhile, other momentous events were gathering pace elsewhere. The rebel barons had finally come into the open and presented the king with their demands for the restoration of what they called their 'ancient and accustomed liberties'. Needless to say, John was not about to grant these without a struggle. Indeed, for a while he looked as though he might even win this particular battle. The barons were by no means united in their purpose. Those I had seen assembled in the abbey church on Saint Edmund's Feast represented barely a quarter of England's nobility, the rest preferring to wait to see how events unfolded before committing themselves one way or the other. And John was not without powerful allies of his own. Having accepted the formal surrender of John's kingdom under bond of fealty and homage, Pope Innocent was outraged that his chief vassal should be treated with such impertinence by a ragbag of disgruntled nobility. He therefore issued letters denouncing the rebels and even threatening them with excommunication if they did not desist in their undertaking.

And then John played his masterstroke. In March he took an oath to go on crusade to the Holy Land, a project dear to Innocent's heart. There was now no question of the pope supporting the barons over his most favoured Christian son and called upon all Christendom to rally to John's aid. But John was still too weak to win the argument outright and in June he agreed to meet the barons' representatives and to seek a solution to the impasse. The basis of the negotiations was to be their charter – the document I had seen lain out on my mother's table at Ixworth Hall. And this, you see, is what I mean when I say John was a reasonable man to deal with. Nobody would have expected his brother to have been so obliging. King Richard would have gouged out the eyes of any mutinous vassals, drowned their progeny and then castrated them so they couldn't produce any more. The one thing he would not have done was sit down in the middle of a damp field and parley with them. But that is precisely what John now proposed to do.

How do I know all this? Because quite unexpectedly I found myself witness to the great event - along with five of my brother monks. The reason was the still-unresolved problem of who was going to be our next abbot. And here I'm afraid John did have to concede defeat. Most favoured son he may be, but Pope Innocent had lost patience with him over this particular vexed question. He made it clear to John that if he was to continue to receive papal support over the matter of the charter then he would have to submit to other of Innocent's wishes, and that included accepting Hugh Northwold as Abbot of Saint Edmund's. John reluctantly agreed but, petulant as ever, he made Hugh come to him to receive the abbatial mitre and ring, and at that moment John was at Windsor awaiting the approach of the barons. So to Windsor was where we went.

Having me along was not part of the original plan at all. Ironically, it was Prior Herbert who requested my presence - not because we had resolved our differences; far from it. When he heard the full details of my exploits from chasing around Bury in pursuit of Effie's murderer, hiding out in the forest with a gang of outlaws and the further bloodshed at Ixworth Hall, Herbert was quite prepared to have me defrocked and thrown out of the abbey. However, a quiet word from the Prior of Ixworth Abbey, who happened to be a close friend of my mother, over his secret collusion with Geoffrey de Saye mollified his tone somewhat. In the end it was thought best we call a truce, put the recent past behind us and begin our relationship anew. However, all was not quite joy and harmony between us. I fear there may be trouble again from that quarter at some time in the future.

So no, it was not love of me that persuaded Herbert to take me with him to Windsor, but his sweet tooth. Herbert had always had a penchant for sugary confections. Unfortunately that particular tooth had gone bad and was causing him considerable discomfort. The answer, of course, was to remove it but for some reason Herbert shied away from that suggestion. I don't know why, the procedure is simple enough: The patient is strapped in a sturdy chair with one end of a length of twine attached to the offending molar and the other to the handle of an open door. At a given signal the door is slammed shut thus extracting the painful appendage in one easy, if rather violent, movement. Something about the procedure seemed to disturb Herbert and he preferred instead to be dosed with palliatives

FULL SPEED TO RUNNYMEDE 285

from my herb collection – I recommended chewing on a piece of Monkshood root for best relief or cloves when available. But relief is all it is, not a cure. Ultimately, extraction is the only permanent solution. Herbert said that if all else failed he would undergo the operation once he had returned from seeing the king, but in the meantime he required my constant attention. I readily agreed. An entire fortnight of watching Prior Herbert suffer unrelieved agonies - how could I refuse?

Thus it was that I joined the small band of brothers that accompanied Abbot-elect Hugh on the Feast of Saint Boniface to ride the ninety miles to Windsor. And frankly, I was not sorry to be going. Two days earlier there had been a great fire that destroyed a large area of the vill and the air was still thick with choking smoke and cinders. As a result there were many funerals that week and just as we were about to set off our journey there was a particularly sorry little affair trundling its way to the Great Cemetery with no mourners other than the priest and two monks. I was told it was the funeral of an old medicine woman which put me in mind once again of Mother Han. I still hadn't managed to find out what happened to her. So with a sad nod to the coffin and a silent prayer I turned my mule's head and set off through the west gate of the town on the first leg of our journey.

For comfort and convenience, the king had suggested his palatial castle of Windsor on the banks of the River Thames as the venue for the negotiations. But sensing a trap, the barons preferred more neutral ground. It was therefore proposed the meeting take place in open country half way between the king's camp at Windsor and the barons' at Staines, upon the little meadow known as Runnymede. Why Runnymede? I suppose the answer is its geography. Here the river snakes along one side with marshland the other leaving a low island in between. It is a well-known assembly point particularly for warring parties since with only two ways in it offers little opportunity for ambush. I could not but reflect what a sad commentary it was on the level of mistrust between sovereign and subjects to which our country had sunk.

Naturally our little party had no knowledge of these new arrangements and so we went straight to the castle expecting to meet the king there. We arrived late in the evening only to be told the king was in conference with Archbishop Langton and we were to present ourselves to him the following day at Staines meadow. Upon reflection we decided to go that same night: After so long a wait and with our goal at last in sight we wanted to leave nothing to chance. Hugh therefore remained alone at Windsor as the guest of the king while the rest of us journeyed the last five miles without him.

Now, anyone who has not been to Runnymede meadow will not know how cramped for space it is and never more so than on that sultry June night. Pavilions and marquees were being frantically erected in preparation for the following day's extravaganza and we were squeezed into one tiny corner - six of us in a tent that was scarcely big enough for two. It was already late when we arrived and we hurriedly intoned the office of compline followed by a light supper of cold pea soup and warm beer and then settled down for the night. But it was not to be a restful one. The soup had predictable effects on Richard's weak constitution and he filled the tent with his noisy and odorous emissions. What with that, the hammering, shouting and sawing outside, Herbert's groaning, Nicholas's feet in my face if I turned one way and Robert's if I turned the other, I got hardly any sleep. Under such squalid conditions are the great matters of state decided.

When we emerged the following morning the sight that greeted our eyes was wondrous to behold. The engineers had been busy all night and had achieved miracles in such a short space of time. It was a sunny June morning, the tenth of that month I think and, with pendants flying, all was colour and spectacle and noise. The King's party had already arrived and occupied the western end of the meadow while the barons had the east. In between were amassed the opposing garrisons, each eyeing the other warily across the few yards that separated them with one large open-sided marquee right in the middle. It was beneath this marquee, I was told, that the signing ceremony was to take place. Hugh rejoined us saying he would be seeing the King again after the main business of the day which was, of course, the king signing the charter.

I say "sign" but in fact John signed nothing. The great seal of state was simply affixed to the bottom of the document to authenticate it, most of the actual details having been agreed days in advance. And thus it was that with a flourish of fanfares and a flurry of flags the great deed was done. Unlike most of his opponents that day John could actually have read and understood the words contained in the charter had he a mind to, although I doubt if he bothered. It was a preposterous document and hardly worth the effort. But he did make a pretty little speech to the effect that he had always held to the principles etcetera set out in the document etcetera and thanked the men who drew them up for reminding him etcetera of his regal obligations etcetera etcetera... Remembering our conversation of six months earlier I was amazed he was able to keep a straight face. Such is the way with politics – a grubby business; I cannot think why my mother is attracted to it. Once the ceremony was out of the way the warring parties withdrew to their own sides of the field to congratulate or commiserate as they saw fit.

And then it was our turn.

We six went with solemn approach into the king's private tent singing the *Te Deum* and stood around as Hugh knelt before his monarch. With little ado John placed the mitre on Hugh's head and the ring on his finger, kissed him fully on the mouth and confirmed him as the next Abbot of Saint Edmundsbury – done in less than two minutes. It was a small moment to savour. At last after nearly two years of mutual recrimination, obfuscation and confusion we had our pastor back. Tears of joy filled Hugh's eyes as he placed his hands between the king's in a gesture of fealty and homage. As he did so, I could not but wonder how much John knew of his new abbot's loyalties over the matter of the charter. I suspect from the twinkle in his eye that he knew only too well. Having kissed the king's feet, the new Abbot of Saint Edmund's went off to give thanks and to celebrate mass with the Archbishop singing Psalm 51 as he went: "Have mercy upon me, Oh God, and wipe away my faults". His business concluded, however, he was in no immediate hurry to start back for Suffolk. As the newly-enthroned Baron of the Liberty of Saint Edmund, Hugh was keen to have his copy of the new charter. Every shire in the country was to be issued with one, apparently, the work for which would keep the royal scribes busy for weeks. So we waited for ours to be drafted so that we could take it with us rather than have the clerks send it out by messenger, and then we left for Bury.

One final ironic twist to this saga needs to be told. Important as the charter was, more important still was the oath to be taken by all free men to the committee of twenty-five barons charged with ensuring the king did not renege on his commitments contained therein. Among these twenty-five 'surety barons' as they were to be called was none other than my old enemy, Geoffrey de Saye. I permitted myself a brief snort of contempt when I heard the news for having Geoffrey de Saye police the liberties of England was like putting the fox in charge of the chicken coop. But what goes around comes around and within a few short years many of the rebels would be dead including Archbishop Langton and, sadly for me, my mother. Some say this was God's judgment wrought upon the ungodly. I leave that for others to decide.

*

All of which is a matter of record to be nit-picked and crawled over endlessly by future historians. But now I am going to reveal something that you will not find in any of the history books:

Just after Hugh had been confirmed in his position as abbot and my brother monks were filing out of the royal enclosure, King John indicated that I should remain. The others, Prior Herbert in particular, looked on in annoyance I'm pleased to say, but what could I do but shrug and obey my sovereign's command? John again dismissed his guard leaving just the two of us alone in his tent. I say 'tent' — it was more substantial than many a burgess's dwelling with rushes on the floor, hanging tapestries and couches to recline upon. He took off his coronet and gloves, laid aside the sword of state and poured himself a goblet of wine.

'Well Bumble, what did you make of that?'

I eyed the goblet covetously and cleared my parched throat. 'Sire, I'm sure I speak for all my brother monks when I say I welcome the appointment of our new abbot.'

'Not that, you fool, I meant the charter. Have you read it?'

I demurred. 'Some of it.'

'Yes,' he nodded. 'The parts your mother had a hand in. Oh don't look so surprised — you think I don't know of Lady Isabel's predilections? Or about the barons' meeting in the abbey church? I should have surrounded the place and burnt it to the ground and that lot with it. Save me a lot of trouble.' He waved a dismissive hand towards the barons. 'But the pope wouldn't have liked that. He sees your abbey as something of a milch-cow - and who would there be left to collect my taxes if half my barons were slaughtered?'

'I am much relieved to hear it sire.'

'Why? Because you were inside too?' he asked sardonically.

I felt the blood drain from my face. 'Not on the ground floor, sire.'

'No, up in the air where you always are, Bumble, up in the air.' He flopped down on one of the couches. 'So, what do you think. Should I have signed or not?'

I took a deep breath. 'No sire. Definitely not. It was so... demeaning. It made you no better than they are.'

He nodded gravely. 'Nicely said, Bumble. No different from them, certainly. Maybe I should have made you Abbot of Edmundsbury instead of Hugh Northwold. I could do with a few friends around.' He took a long draught of his wine.

'Oh sire,' I simpered, 'you have many friends.'

He shook his head. 'Kings don't have friends, Bumble, they have allies, associates, collaborators.'

'I like to think I'm your friend, sire.'

He smiled and patted me on the head like a pet dog. 'Fret not, Bumble. I haven't lost yet. That *thing* I signed this morning - anyone can see it will never work. Under its terms they have the right to take up arms against me for any infringement I make however trivial. So I'll simply commit some minor indiscretion and they'll mobilize their forces. I'll back down and they'll *de*-mobilize. Then I'll do something else that upsets them, they'll mobilize again. I'll retreat...and so on. They'll soon get sick of putting on their armour every time one of their fellows decides he's been badly done by. Sooner or later they'll get fed up, we'll have another Runnymede and then it'll be me dictating the terms. You'll see. I can't lose - unless of course I die beforehand which isn't very likely. I'm not yet fifty and strong as an ox. Even my father was fifty-six when he died and my mother was over eighty. I've got years ahead of me yet. And in the meantime more of them will come over to me. Then when I've got enough I'll crush them and consign their precious charter to the dunghill of history where it belongs.' He crushed his fist by way of demonstration.

I could see he was in earnest, the anger simmering barely below the surface. But he seemed to have better control over his temper these days able to bide his time rather than burst into a rage as he once would have done. Still, I did not envy the barons who continued to oppose him - and that included Geoffrey de Saye. Well, they say every cloud has its silver lining.

'By the way, Bumble,' he said pouring himself a refill of

wine. 'How did you get on with that murder? Did you find the culprit?'

'I did, sire - eventually.'

'All stuff and nonsense, wasn't it? That boy needn't have run for France. I knew everything he knew before he did. A total waste of time.'

And thus in a sentence did he dismiss the lives of Effie, Raoul, Hervey and Mother Han, not to mention Eusebius in his bricked-up cell.

'How...erm...did you know?'

He smiled. 'Remember those two young men, pilgrims on their way to visit the shrine of Our Lady of Walsingham?' He chuckled. 'You really shouldn't take everyone at face value, my overly-trusting friend.'

*

Those were the last words the king ever spoke to me. I did see him one more time - briefly, the following spring as he passed through Bury on his way to lay siege to Earl Bigod's castle at Framlingham. But he was a soldier then at the head of an army and had little time for monks. The castle surrendered almost immediately but seven months later despite his predictions to the contrary King John was dead – dying, strangely enough, at the time of the next Blood Moon.

Hugh showed me our copy of the charter when we finally got it home. It seems I got my way over the inclusion of forestry law reform. Clause 48 of the charter provided for twelve knights of the shire to investigate the 'evil practises and customs' in the old forest laws. Under their auspices all royal woodlands enclosed since the time of John's father, King Harry, were deforested and all those outlawed for breaches of the forest law were pardoned. Unfortunately for Gil the amnesty did not go so far as to pardon him for the murder of his lord's son, nor did it restore to Lena her virginity, Will Conyer his family, Fra William his living or Fitchet his nose. What happened to them I never discovered. I can only hope that, since I never heard the name Gil of Nayland mentioned again, he managed to survive my blundering into his camp and lives still in his comfortable forest hideaway.

Eventually the forestry reforms became so many they were given their own separate *Charter of the Forest* while everything else was put into the bigger one which became known as the *Great Charter* - or to give it its Latin name, *Magna Carta* in order to differentiate between the two. I like to think the name-change was my personal contribution to the business. Not that I ever dreamed it would survive, but survive it has despite civil war, John's death and the enthronement of his son, Henry - the little boy who I had last seen holding his mother's hand in the abbot's palace. At least we have the blessing that he was not called Louis.

And one last word before I lay down my pen. Once back in Bury, Prior Herbert still did not manage to find the courage to have his bad tooth removed. He suffered agonies for most of the time he was away despite my ministrations, I'm happy to say, and in fact his problems in that quarter seemed to be getting worse. A few days after our return I saw him creeping across the cloister garth holding his mouth and looking very sorry for himself. Once I'd managed to persuade him to remove the hand I saw that he had burns all over his chin and lips. When I enquired how he got them he explained that an old medicine woman had told him to hold the naked flame of a candle beneath the painful tooth and a bowl of cold water beneath that. The worms that were gnawing at the tooth would then drop into the cool water to escape the heat and thus the toothache would be cured.

'Did it work?' I asked struggling to keep a straight face.

'Does it look like it?' he groaned.

Such invention! Such audacity! Such nonsense! It could only be the work of one person. It seems that Mother Han didn't die at the hand of Eusebius after all and I wondered, as I laughed myself to sleep that night, when or even whether I would be seeing the old miscreant again.

HISTORICAL NOTE

King John has had a bad press. That's because most of his obituaries have been written by churchmen who didn't like him very much. But he was probably a better king of England than his brother Richard who had contempt for all things English and didn't even speak the language. John's monument is not a bronze statue of a sword-wielding crusader sitting astride his charger outside the Houses of Parliament but a two-foot square piece of parchment written in archaic Medieval Latin.

The name *Magna Carta*, or Great Charter, has almost magical resonances today but it was only called that in order to differentiate it from the smaller *Charter of the Forest* which accompanied it. Americans in particular seem to revere the document as a precursor to their own constitution. In fact Magna Carta was little more than a negotiating tool and a thoroughly unworkable one since it institutionalized rebellion and ensured permanent civil war. It was revised many times before it was finalized and the document we have today is not the one John signed at Runnymede in June 1215. Nevertheless that first attempt set out certain principles which have been expanded upon over the eight hundred years since it was drafted and which form the basis of modern western democratic government particularly in Anglo-Saxon countries. John did not sign it willingly. In fact the greatest service he did this country was to die before he had a chance to revoke it leaving a nine-year-old child on the throne and the barons thereby free to enact its principles.

Most of the characters in this novel were real people and many of the events actually happened. Prior Herbert was the prior of Bury during the interregnum between the death of Abbot Samson and the election of Hugh Northwold. Geoffrey de Saye did become a member of the committee of twenty-five 'Surety Barons' whose job it was to enforce the terms of the charter. He later went on pilgrimage to the Holy Land to atone for a lifetime of sin and died in Poitou in August 1230, aged seventy-five. King John did come to Bury St Edmunds in November 1214 to impose his own candidate for the vacant abbacy only to be sent away by the monks with a flea in his ear. Hugh Northwold was eventually confirmed by John as the eleventh abbot of Saint Edmund's at Runnymede the day after the signing of Magna Carta. He went on to become Bishop of Ely Cathedral where his tomb can be seen today in the presbytery that he built there. Bishop John de Gray did die in France on his way back from seeing the pope and his bones are buried in Norwich Cathedral.

He may well have had a nephew who could have got wind of the barons' rebellion and tried to get to France to warn his uncle - dressing as a woman was a favourite ruse of fleeing fugitives in those days. There is some question as to whether the barons' meeting in the abbey church of Bury St Edmunds actually took place, but they must have met somewhere at sometime in the months before Runnymede to agree their strategy, and where better than before the high altar of England's greatest abbey on the feast day of its saint?

Stephen Wheeler was born in London in 1952 and graduated from the University of Wales. He studied and worked in England, Canada, Australia and Southern Africa, mostly in the retail industry but also as a teacher, driving instructor, ambulance technician and organist. He also writes music and short stories, some of which have been published. Since 1984 he has lived in Norfolk.

Blood Moon is the second novel featuring Brother Walter. The first, Unholy Innocence, is also published by The Erskine Press.